I0785417

HIMBO

Elite 8 Studios Book 4

Emmy Sanders

Copyright © 2023 by Emmy Sanders

All rights reserved.

The names, characters, businesses, places, and incidents portrayed in this book are either the product of the author's imagination or used in a fictitious manner. Any similarity to actual persons, living or dead, events, or locales is coincidental and not intended by the author.

No part of this book may be reproduced in any form or by any electrical or mechanical means, including information storage and retrieval systems, without written permission from the author, except for the use of brief quotations in a book review.

Beta Reading by Georgia Johnson, Jen & Maxie of Smut Readers Society, Lauren, and Leigh

Editing by M.A. Hinkle

Proofreading by Ky

Cover Design by Natasha Snow Designs

ISBN: 9781967130030

Content Warning: This book contains mention of past parental death as well as subject matter pertaining to a degenerative nerve disease. Please take caution if this may be triggering for you.

This one goes out to my brothers, who taught me about the undertoads. Love you guys.

Contents

Chapter 1

CAS

You think I'd be used to feeling like an impostor by now, having had twenty-five years to perfect the experience, but you'd be wrong. With each squeak of my tennis shoes against the smooth marble floor, I feel like I'm walking where I don't belong.

And yet I grew up within these wide, echoing halls. In this house that looks more showroom than family home. Me and my siblings are adults now and moved out long ago, but even in my earliest memories, I can't recall a single area in this house looking anything but pristine. That probably had something to do with the staff that followed us around like personal vacuum cleaners, making sure our trail was spotless.

I never understood who we were trying to impress. Why we had to be perfect *all* the time. Even now, my parents only host guests on occasion. Most days, the only ones here are my mom, my dad, and their army of waitstaff.

And, well, me. At least this morning.

But Kinsleys pride themselves on appearances. Hence the mansion.

"Brenda, I'll call you back shortly," my dad says as I step into the expansive dining room. His ever-present Bluetooth is in his ear, and he dabs his mouth with a cloth napkin. "My son just arrived."

I head toward the table, eyes skipping over the large outdoor pool visible through the wall of southern-facing windows. Early as it is, the sun is just catching the top of the water, painting it in orange more than blue.

As I take a seat at the table that could easily fit sixteen, my dad finishes his call with his assistant. He gives me a smile before cutting into his half-eaten eggs Benedict.

"Good morning, Cassius."

I open my mouth to respond but startle somewhat when one of the waitstaff appears out of thin air to set a crisp white napkin across my lap. I thank them before answering my dad. "Morning."

"Thank you for making the trip today."

Shrugging a little, I take a sip of my fresh orange juice. "It's no trouble."

The drive to my parents' palatial home in Las Vegas, Nevada only takes fifteen minutes on a slow day. I didn't move far from where I was raised, although my own cramped one-bedroom apartment might as well be in an entirely different world for how *other* it feels from this place.

Regardless, I visit when I can. I love my family, even if, at times, I feel like one of those birds that was dropped into the wrong nest as an egg.

"Mom still upstairs?" I ask.

My dad nods, making his way efficiently yet cleanly through his breakfast. Mom isn't as early of a riser as the rest of us. The times I do stop by for breakfast, I usually miss her.

"I'll send your regards," my dad says, reading the unsaid.

I thank the staff member who sets a plate in front of me and glance forlornly down at the decadent Hollandaise-slathered egg-and-muffin dish. There's no way I can eat all of this, not unless I want to be puking up my guts at the gym in a half hour. I'm fairly certain my coworker wouldn't appreciate that. *Nor would I.*

Not wanting to waste the food, I take a small bite as my dad sets his napkin atop his empty plate.

"Dorian said you had some trouble settling in last week," he says, watching me carefully.

I sigh, setting down my fork and offering a wan smile. I didn't realize I was here for an inquisition. "Did you really expect otherwise?"

My dad's lips twist, a furrow appearing in his brow. For how imposing of a man Tiberius Kinsley can be—both in size and station—I've never felt uneasy in the presence of my father. Even now, as he sets in to grill me, there's only concern on his face. Concern for *me.*

He loves me. Unconditionally. It makes me feel bad that the only thing I seem able to offer in return is disappointment.

"Cassius, give it some time," he says. "Maybe Human Resources will work out for you. If not, we'll find the right fit."

I hold in my laugh. "We both know I don't fit at your company."

"*Our,*" my dad replies.

"I'm no more useful in Human Resources than I was in Design," I point out, ignoring his comment. "You might as well put me to use running coffee."

My dad frowns, settling his hands one atop the other as he leans toward me. "We'll find the right fit."

Maybe I don't want to fit.

The words sit at the tip of my tongue, but I don't say them. I can't bear to. My dad has been my relentless cheerleader my entire life. When I struggled through grade school, he hired tutors to help. When I scraped by in college, barely managing to come out with a degree dangling off my belt, he told me how proud of me he was. And in the two years since, as he's tried to insert me into the family business without success, he won't hear a negative word from anybody about my failures.

Leonidas, my brother, is a senior architect. Charlotte, my sister, manages the back office IT team. Both of my older siblings have found permanent positions at my dad's architecture firm. They've earned their spots through skill and training.

But me? I have nothing to contribute.

"Cassius," my dad starts, but I shake my head. I don't want to do this. Not today.

"Look, I should get going. I'm meeting a friend," I say, checking the time on my phone. It's not exactly a lie. "I'll stop by your office soon, and we can talk about it, okay? I'll make an appointment with Brenda."

My dad sighs. It's barely there, just a quick, soft inhalation, but I catch it all the same. "Of course."

"Thanks for breakfast," I add, standing up and setting my cloth napkin beside my plate.

My dad looks down at my mostly untouched eggs Benedict with a frown. "Have a good day, Cassius. I love you."

"Love you, too, Dad," I say, managing a small smile before I go.

My shoes squeak on the walk back down the marble hall, and my eyes drift along the many framed pictures on the walls. Some are professionally done, the five of us sitting in perfect arrangement with muted smiles on our faces. Others are candid shots with big, beaming grins and imperfect hair. I like those best. The real moments.

The early morning sun is painting the air in a hazy glow when I jog down the handful of steps at the front of the house and get into my car. It clunks before turning over, and I glance back, half afraid my dad will be standing there, having caught the hesitation of my old, used vehicle to start. The last thing I need is a new Mercedes turning up on my doorstep. Luckily, it's only me and a groundskeeper out front.

After waving a goodbye to the man, I pull around the circle drive, passing the palo verde tree that's long past its blooming season—the yellow flowers were always my favorite—and it only takes ten minutes from there to arrive at the gym where I'm meeting Dixon, one of my coworkers.

Like usual, a curl of guilt hits my stomach when I think about my side job. No one—and I mean *no one*—in my family knows about it. I don't like keeping secrets, but I shove the guilt away. I *like* working at Elite 8 Studios. Sure, it may be a rather unconventional job choice, and it's not like I actually need the money, but it feels like something that's finally just for me. I refuse to feel bad about that.

Dixon is inside the gym when I arrive, his large frame easily visible from a distance. I give him a wave, hold up my bag with my change of clothes, and head toward the locker room. When I get back to the main part of the gym, Dixon is on a treadmill. I hop onto the one next to him.

"Good morning," I say.

Dixon grunts a little. "Is it?"

Dixon, aka Dix at the studio where we work, is, at first glance, an intimidating person. He's a few inches above my own five-eleven frame, easily twice my width, and he wears a perma-scowl like a shield. But I don't take his gruff demeanor to heart. I know it has nothing to do with me.

"I think so," I tell him, my mood already improving, despite the somewhat uncomfortable start to my day. It's hard not to be in a good mood at the gym. The promise of physical exertion always lifts my spirits. "Thanks for letting me tag along."

Dixon's response is a stilted hum. I let it be, and the two of us are quiet as we warm up for our workout. When Dixon moves off toward the leg press, I follow, watching in amusement as he loads the weights higher than I would dare. It's not exactly surprising, though. The man is a beast.

"Gonna watch me all day?" he asks, starting his reps, leg muscles bunching.

I huff a laugh, setting up the machine beside him. "Just admiring."

His brow furrows at that, and he pauses. "I thought we already covered this."

"Covered what?"

He offers me a blank look. "The flirting."

Oh. That.

I roll my eyes, getting into place next to him, knees bent up toward my chest. "I'm not coming on to you, Dixon," I tell the man, pressing the weights up with my legs. "I know you're not interested."

I'm well aware Dixon is happily taken because his boyfriend and another of our coworkers, Niko, already set me straight on that front when I started at Elite 8. Granted, it was Niko I was flirting with at the time. But no one—and I firmly hold my stance on this—would blame me for flirting with Niko. Known on set as Adonis, the man is a literal god in human form, with his olive skin and long, curly dark hair. He moves and talks like sex incarnate. Dixon is no slouch either, with his ridiculously muscular body, dark brown skin, and truly porn-worthy cock. I have firsthand experience with that cock considering, well, our business *is* porn.

But I don't flirt with men who are off-limits. That doesn't mean I can't admire my coworker's impressive workout routine. It's my first time at the gym with him.

"You seeing anybody?" Dixon asks as he finishes up on the leg press.

The question brings a smile to my face. Not because of the subject matter, but because it's the first time Dixon has prompted a conversation with me that falls on personal ground. Usually, the questions he asks occur while I'm on my back, running along the lines of *are you stretched enough?* or *is this angle uncomfortable for you?*

Asking after my dating life is new.

"No, still single," I answer, dropping my feet to the ground and sitting upright. "Not for lack of trying, though."

And it's not that there aren't interested parties. It's just that, well, I want a partner on *my* terms this time. Someone I've picked, not someone who's only after a good time.

Dixon grunts, wiping down his machine. I do the same and follow him over to the barbells.

"Unless you want a personal matchmaker up your ass twenty-four-seven, do *not* let Alex hear you say that," he cautions. "The man is a menace."

Alex, aka Tink, is another of our costars. He and Dixon are good friends, although I'm fairly certain Dixon would deny such vehemently, and although I haven't known Alex long, the little blonde does seem like a well-intentioned shit-stirrer.

I wonder if I should tell Dixon it was Alex who suggested I come along with him to the gym in the first place. Although surely he wasn't trying to match me and Dixon. I shrug it off, following Dixon through a rather grueling workout.

A good forty minutes later, after we're both sweaty and sore, he says, "Come on. I need caffeine."

"Sure, let's do it," I agree, wiping the sweat off my face with a towel.

Dixon and I pack up our things, and, bag over my shoulder, I follow him a short ways down the street to Hyped, a local coffee joint. The woman at the register looks up as we enter, a smile jumping to her face when she spots Dixon. Her eyes trail to me next, and with a quick raise of her eyebrow, she shifts a glance toward the espresso machines.

I check out the specials board as Dixon and I wait in line. The sounds of a coffee grinder and frothing milk rise above the gentle chatter in the shop, and the smell of bitter roast permeates the air. It's not terribly busy, but I notice a couple of people off to one corner, nursing their drinks, and a guy about my age alone at a table nearby, a laptop out in front of him.

When Dixon and I reach the front of the line, he greets the woman behind the register. She's pretty, but pretty women have never been my type. I tried it a couple times just to make sure, but nope. I'm firmly in *camp dick*.

"Marley, fancy seeing you here," Dixon says, tone dry.

Marley snorts a laugh. "Uh-huh. Real shocker that my most routine customer showed up for his morning hazelnut latte fix at the same time he does *every* morning," she intones, to which Dixon audibly rolls his eyes. She ignores him in favor of giving me a once-over, her pierced eyebrow rising as she smiles. "And who's this?"

"This is Cas," Dixon replies, waving a hand my way.

"Cas," Marley says, grin bordering on manic. "How nice. Hear that, Jason?" she calls out loudly, eyes panning slowly toward the espresso machines again. "Dixon brought us another *friend*."

A head peeks out from around the machinery, a dark beanie in place over blonde hair. The guy's eyes widen, shifting first to Dixon and then slowly over to me. He blinks, all boyish charm and something endearingly innocent flashing in his expression, and suddenly, I wonder if maybe Alex *was* matchmaking, after all.

Jason is cute, maybe a little shy, almost certainly queer if that rising blush is any indication, and although I can't say I have a specific type, those big, guileless eyes have me stepping forward without hesitation.

"Hi," I say, giving the guy my best smile. "I'm Cas."

Jason inhales sharply, muttering out something like, "I, uh," and then he disappears before I can get another word out. Marley chuckles under her breath, pressing a few buttons on the tablet in front of her as my smile slips into a frown.

"Don't take it personally," she says quietly, voice barely rising above the hisses of the espresso machine. "He's a skittish kitten."

A kitten. I can work with that.

"One large hazelnut latte for our regular," she says without looking at Dixon. Her smile for me is more subdued. "And what'll you have, sweetheart?"

Someone honest and kind? A man who'll love me for who I am, despite my many faults? Someone real who doesn't look at me like I'm good for one thing and one thing alone?

If only I could order a boyfriend as easily as a latte.

"Vanilla, please," I tell her, doing my best to peek around the large espresso machines. All I can see is a hint of blonde, but it's enough to have me wondering.

Chapter 2

JASON

Oh my God. Oh my *God.*

My hand shakes as I pour whole milk into the little metal carafe for steaming.

There's two of them today. *Two.* I can barely manage to look Dixon in the eye when he comes in each morning for his hazelnut latte, and now he's dragged along Himbo—no, Cas. Which means the only thing standing between me and two porn stars is this hunk of coffee beans and metal.

Oh. My God.

Marley shoots me a little grin, and I flip her off. She laughs, facing forward and taking the next customer's order.

Focus. Large hazelnut latte. Large vanilla latte.

I finish Dixon's drink first, capping the paper cup with a lid before sliding it across the counter. My eyes skitter over to Cas, who's watching me with the same unnerving focus and large smile he's had ever since introducing himself. *Holy fuckballs*, the guy is ridiculously pretty.

I avert my gaze as Dixon accepts his latte.

"Thanks, Jason," the bigger man drawls.

I give him a clipped nod before disappearing again, just able to make out his conversation with Cas as Marley calls in an order of frappuccinos.

"—don't need to stick around," Cas is saying. "I'll catch you later at work."

"Yeah, all right," Dixon replies. "See ya."

My hands shake even harder, and I force calm through my body, closing my eyes for three seconds and breathing long and low. When I'm done, I'm steadier, and I set another couple espressos to brew as I steam the milk for Cas's vanilla latte.

Why am I so nervous?

Psht, my brain admonishes. *Because you're a damn virgin standing in front of a porn star. Of course you're nervous.*

Yeah, that'll do it.

Regardless, I tell my brain to fuck off, *please and thanks*, and focus on my orders. It works, for a minute. Right up until I sidestep the machines to grab a can of whipped cream for the frappuccinos and Cas's eyes latch back onto mine.

Can he tell? Does he *know*?

His mouth twists up into a smile, and I nearly fumble the whipped cream as I grab it from the mini-fridge. *Fucking fuck*. Get it together, Jason.

"Have you worked here long?" Cas asks.

It takes me an extended moment to realize he's talking to me. When I glance up again, he's leaned against the counter, his upper body hanging far enough over it that he can see me behind the espresso machines. He grins my way.

"I, uh...three years," I answer, mentally kicking myself for my awkwardness.

He nods, arms crossed in a position that shouldn't look casual, and yet he manages it. "I work with Dixon."

My hand jerks as I pour piping-hot milk over the espresso and vanilla in his cup. "Uh, yeah," I manage, certain my face is flaming.

Does he *know* I know what he and Dixon do?

Stop thinking about the man having sex.

I take a moment to look at him as I secure a lid on his cup. He's still smiling at me, his chestnut-brown hair wet and messy over his forehead. He probably came from the gym—that's Dixon's routine, at least. His eyes are the color of whiskey, rich and amber brown. He has the sort of chiseled face that universally screams *attractive* and just a touch of barely there stubble along his jaw. His features are symmetrical and beautiful, and I know from his videos he has a body to match.

But it's his lips. Those damn lips that make me think this man should be immortalized as a statue or priceless work of art. They're full and pouty and even prettier in person.

He is, in a word, breathtaking.

"Are you single, Jason?" those lips ask.

I jolt hard at the question, not having expected it in the least, and the latte I was setting in front of Cas tips right out of my hand. The lid pops off the moment the cup lands on its side, and, like a slow-motion nightmare, coffee sloshes across the counter toward Cas. He raises his arms, scrambling back, and I reach forward to do *something*, but neither of us moves quickly enough to stop the drink from saturating his shirt.

Cas moves fast, whipping his t-shirt over his head before the hot liquid has time to burn his skin. I stand there, staring, mute, as he comes jogging around the counter toward me.

"You okay?" he asks, dropping to his knees at my feet. I'm immobilized from shock, so it takes me a minute to realize what his concern is. Some of the latte soaked into my apron.

I open my mouth to tell him I'm fine—*I think*—but my brain has gone completely offline. Because Cas is on his knees. In front of me. Shirtless. Wiping at the spill near my groin with his discarded t-shirt.

The entire coffee shop has gone silent, and when I look up, Marley is staring at me with wide eyes, and my friend Brad, who's sitting at a nearby table with his laptop, has a massive grin on his face.

"Uh...yeah, I'm fine," I manage to eke out as Cas continues to rub perilously close to my dick.

Is this happening? Is a half-naked porn star kneeling at my feet, giving me a veritable rubdown in front of the entirety of the coffee shop?

As soon as my brain clicks into gear, I reach out to stop him, only to realize there's a can of whipped cream in my hand. I use the other to halt his movements.

"I'm fine," I assure him. "It didn't go through to my clothes."

Cas sits back on his heels, looking relieved and painfully adorable as he smiles up at me. "Okay, good." And then, either oblivious to the fact that all eyes are on us or not caring one bit, he says, "So...are you single?"

I think I squeak.

"He's single," Brad calls out, the absolute asshole.

Cas doesn't look away from me once. "Can I take you out, Jason?"

My hand flexes in surprise, and whipped cream sprays across Cas's face.

He freezes. I freeze.

And my soul goddamn leaves my body.

Brad starts laughing as I spin quickly around, looking for a towel. "Holy shit," I mutter to myself, vaguely registering my friend sounding as if he's struggling to breathe through his laughter. *Good. I hope you choke on it, Brad.*

Finding a hand towel, I spin back around in time to catch Cas bringing a whipped cream-covered finger into his mouth.

Ho-ly shit. I creamed his face.

I hold the towel out weakly. "I...I'm *so* sorry," I tell him.

Cas doesn't look the least bit upset. He rises to his feet smoothly and accepts the towel, wiping it over his face and catching most but not all of the whipped cream.

"Did I get it?" he asks, a rueful smile on his lips.

"Uh, no," I answer truthfully, holding out my hand.

Cas hands me back the towel, and I step close, using the corner to clean up his cheek and bottom lip. He's taller than me by a couple inches, and he watches me patiently as I complete the task.

I swallow roughly, stepping back, eyes sweeping down his torso to confirm he didn't sustain any damage. He looks fine, skin smooth and unblemished.

"Everything okay?" Marley asks, coming over and helping clean up the counter with a bundle of paper towels.

A nod is all I can manage.

"Need a shirt, Cas?" she asks lightly.

He shakes his head, tucking his soiled t-shirt into his waistband. "Nah, that's all right. Thanks, though."

It takes me a moment to catch onto the fact that Cas is still watching me, and I realize I never answered his question.

"I, uh..." I start, having no clue what to say. What *does* one say to a porn star asking for a date?

My head spins, but luckily, Cas seems to sense my discomfort.

"Tell you what," he says, leaning a hip against the counter. He's still behind it, in my space but not crowding me. "How about I come back tomorrow for my vanilla latte and you can answer me then?"

I nod, eyes skipping to the customers who are waiting for their drinks. Marley is manning the machines now, filling orders.

"Okay, great," Cas says cheerfully. "I'll see you tomorrow. Have a good day, Jason."

"Uh, yeah. You, too."

Cas gives me a grin before walking around the counter. He stops to swipe his gym bag off the floor, and then, still shirtless, he exits the coffee shop, an effortless swagger to his step. It's quiet for a solid five seconds before Brad starts to slow clap. I groan, but a few other customers join in.

"Thanks for the free show, Jason," Marley says wryly, her eyes dancing with humor.

I shake my head, scrubbing my hand across my face before I hop into action. I take over behind the espresso machines, and Marley heads back to the register. Apart from calling orders, we work in relative silence for the next half hour until the morning rush dies down, and then Marley comes over and gives my shoulder a squeeze.

"Take fifteen," she tells me. "You look like you could use it."

"Yeah, thanks," I mumble, untying my apron and setting it aside before I walk out from behind the counter. Brad looks up expectantly as I approach, and I slump into a chair across from him, banging my head onto the table.

"That was, quite possibly, the most beautiful thing I've ever witnessed," he says, ignoring my answering groan. "Pure art."

"Brad," I mutter, contemplating ways I can exact my revenge. We live together, so it shouldn't be hard to come up with something. Rubber tarantula in his bed?

Brad pats me on the head, mussing up my beanie. "There, there."

"Thanks so much for your sympathy," I say, sitting upright and fixing my hair before I replace my cap. The beanie is a staple of my wardrobe. I'm always cold.

"You know," Brad says, humor lacing his tone, "I've seen you do that nervous stuttering thing before, but never that bad. Was it because he's so pretty?"

I sigh, keeping my voice low even though the shop is mostly empty at the moment. "Not just that," I tell my friend. "He's a gay porn star."

Well, maybe *star* isn't an appropriate word. Cas, known as Himbo, is new at Elite 8 Studios—a huge producer of gay porn. I happen to pay for a membership. But still, even if Cas isn't at star level, the intent stands. And by Brad's widening eyes, I can tell I've surprised him.

"Well, shit," he says succinctly before a slow smile spreads across his face. "So that's why you were flustered."

I groan again, rubbing my forehead. "Brad..."

"He *is* pretty, though, right?" he asks, genuinely questioning me. Brad is straight, but honestly, *anyone* would be hard-pressed not to call Cas pretty.

"Yeah, he is," I agree.

Brad nods. "So you're going to go out with him?"

"Uh...no."

"Why not?" he asks, clearly confused.

"Gay porn star," I repeat, pointing toward the door, even though Cas left long ago. I point to myself next. "Twenty-four-year-old virgin."

"So?" Brad says. "I'm not saying you should sit on his face, but why not go out with the guy?"

"Sit on his... Jesus, Brad," I moan.

He laughs at me.

"You know it's not that simple for me," I say, and my friend immediately quiets.

"I know," he says softly. "And I'm not making light of that, Birdie."

I roll my eyes at Brad's affectionate usage of the nickname he's held for me ever since we were young. My parents used to call me Jaybird, and for a while, I thought that was my real name. I introduced myself to Brad as such in kindergarten, and I've been Birdie to him ever since.

"But Jason, come on," Brad continues. "You're demisexual, not a nun. If you don't give him a chance, you'll never know if it could be more."

"I *really* hate when you make sense, you know that?"

"I'm wise, and we both know it," he replies, modest as ever.

"Uh-huh." I pick at my shirtsleeve. "I can't date him, Bee. He'll expect things."

And yeah, yeah. Birdie and Bee. We're adorable.

"You don't know that," Brad shoots back, taking a sip of his third coffee of the day. I may need to cut him off soon. His habit has been getting out of control lately, and I'm nothing but his caffeine-toting enabler. "He could be a perfect gentleman."

"That's true," I allow. "But dating strangers *sucks*. Do you know how many people want to see me again when I tell them, 'Hey, I don't want to have sex with you, and I might not ever, but we'll have to keep dating to find out for sure?' It's not a conversation that goes over well."

"But if you don't try—" he starts, and I nod, cutting him off. He doesn't need to finish his sentence.

If I don't try, I might not *ever* find someone I'm attracted to. It's only happened twice, and only once I knew them for a long time. Months. As far as I know, attraction doesn't happen quickly for me.

Yes, Cas is beautiful—so lovely it almost *hurts* to look at him. Aesthetically, he's quite appealing, but that doesn't mean I'm sexually attracted to him. When he was rubbing my crotch, there was nothing but mortification.

Sure, I've gotten off to his videos before, but that's a matter of fulfilling a physical need. And yes, watching sex turns me on when it's me and my hand. But it doesn't have anything to do with Cas or the other performers specifically, and it didn't translate into me wanting to bed the man who dropped in front of me like a sweaty, shirtless angel.

I need to know someone, as far as I can tell. Attraction comes after affection. *Wanting* someone is deeper for me than a pretty face. And there's no guessing who or when it will be. Like I said, it's only happened twice.

It's a bitch, if I'm being honest, and there's every chance I'll never be attracted to Cas. But Brad is right. I'll never know if I don't try.

So how the hell do I tell a porn star I don't want to have sex with him?

Chapter 3
Cas

"Good day, brother. I hope the morning is treating you well."

"Hey, Leo," I reply, stopping near my front door, phone at my ear. "What's up?"

Leonidas snorts, likely at my informal greeting. "I'm calling to see if you'll be at the office later."

"Yep, I will. Why?"

"Char and I were hoping to take you to lunch," he says, talking about our sister Charlotte. "Mom and Dad's anniversary is coming up in a few months, and we thought it would be nice to plan an elaborate soiree. Forty years is somewhat of a big deal, after all."

I keep my groan to myself. My parents will love a fancy party in their name. I seem to be the only one who doesn't much care for the fanfare.

"Sure," I tell my brother. "I'll help however I can."

"That's the spirit," he says, sounding far older than his thirty-six years. "We'll collect you at noon."

My brother clicks off the call before I can chide him for treating me as if I'm a wayward child, and I tuck my phone back into my pocket. Despite the early hour, there's an undeniable pep in my step as I head out of my apartment and take the stairs down to ground level parking, my mind tumbling over what little I know of the barista I'm on my way to visit.

Name: Jason. Hair color: sandy blonde. Eye color: hazel. Height: maybe five foot eight. Build: slim. Cheeks: adorably bright.

It's all physical, but I don't know anything else about the man, apart from the fact that his aim with a whipped cream can is impeccable. But that's what dating is for, right? Getting to know a person.

And I have a good feeling about Jason. I just hope my instincts aren't wrong this time.

Hyped is busy when I push through the door, and Marley gives me a brief up-nod from behind the register. I take my place in line, watching the espresso machines and catching glimpses of the barista behind it. I get my first full view when Jason steps to the side to hand someone their drink order.

He's wearing a beanie again today, his hair falling in shaggy clumps around his face below it. His shirt is long-sleeved and red, and an apron is tied around his waist. He doesn't see me in line as he works, but Marley is all smiles when I step up to the front.

"Large vanilla latte," she calls before I've said a word.

Jason peeks his head out, gaze wide, and I give him a wave. He disappears again, and Marley snorts.

"Welcome back," she says. "Your drink is all set, since we owe you for yesterday."

"Thanks," I reply, dropping a couple bucks in the tip jar.

Marley gives me a salute, and I move down from the register. There are a few people waiting at the pickup counter in front of me, but as soon as they're gone, I stretch over the surface to get a glimpse of the cute barista.

"Hey, Jason," I say.

He startles slightly before his eyes raise to mine, looking mostly brown from this distance, but I know there's green in there, too. "Uh, hey."

"Having a good morning?" I ask.

His hands move quickly as he multitasks drink orders. "Um, sure," he answers slowly, and then finally, "You?"

"Uh-huh. You look nice today."

He nearly fumbles the shot of espresso in his hand. "I, uh...thanks?"

"You're welcome. Red suits you."

His cheeks brighten—proving my point—and my cock shifts. *Huh*. Do I like shyness in a guy? Or is it just him?

"Here's your vanilla latte," Jason says, sliding the lidded cup over to me with extra care. "Sorry again about yesterday."

"No problem," I reply, grabbing the drink. "It gave me a reason to see you again."

He blinks at me before dropping his gaze to the counter and mumbling, "Uh."

The line behind me is long, so I step out of the way, and Jason's eyes lift. "I know you're busy," I tell him, "but I'll be here for a bit. If you have a couple minutes, could we talk?"

His mouth opens and closes once, then twice, before he says, "Okay."

I give him a grin. "Great! See you soon."

Jason blinks at me, and I turn to head toward an empty table near the wall. A woman drops her coat as I'm passing, so I stop to hand it over, politely declining her invite to join her at her table. As I wait for Jason at my own, I think about what kind of date he might like. Probably not coffee. Maybe drinks if he's over twenty-one? Surely he is. Would he like something active, like walking around a park? Or something more intimate, like dinner at an expensive restaurant? Most of the people I've dated preferred being dined.

I mull the possibilities over as I sip my latte. It's just the right amount of sweet on top of bitter, and even though I've never been a huge coffee drinker, I savor it as I pull out my phone. Since I have time, I scroll through the responsibility list Dorian, the head of Human Resources at my dad's firm, gave me at the end of last week. I don't know the first thing about administrative work, but my dad has tried putting me in just about every other department to no avail. It's clear, at this point, I'm never going to hack it in the Design sector of the business. I had to drop my architecture major for a reason; the concepts are over my head. In theory, sitting at a desk in Human Resources doing entry-level office work should be easy enough, but computers have never been my thing, either, and it was obvious Dorian was getting frustrated with my lack of knowledge after the two brief training sessions we had last week. I'm not expecting much better today.

I try. I really do. But I'm simply not cut out for this stuff. I didn't get accepted into a prestigious college like my brother. I don't have a specialized skill set like my sister. I'm just me, barely scraping by at every turn, so unlike the rest of my family it's not even funny.

I feel like I'm stuck bumbling my way through a legacy I'm supposed to want but *don't*. But how could I possibly admit that without sounding ungrateful?

When I look up from my phone, I catch sight of Marley giving Jason a little shove out from behind the counter. He unties his apron, setting it down before coming my way, eyes on his feet as he walks. Hopping up, I pull out the chair on the other side of the table. Jason gives me a startled look before sitting down.

I retake my own seat, offering a smile. "Hey."

"Uh, hi. Again," he says, rubbing his hand over his beanie and making his hair ruffle a bit.

Is he nervous? *Good* nervous or *bad* nervous?

"You wanted to talk?" he prompts.

I lean forward a bit, elbows on the table, so I can see the green in his eyes better. "Can I take you on a date, Jason?"

He blinks at me, one big slow motion. "Why?"

"Why?" I repeat. Isn't it obvious? Although, maybe not. I suppose there are plenty of reasons for people to want to date one another. "Because... I think you're attractive, and I'd like to get to know you better."

His face scrunches into the briefest of winces before his expression smooths back out. My stomach sinks, but I hold my smile in place, even though it feels a little frayed at the edges.

"It's okay if you're not interested," I say. "You can tell me no." Even though the idea stings.

He doesn't shut me down, though. Not exactly. "It's not..." He makes a small sound. "One date."

"Really?" I ask, perking up.

"Yeah. We'll see how it goes," he says, pulling his shirt-sleeve over his hand and fidgeting with the fabric.

I nod emphatically. "Okay, yeah. What do you like? Have you ever had crab pithivier? I know this place—"

"How about tacos?" he says, meeting my gaze a little unsurely.

I let out a breath. That sounds... "Perfect. Tomorrow night?"

"Uh." He winces again. "I can't do tomorrow. Saturday?"

"Yeah, that works," I say, grabbing my phone. "Can I have your number?"

He nods, that blush rising again, and I hand the device over. Jason licks his lips as he enters his digits. "Here you go. And, uh, Cas?"

"Yeah?" I ask, taking my phone back.

"You look nice, too. Your shirt, uh...fits...well," he says, eyes widening with each word he speaks before he closes them entirely and breathes out.

"Thanks," I say, smoothing a hand over my shirt. I don't love wearing button-downs—I much prefer comfortable tees and sweatshirts—but dressing professionally is a necessity on the days I'm heading to the firm. I thought this particular shirt was a little on the tight side, but if Jason thinks it looks nice, maybe I can find something similar to wear on our date night.

"Uh, anyways, I should get back to work," Jason says, standing up.

I stand, too, grabbing my empty cup. "Have a good day, Jason. See you Saturday."

"Yeah. Okay, bye."

With that, Jason spins and heads off, and I pocket my phone before making my way toward the door. I toss my cup on the way out, a smile on my face as I walk toward the parking lot.

It's been months since I've dated. Nearly six, now that I think about it. I've always been a bit hopeless and a romantic—different than a hopeless romantic, as my sister Char likes to say—so I've missed the intimacy of it. The longing glances and anticipation of that first touch. The fizzing in my gut and that moment bodies finally come together. Finding small ways to make my partner smile. Learning what makes them scream.

But, most of all, feeling wanted. Cared for. Showing someone how much I'm capable of caring in return. That's what I miss.

And that's what, in the past, has been missing. Because I don't think a single boyfriend—or girlfriend, when I was still trying that—cared about what I could give them beyond my body or the capabilities of my checkbook. They didn't care about *me*.

Is it too much to ask that someone see me? That someone want what *I* have to offer?

I wouldn't think so, and yet, time and time again, I've been proven wrong. So, hopeless? Maybe. A romantic? Yes, still that. Probably always.

But one of these days, I'm bound to find the right guy. Right?

My dad's firm, Kinsley Richman, is busy when I enter the lobby shortly before nine in the morning. One of the receptionists gives me a smile and a wave as I pass, and I return the gesture before stepping in line at the elevators.

Dorian, my reluctant trainer, is waiting for me in Human Resources on the third floor, a cup of coffee in his hand, an unhappy look on his face. He doesn't want me to be here any more than *I* want to be here. But when the boss-man makes demands, his workers follow.

"Morning," I greet, hoping a little kindness will pave the way for a good training session.

He doesn't look enthused. "Follow me," he says, leading the way into a small, private office. Per usual, we sit side by side in front of three computer monitors, and my mind spins looking at all the forms and spreadsheets in front of me. Dorian goes through the process for payroll, but even by the third time, I'm no closer to remembering it.

"Do you have printed instructions?" I ask, thinking it might be easier if I can see the steps written out in front of me.

Dorian sighs before standing. "Give me a minute."

I scrub a hand through my hair as he steps out. Dorian closes the door, or at least tries, but it rebounds at the last moment, leaving it cracked open an inch. Which is why I hear my new boss talking to someone in the hall.

"—even more work to teach someone who can't learn," he's saying. "I swear, the boy's got air for brains."

My chest aches, a burn that crawls along my sternum. I can't make out the rest of his conversation, but I heard enough. When Dorian steps into the room, I blink back the sting and sit up taller.

"Melanie is writing up instructions," he says, retaking his seat. "In the meantime, let's go over new hire forms."

I give Dorian a nod, wondering why they don't already have instructions made up for standard job procedures. Not my place. I do my best to listen, focusing on the screens in front of me, but my heart...

My heart doesn't belong in this room.

Chapter 4

JASON

"You're freaking out," Brad says.

"No shit, I'm freaking out," I tell him, tossing my shirt back into my closet, not caring where it lands. I grab another, tugging it over my head. "I'm going on a date with a *porn star*."

"You're still on that?" my friend asks.

I grab a pair of scrubs from my hamper and throw them at his head. Brad laughs, and I wrestle my shirt on.

"Ugh," I complain, flopping onto my bed, shirt still stuck over my face. "What do I say to him?"

"You say, 'Hi, I'm Jason. Barista by day, nurse extraordinaire by night. I'm twenty-four, I like cheese more than any one person should, and you have nice nipples.'"

"Oh my *God*," I groan. "I'm not going to be seeing his nipples."

"Haven't you already seen his nipples?" Brad asks.

"Not the point," I grumble, tugging my shirt down.

Brad's amused smirk shifts into something gentler, possibly concern. "It'll be okay, Birdie. It's just a date."

"He's too pretty for me," I say.

"Nah."

"Too sexy," I point out.

Brad shrugs. "You can be sexy."

I roll my head toward him, raising a dubious eyebrow. "I don't do sexy."

"Yeah, you do," he says. "Remember that one guy you dated briefly from the hospital?" He snaps his fingers. "Zeek."

"Yeah?" I ask, sitting upright. "What about him?"

"He used to stare at your stomach, like, all the time," Brad says. "He'd stare and lick his lips. It was borderline creepy."

"I don't have a sexy stomach," I say, sure my face is mirroring my confusion. "What even is that?"

He shrugs. "I don't know, man, but I'm telling you. Use your stomach."

"That's not a *thing*."

Brad's lips purse before he reaches for my shirt. "Let me see."

"What?" I squawk, batting his hand away. "No."

"C'mon, you were just changing in front of me," he says, making another grab.

"I swear to God, Brad, if you lift my shirt, I'm going to wait until you're asleep and *kick you in the balls*."

Brad reclaims his hand in a quick snap, and I groan again, flopping flat on my back. How is this my best friend?

A knock at the door makes me freeze. "Shit," I chirp.

"I'll get it," Brad sings, popping off my bed.

"Buy me five minutes," I whisper urgently.

He grins, leaving my door wide open, and I dash over, closing it to a crack before I hear the front door click. Brad says something surely annoying. Cas's tone is polite. Brad laughs. *Ugh*.

Hastily, I step in front of my mirror, examining my long-sleeved shirt. It's not red, but the soft blue looks nice.

I hope. Jeans will have to do. Grabbing a dark gray beanie, I pop it on my head and make for the door. Brad has Cas in the living room, looking through his extensive collection of video games.

Cas's head swivels when I walk out of the hallway, and a smile leaps onto his face.

Too pretty. Too…

Is that shirt *painted* on?

Brad stands behind Cas, grinning at me maniacally and pointing to Cas with both hands, as if I can't see the man. Anyone with eyes would see the man. And his nipples. Which are visible. Little buds outlined through his tight black shirt.

Ho-ly shitballs.

It takes every ounce of my willpower not to blurt, "I like your nipples!"—*damn it, Brad.* Luckily, I manage to keep my mouth shut as I step toward the duo.

"Hey," Cas says happily, as if he's truly pleased to see me.

"Yeah," I manage. "You, too."

Fuck. Me. Now.

Not literally.

Christ, he can't hear your thoughts, Jason.

"You, uh, tacos?" I ask.

Brad's grin widens.

"You ready to get tacos?" I amend, wishing our second-floor apartment would grow a sinkhole to swallow me down. Anything would be better than this.

"Yeah, let's do it," Cas says, turning to shake Brad's hand. "Nice to meet you."

"You, too, man," Brad says.

Cas heads toward the door, and I stop to grab a lightweight jacket. It's treading into fall now, and although the weather isn't cool yet in Las Vegas, it's enough for me to layer. Cas gives me a curious look when I tug the jacket on, but he doesn't comment, only holds the door for me to go through.

"Have fun!" Brad calls out.

"Die by a swarm of bees, Brad!" I call back, stepping into the hall.

Again, Cas looks at me curiously, but I wave it off, shutting the door.

"Shall we?" I ask.

"Yeah," he says, grabbing my hand and threading our fingers together. I nearly fall down, shocked by the gesture, but Cas doesn't notice. He tugs me gently down the hall toward the exit. "I figured I'd drive," he says, "unless you want to."

"That's fine," I reply, swallowing, my heart beating fast.

"Okay." He smiles wide.

I blow out a breath.

The trip to the restaurant passes quickly, Cas keeping the conversation flowing with chitchat about the weather and living in Las Vegas, which we both have our entire lives. He makes it easy—or at least relatively easy—to talk back. For a minute, I almost forget who I'm in the car with.

That is, until we arrive at the restaurant and the first person we pass on the sidewalk nearly runs into a pole trying to keep her eyes on Cas. He doesn't even seem to notice the woman ogling him shamelessly, but I shoot her an entirely ineffectual glare. Ineffectual because she never once looks at me.

It's the lips. I swear it's the lips. They just *look* like they'd feel good. And this coming from a guy on the ace spectrum.

The woman eventually turns away just as we arrive at the door, and Cas hustles a step ahead, grabbing it for an elderly couple getting ready to walk through. He gives them a smile and a hello, and I watch him, feeling like I'm observing some sort of unicorn in the wild.

Once the other couple is through, Cas motions me forward, and I step inside, my breath catching when Cas's palm lands solid and warm against my lower back. There's no way I can feel the warmth of his hand through two layers—I know that—and yet, the sensation is still there.

The hostess leads us to a table after seating the older couple, and Cas once again pulls out my chair before I have the chance to.

"Want anything to drink?" he asks me, taking a seat across the table and handing over the cocktail menu. "You're old enough to drink, right?"

I huff a laugh, accepting the laminated sheet. "Yeah. I'm twenty-four," I tell him, not the least bit offended he had to ask. I'm well aware I look perpetually eighteen and have since the moment I turned, well, twenty.

Cas gives me a smile, and I maneuver out of my jacket. I order a margarita when the waitress arrives, and Cas does the same.

"I'm twenty-five. Youngest of three," Cas tells me, offering the information freely. "My family is pretty great most of the time."

Most of the time?

"And when they're not?" I ask, curious about the way in which he worded that.

He shrugs a little. "It's not their fault we're so different. Do you have family?"

"I, uh, yeah. My mom lives close," I tell him, throat tightening. "My dad passed away a few years back."

"Sorry, Jason," he says, those whiskey eyes soft like he means it.

"Thanks," I mumble.

Thankfully, the waitress comes back with our drinks and takes our order. I get the steak and romano cheese tacos that sound too intriguing to pass up, as well as street corn with queso fresco. Cas orders a variety plate with a bunch of different tacos.

When the waitress goes, Cas takes a sip of his drink, eyes on me. I can't tell what he's thinking, but the attention makes me nervous enough to blurt, "You know I'm aware you work in porn, right?"

I wince, but luckily, my voice didn't travel.

Cas smiles almost serenely, setting down his margarita. "I wasn't sure, but you seemed to know Dixon, so..." He shrugs, and I nod.

"Yeah, uh. Yeah," I say.

Jesus fucking eloquent Christ on a cracker.

"You're okay with that?" Cas asks.

I nod quickly. "Yeah, of course."

"Okay," he says simply. "I work for my father's company part-time, too. But I don't know..."

"Don't know what?" I ask when he trails off.

"I don't know that I want to be there," he says before shaking his head. "No, I *know* I don't want to be there."

I'm not sure what to make of that, but Cas goes on.

"I like people, you know? And there are so many people in that building, but you're not working with them. It's about building mega-mansions and designing the perfect modern aesthetic, and I just couldn't care less about all that. I'm not *good* at it, either." He smiles at me almost sadly. "I know I shouldn't complain. Not everyone is lucky enough to have a job in the first place, but I just... I just wish I was doing something to actually help people. Probably sounds pretty stupid, huh?"

"No," I say, voice a little hoarse. "No, it doesn't. I, uh, I'm a nurse."

"You are?" he asks, eyes lighting. They ping between my own, his focus absolute. It's unnerving, but...not.

"Well, almost," I say. "I'm in my fourth year in a BSN program nearby. Uh, Bachelor of Science in Nursing," I explain when Cas gives me an uncertain look. "I take classes at night and do my clinical rotations at one of the local hospitals."

"Holy crap," Cas says, sounding awed. He reaches forward and squeezes my arm, his fingers drifting over my sleeve in a soothing manner. "That's awesome, Jason. How the hell do you manage all that?"

"Yeah, um, I don't get out much?" I admit.

He huffs a laugh, fingers still on my arm. It's...nice.

"I'm impressed," he says, moving out of the way when the waitress returns with our food. He gives her a smile, and she nearly drops my plate of corn. *Get in line, lady.* Once she's gone, Cas returns his attention to me. "Have you always wanted to be a nurse?"

Cas picks up a taco after his question, biting into it with a happy little moan, and my mind drifts to my dad. Not quite ready to get into that yet, I simply nod and tell him, "Yeah, for the most part."

"That's nice," he says. "I've never really had that one thing I wanted to do. Porn is okay, though."

I nearly spit out my mouthful of steak and cheese. "Um."

"Do you have a favorite season?" he asks, nudging my water closer to me.

I pick it up, grateful for the cooling liquid. *And topic change.* "Uh. Summer, I guess?"

He nods. "I like the colors in the spring and summer. All the flowers. But I think winter is my favorite."

"Why's that?" I ask, ever so curious. Nothing about this man, thus far, has been what I was expecting.

"Have you ever just stood outside and watched the snow?" he asks, a little smile on his face. "It's so uncommon here, but every once in a while, those flakes come down, and... I dunno. I guess I like watching something so rare. You blink, and it's gone. Melted. The idea that I might be the only person in the entire world to see that one unique snowflake before it's gone?" He shrugs. "It makes me feel...important, I guess."

Who. The *fuck*. Is this man?

My heart does a very complicated roll inside my chest as I watch Cas, trying to come up with something to say. *Any* words would be good. Any words at all. But how do I even respond to that?

I have never, not once, contemplated the longevity of a snowflake. And my prevailing thought, amongst all others, is that I want him to look at me like that. I want him to see *me* before I have a chance to pass from his life.

I swallow roughly, taking a sip of my drink to stall. Cas doesn't seem to mind the silence. He continues eating his tacos, as if he didn't just bare some profound piece of his soul to me.

"The food here is really good," I finally manage to say. Not my best talking point, but Cas smiles in return.

"Yeah, it is. I'm having a nice time. Thanks for coming out with me, Jason."

"Uh, yeah," I respond, unable to look away from those sincere whiskey-amber eyes.

When Cas and I are finished with our food and the waitress brings our check, Cas grabs it. I open my mouth to protest, but he cuts me off. "You can pay next time," he says, giving me a wink.

The waitress garbles something unintelligible before strolling off.

When we exit the restaurant, Cas grabs my hand. I shiver, the result of his smooth skin on mine and the light breeze in the air, and Cas comes to a stop, frowning.

"Are you cold?" he asks, straightening out the collar of my jacket so it's up against my neck.

"I, uh, a little," I admit, feeling ridiculous considering it's still in the sixties and Cas is wearing a short-sleeved shirt. My eyes ping down to his nipples without my permission, and I look up quickly, landing on his lips. *Not better.*

Cas grabs my hands between his, rubbing them as if it's actually winter, and I can't find it in me to stop him.

"We should probably get you home, then, huh?" he says, wrapping his hand around mine again and giving a tug. "Come on."

Cas turns the heat on in his car before pulling onto the road. He asks me about my life as we drive. About where my mom lives and about Brad. About the nursing program and my shifts at the hospital. About making coffee and whether I'm a light roast or dark roast kind of person. And he listens to every answer like he cares.

When we get back to my place, Cas insists on walking me to the door. His hand stays in mine the entire time on the short journey, and he smiles at each person we pass: one of my neighbors in the lobby, collecting her mail, and a food delivery person with pizza boxes in his hands. He even holds the door for the latter.

By the time we reach my apartment, I wonder if I've ever met someone as naturally charismatic and kind-natured as Cas. I don't think I have.

It makes me want to hold onto him a little bit tighter.

When we come to a stop at my door, I let Cas's hand go, my heart thudding. He's so close, his dark hair artfully tousled, his lips plump and *there*.

Is he going to kiss me? Do I want him to?

"Can I kiss you, Jason?"

Of course he asks. Of *course* he does.

My instinct is to say no. Kissing leads to other things. *More.* And I'm not ready for sex with this man. I might not ever be.

But my head is nodding before my brain catches up with the motion, and Cas grins like I just handed him the key to immortal life. His hand settles at my jaw, thumb stroking over my cheek, and he leans close, aftershave or cologne or something distinctly warm and spicy tickling my nose. And then his lips—*those* lips—brush ever so slightly against the corner of my mouth.

It's a blip. The kiss of a feather. But it's quite possibly the best thing I've ever felt in my life.

Cas leans back with a happy little hum, and his thumb brushes my skin again. "Can I take you on a second date?" he asks.

"Yeah," I breathe.

And there's that smile again.

"Okay," he says. "I'll call you, then."

"'Kay."

"Have a good night, Jason."

"Yeah."

Cas gives me one last smile before walking off, and eventually, I have the wherewithal to open my door and head inside.

What...was that?

Chapter 5
CAS

"Well, well, look at that li'l smile," Alex says, flopping onto a couch next to me in the break room at Elite 8 Studios. "Have a good scene, boo?"

I snort, finishing my bottled water before answering. "It was fine."

Alex raises a brow. "Just fine? I'd think being the filling in a Teddy-and-Felix sandwich would be more than fine."

I huff a laugh. The orgasm was good, sure, but... "I had a date Saturday night."

Alex gasps, flipping onto his stomach to see me better. "Do tell."

A grin takes over my face as I think about a certain barista-slash-nurse. "I went to the gym with Dixon last week, like you suggested."

Alex's expression turns thoughtful. "Aaand?"

"And then we went for coffee."

A smirk lifts the corner of his lips. "Aaand?"

"And I met Jason."

"A-ha!" he says, springing onto his knees and leaning toward me over the arm of the couch. "I knew it! Tell me *everything*, sugar beau."

"How did you know?" I ask, chuckling as Alex bounces in his seat. "That I'd like him, I mean."

I wasn't entirely certain Alex's intention *was* to set me up, but he's all but confirmed it now.

Alex waves a hand through the air. "Psht. I know these things. Now give Mama the goods."

He moves his hand in a *gimme* gesture, and I huff another laugh, twirling the cap of my water bottle between my fingers as my mind drifts over the events of Saturday night. "We've only gone on one date, but I'm seeing him again tomorrow. He's...nice," I say. "I like that."

"Nice," Alex repeats, looking at me a little dubiously. "*Just* nice?"

"That's not what I mean," I say, trying to find the right words. "The date was more than nice, but he's...he feels good, you know? It doesn't feel like he has ulterior motives when he looks at me."

Alex's face falls slightly. "Oh, honey."

"What?" I ask, my heart rate kicking up.

My coworker swings his feet to the ground, and then he's closing the couple steps between us and wrapping his arms around me. He hugs me surprisingly tightly for such a small person. "I'm sorry you've had that happen to you. No one deserves to be used."

His words hit sharply. Is that what it was? People using me?

I knew that, in a way. That people wanted me for my face or my body or my family's connections, even. But it's different hearing it broken down into one small, succinct word.

Used.

"Thanks, Alex," I finally say, wondering why he's the first person to ever tell me he's sorry for it. My throat burns a little as he steps back.

"You deserve more, okay?" he says, giving my arm a squeeze. "Don't settle for less than you're worth."

And what am I worth?

It's not a question I'm sure I know the answer to.

"I need to get going," I tell Alex, checking the time. I want to swing by Hyped before Jason's shift ends.

"Fine, fine," he says, sprawling back onto his couch as I get out of my chair. "But you better let me know how things go with that cute barista. Don't make me come after you, boo."

"Wouldn't dream of it," I say with a chuckle.

Alex blows me a kiss as I walk out of the break room, and I smile to myself. The guys here are pretty great.

As I'm making my way down the hall toward the front of the building, Teddy steps out from the small on-site gym. "Hey, Cas," he calls, beelining my way.

I stop and wait. "Hey, Teddy. What's up?"

Teddy, whose moniker and real name are one and the same, comes over with a towel around his neck. He looks every bit the part of a teddy bear, from his bigger stature to his brown hair, beard, and furry chest. The guy has worked here for years, and he's been genuinely nice to me ever since I started up half a year ago.

He's the type of person who can set someone at ease with a smile. Like he does now.

"I wanted to make sure you're feeling okay," he says.

I blink. "I'm fine," I answer slowly. "Why wouldn't I be?"

His smile is gentle, but his brow lifts slightly. "I went kind of hard on you today. Are you sore at all?"

"Oh," I say, realizing what he's asking. A laugh breaks free. "No, my asshole is fine. Thanks for checking."

"All right, good," he says, chuckling with me. "In that case, I'll see you later?"

"Yeah, have a good one."

"You, too," Teddy says, squeezing my shoulder before walking off toward the locker room.

I shake my head. Who would have thought I'd end up working in porn, of all things, with a bunch of guys who are so thoughtful and nice?

And what would they *think if they knew?*

My stomach bunches. My parents, my siblings...would they be disappointed in me yet again? Do I really care at this point? I like working at the studio. The people inside this building have been more accepting of me than the whole of my dad's company. I don't feel out of place here. I don't feel like I have to live up to some impossible standard.

I won't feel guilty about that.

When I get outside, my car takes a minute to start, and I briefly wonder if I'm going to have to replace it soon. But then it roars to life and I'm on my way, swinging by a small meat and cheese shop nearby. I pick out a round of brie and some nice-looking crackers and get back on the road. Ten minutes later, I'm parking behind Hyped, anticipation making my insides bubble as I think about the barista within.

I don't see him at first when I step into the coffee shop. It's early afternoon, so the place isn't particularly busy, but there are a couple people seated nearby, working on laptops, and the rich scent of coffee fills my nose. Marley gives me a smile as I approach the counter and says something too quietly for me to hear. But then, there he is—Jason—turning around with a carton of milk in his hand. His eyes widen when he catches sight of me, gaze dropping to my lips as I give him a grin.

"Hi, Jason," I say, leaning up against the counter.

"Um, hey," he responds, brushing his bangs aside. His beanie is dark green today, and it brings out the color of his eyes. It looks nice.

"I brought you something," I tell him, holding out the brie and small package of crackers.

His head rocks back, and he looks...stunned. I frown, but then he steps forward, hand hovering over mine for a moment before he takes the gift. "I, uh...you got these for me?"

"Yeah," I answer. "You ordered two dishes with cheese on Saturday night, so I took a gamble. Thought you might like it."

He blinks down at the brie. "Yeah," he says quietly. "I, uh... I do like cheese."

"Good," I breathe out, relieved to hear I got it right. "You look nice in green, by the way. We still on for tomorrow night?" It's the one night a week, apart from weekends, that Jason doesn't have class, lab, or clinicals.

He swallows before meeting my gaze. "Yeah. Tomorrow."

"Great. Have a good day, Jason. Marley," I add, giving the woman a nod and a smile. Her lips are tucked between her teeth.

I'm halfway to the door when Jason calls out, "Cas. Your pants. They, uh, that's a nice wash."

When I turn back around, Jason's head is down, hand over his eyes. I give him a big smile, even if he can't see it. "Thanks, Jason. See you later."

He waves, staring at his shoes, and then I'm out the door. Today isn't one of the days I head to the firm. I work three days a week at Kinsley Richman and film a handful of scenes a month at Elite 8 Studios. I'm not exactly raking in the cash, but

I've never cared about that. I'm perfectly content in my small apartment, making do with my small paycheck. I *could* live off the balance in my bank account and not bother working at all, but I try not to touch that money, seeing as I've done nothing to deserve it apart from being born to rich parents. It's there if I need it, but I can't decide if that's reassuring or...a guilty burden I never agreed to carry.

Since I don't have work this afternoon, I head to one of my favorite places. Neddy's Rec is a community space open to teens and volunteering adults. The first time I stumbled there was by accident. I saw the basketball courts outside, went to ask about a membership, and was laughed kindly at by the woman up front who told me I didn't have to pay a thing, so long as I was a decent person with a clean record.

Queenie, Neddy's daughter, is here again as I walk through the front door. Her box braids shift over her shoulders as she raises her head, and purple-painted lips rise into a smile.

"Well, if it isn't my favorite person," she says, her voice booming through the lobby.

I shake my head, although there's a smile on my face as I walk closer. "Your favorite?" I challenge, positive that's not true. I only see the rec center's manager once a week at most.

"Accept the compliment, love," she says, reaching over the counter once I'm close enough.

I embrace her arm, hand near her elbow, as has become tradition, and she squeezes my forearm in kind before letting go.

"Hoops today?" she asks, eyes slipping down to the gym bag in my hand.

"Yep. I have some energy to spare, so..." I shrug, and Queenie laughs.

"You boys always have energy to spare," she says. "Get on, then." I'm a few steps away when she adds, "Marshall is here today."

"Thanks for the heads-up," I tell her, heading off down the hall toward the locker room. The space is empty, and I plop my bag onto a bench before unzipping it so I can change into my workout clothes. Once ready, I shove the bag into an empty locker and snap a padlock into place, fingers grazing over the peeling metal on the locker door. The entire bank of lockers is a little rusty, in fact, and the bench seat nearby is pulling from the ground, the bottom having eroded around the bolts securing it to the floor.

Deciding to swing by the front again before heading out back to the basketball courts, I find Queenie where I left her.

"Hey, Queenie?" I ask cautiously.

She looks up at me, a frown on her face. "What is it?"

"Do you..." I pause, hoping my question isn't rude. "Do you accept donations?"

Her frown turns pensive. "Of course. We operate primarily through donor funding, as well as some grants."

"How would I go about making a donation?"

Queenie's expression smooths out, and she gives me a soft smile. "We have a form. Here," she says, pulling one from the desk and setting it on the surface, turning it toward me as I approach. "You can fill this out, and I'll make a copy for your taxes."

"Great, thanks," I tell her, accepting a pen. "I can write the check before I go."

"That's fine, love," she tells me, giving my hand a pat.

Once I've filled out the form, I pass it back her way. Queenie stares at it for a long moment, not saying a word, and I crane my neck to look at the paper, trying to make sure I didn't miss something.

"Is this right?" she asks me, turning it back my way and pointing to the dollar amount I filled in.

"Yes?" I say.

She looks at it again and then back at me. "There's not an extra zero. Or two?"

"No," I tell her.

"You can afford this?" she asks me evenly, and I'm not sure if she's concerned about my savings or thinks I might be lying to her.

So I answer, simply, "Yes."

She lets out a big breath before setting down the form and coming around the desk toward me. Queenie towers over me by an inch, but her arms are gentle as she tugs me into a hug. I return the gesture, a little bewildered.

When Queenie steps back, she places her hands on my cheeks. A maternal gesture. "Thank you, sweet boy. We'll be able to do a lot of good with this."

"Yeah?" I ask, warmth suffusing my chest.

"Yes. Now get on out of here before I start crying," she says, stepping back behind the desk.

I chuckle a little, feeling good and a little floaty. The sensation stays with me as I head outside, the desert sun beating atop my head. One of the two basketball courts is occupied by a group of older teens playing streetball, their calls and good-natured jeering rising above the sound of nearby passing cars. The second court has one occupant. Marshall. I head that way, and the teen looks up at me, scowling.

"Hey, Marshall," I call, coming around the tall fence that lines the court.

"Play with the other guys," he calls back, taking a shot from the center line. The ball hits the rim, bounces away from the net, and Marshall jogs after it.

"I'd rather play with you," I tell him, earning another scowl.

Marshall has never been friendly toward me, but he reminds me a lot of Dixon, wearing his attitude as a defense. I don't know enough about the seventeen-year-old to know if I'm right, but his reception doesn't bother me. He doesn't know me, not really. I'm just a guy that comes around to shoot hoops sometimes. Marshall has been coming here for years, as Queenie told me.

Neddy's is a safe space for anyone in town.

"Horse?" I suggest.

He doesn't respond verbally, just takes a shot from the three-point line. When the ball swooshes through the net, he jogs over, grabs it, and tosses it my way.

With a smile on my face, I mimic his position and take my shot.

"H," Marshall says triumphantly when I miss.

"Yeah, yeah," I say lightly. "H. I'm still warming up. Don't count me out yet."

"Whatever," he says, but he takes another shot. And for the next half hour, Marshall and I play. I win once. He wins twice. But that floaty feeling never quite lets up, and when I drop that check off to Queenie at the front desk and get a big, beaming smile in return, I wonder if maybe there *is* a way for me to help people, after all.

Chapter 6

JASON

"Hngh," I groan, smoothing down a piece of my hair that's trying to achieve space flight. "Fuck it."

I grab a beanie—the green one—and smash it over my head.

Brad watches me, amused, from atop my mattress. "This is fascinating."

"You're not helping," I moan.

"You usually have more chill than this," he says. *Unhelpfully*. "You must really like this guy. Or is it the tight clothes?"

I glare at my friend. "You know that's not it."

"Yeah, you've explained as much..." he says contemplatively, rolling onto his back and tossing my pillow into the air. He catches it and tosses it again. "But I can't really relate. If I'm interested in a girl, it's because my dick has given his stamp of approval first."

"I don't even want to know what your dick is stamping," I mutter.

"My body and my brain are in sync, you know?" he goes on.

I sigh, plopping onto the end of the bed. "Such a difficult life for you allosexuals."

Brad abandons his pillow-tossing and rolls toward me, grabbing me around the waist and crushing me in a hug. "It'll be okay, Birdie," he says into my hip. "You'll find that person your dick approves of. The one who will return your interest."

"That was...almost sweet," I admit, throat stupidly tight.

Brad squeezes me harder. "And then you'll *bone*," he whispers.

I shove him off me, ignoring his cackling as I get up and check my reflection in the mirror. *Shit*, is that a pimple? No, just a smudge. *Thank God*.

"Be honest with me," Brad says, suddenly at my back. He looks at me in the mirror, hands on my shoulders. "Is the potential there? With Cas?"

"Yeah," I say, blowing out a breath. "The potential is there."

Brad nods, giving me a squeeze before backing off. When there's a knock at the door, I barely jump.

"I got it," I say.

"Need me to feed Amadeus tonight?" he asks.

"No, he ate earlier," I tell my friend on my way out of the room.

When I open the front door, Cas is standing on the other side of the threshold, a smile on his handsome face and a scarf looped loosely around his neck. He's wearing a long-sleeved shirt today and gray jeans, and I'm *fairly* certain I can see his dick print. So as soon as Brad appears in my peripheral vision, coming toward the door, I grab my jacket and barrel out of the apartment, essentially plastering myself against Cas's front.

"Hi," he says in happy surprise, hands grabbing my arms.

"Hi," I squeak, regaining my equilibrium and taking a small step back. I hastily shut the door before pulling on my jacket. "Ready to go?"

Cas nods, and, taking my hand, we walk down the hall. My heart starts to calm as soon as Cas's fingers thread through mine, and he looks over at me, eyes skimming up and down. It doesn't feel as...*blatant* as some once-overs do. His assessment is softer, and it sets me at ease.

"So this place is just down the road?" Cas asks as we reach the lobby.

I picked the restaurant tonight. A casual mom-and-pop Italian eatery I frequent a few times a month.

"Yeah, a couple blocks," I answer. "That okay?"

He nods quickly, holding the door open while I walk through. It's cooler tonight, dipping into the high fifties, and I shiver a little as the air catches my exposed skin. We've only taken a handful of steps when Cas lets go of my hand to pull the scarf off his neck. Before I can figure out what's happening, he's looping it over my head and settling it against my skin.

"What...what are you doing?" I ask as he stands back, adjusting the tail ends until he's satisfied.

"You looked cold," he answers.

I was, but... "Won't *you* be cold?"

Cas shakes his head, reclaiming my hand. "Nah. I brought it for you."

My world tilts a little to the side as Cas leads me down the sidewalk.

"Where are we going?" he asks after a minute.

I huff a laugh, coming to a stop and turning us in the other direction. "This way."

Cas grins at me. We chat about our day on the short walk to the restaurant. About my shift at Hyped and the shipment of bad milk I had to send back to the supplier. About Cas's siblings, who I learn work at their father's company, same as Cas. Before I know it, we're stepping through the doors.

Mandy, one of the hostesses I recognize, looks up at our arrival, her smile going big and bright. Her eyes latch immediately onto Cas.

"Hi," she says all breathily. "Table for one?"

Oh, Jesus.

I cough, and Mandy's eyes skip over to me.

"Oh! Hi, Jason," she says.

"Mandy," I mutter.

"There's two of us," Cas corrects gently.

She grabs two menus. "Right this way."

Cas's hand lands on my back as we walk, and the tightness in my chest uncorks, just that easily. Mandy leads us to a booth, setting the menus on the table before letting us know a server will be with us shortly. She nearly topples a chair when she backs away, eyes on Cas's ass.

I grit my teeth, but he doesn't even notice, as far as I can tell. He's too busy unwinding my scarf—*his* scarf—from around my neck.

"So, what's good here?" he asks, settling into the booth across from me.

"All the things," I answer seriously. Cas laughs, and it's such a nice, sweet sound that I find myself smiling with him.

As he peruses the menu, however, his expression goes a little...vacant.

"Something wrong?" I ask.

He shakes his head, clearing the expression. "Nah. I was just thinking about my parents' upcoming anniversary. Sorry, it's nothing."

I don't like how easily he dismissed whatever was on his mind. It was clearly troubling him.

"It's not nothing if it's bugging you," I tell him. "Wanna unload?"

Cas looks at me for a moment before setting down his menu. "My siblings and I are planning a party for my parents' fortieth anniversary. And I'm happy to, but…" He cocks his head to the side, as if weighing his words. "It's just so *much*."

"Really fancy?" I guess.

"Like you wouldn't believe. It's so lavish, and sometimes I just wonder *why?* What's the point of it all?" His voice softens when he says, "I don't want my life to be about appearances. I want it to mean something, you know?"

"Yeah," I say a little weakly. "I know what you mean."

He nods, like he's happy enough with that, and the sadness clears off his face. He gives me a smile as he sets his arms on the table, palms close together and facing downward, almost as if he's reaching for me. The moment is interrupted by the waitress arriving with our waters. She takes our order before heading off, but Cas doesn't once move his arms. A little hesitantly, I place my hand on his, and he turns up his palm, smiling widely.

"So, uh, your siblings," I say. "You get along with them?"

"Yeah," Cas says, fingers toying with mine lightly. The sensation sends a shiver down my spine. "Leo's the oldest. Leonidas."

"Wait," I cut in. "Leonidas?"

"Yeah," he says with a huff of laughter. "There's this tradition in our family of really pretentious names."

I laugh at that, and Cas grins.

"Charlotte got off easy," he says. "My mom won naming rights for her over a game of pool."

"You're kidding."

He shakes his head. "Dead serious."

"Then your name…?" I ask, trailing off.

He gives me a rueful smile. "Cassius."

"Holy shit," I mutter.

He laughs again. "I know. It's pretty bad."

"No," I breathe, swallowing. "That's, uh. I like that." *Cassius.*

He smiles at me. "Lucky me, then. Leo's the oldest," he says. "Char's right between us. They're good to me, all things considered."

"What do you mean by that?" I ask, frowning.

He shrugs, the motion jostling my hand in his. "Just—I've always been the odd one out. But they look out for me. They're never cruel."

My heart thumps a little too hard at that. "People are cruel to you?"

"I mean, my family is smart. All of them," he says. "And I'm... I don't *fit.* I never have. And I hear what people say about me, even if they think I don't. I know they think I'm pretty and empty. My name—Cassius? It literally means hollow."

He taps his head, and I bristle. Hard.

"Fuck that," I say a little too loudly.

Cas's eyes widen, and I can feel a few stares on the side of my head, but I don't give a shit.

"You're not *hollow,*" I say, lowering my voice. I realize my hand is clamping his, and I loosen my grip. "You're not... You're..."

"It's okay, Jason," he says lightly. "I know what I am and what I'm not. I'm *not* smart enough to get by in the same world my family runs in. And I'm okay with that."

"Yeah, but people shouldn't talk shit about you just because you..." I don't even know how to finish my sentence. It makes me too mad to even think the words *aren't smart enough,* like that's a measure of a person.

"Because I barely graduated high school?" Cas fills in, not having the same problem as me. "Barely scraped through college? I was supposed to follow Leo's footsteps and become an architect like our dad. But I flunked too many classes for that and had to switch gears. I've failed at plenty in my life."

"It doesn't matter," I say.

"I appreciate that you think that, Jason," he says smoothly, "but to most people, it matters."

"Yeah, well. Fuck that," I mutter.

He chuckles lightly. "You said that already."

"And I mean it."

Cas squeezes my hand, moving out of the way when the waitress arrives with our food. It takes me a minute to find my tongue.

"Did your boss give you the name Himbo?" I ask, my tone tight.

Cas shakes his head, swallowing his bite of pasta before answering. "No, of course not. Jerome is a great guy. The name was there when I applied for the job. I just happened to fit the casting."

I huff an angry noise, and Cas chuckles slightly.

"You're cute when you're growly," he says.

And that shuts me right the hell up. The look Cas gives me when I blush is...a little hot. A little pleased. A lot smug.

"Tell me about your mom," Cas says, and I let the rest of it go. At least for now.

"She's great," I say. "Warm and loving. She lives alone now, but I visit when I can. She never makes me feel guilty when it's been a while, though. She understands how busy I am."

Cas nods for me to go on, and I do. It's effortless, I realize, talking to Cas. It's easier than it has any right to be, considering we barely know one another.

It's a good hour later when Cas and I finally call it quits, our food long gone. We pass Mandy on the way out of the restaurant, and she tells Cas to come again soon. It sounds so suggestive I snarl, just a little. She blinks in shock, and I feel better.

Cas takes my hand once we're on the sidewalk, and we walk in companionable silence. His scarf is a warm, comforting presence around my neck, the same as his hand in mine. But try as I might, I can't get his earlier words out of my head. I vow to keep it to myself, but by the time we're walking up the stairs of my building, I can't hold it in anymore. I stop at the landing between the first and second floors, and Cas comes to a halt a step down from me, looking up at me curiously.

"In the time I've known you," I start, "which hasn't been very long at all, I've seen you hold the door for no less than six people. I've seen you return a twenty-dollar bill that fell out of someone's wallet. I've seen you stop on the street to help an old lady who dropped her cane, and I've seen you smile at every single person you've passed. I don't care what other people say. You are better than them. You're better than *all* of them."

Cas takes a single, slow breath, whiskey eyes dragging between my own. "Thank you, Jason."

"Yeah," I breathe, nodding once before I grab his hand and continue up the stairs.

When we get to my door, my pulse hasn't quite come down, and I'm not ready to let Cas go. He makes me...warm. And off-balance, but not in a bad way. I blame those facts for what comes out of my mouth next.

"Do you want to meet my snake?" I all but blurt.

Cas stops beside me, smile going a little crooked. "Your snake?"

"Yeah." Anything to keep him with me for longer. People like meeting pets, right?

Cas takes a step closer to me, fingers trailing along my—*his*—scarf. "Okay, Jason," he says quietly, eyes on my lips.

"He, uh...he's not very big," I babble. "If you're worried about that."

"I'm not," he says simply, eyes casing my face.

"Okay. Yeah, okay," I mutter, breaking his gaze and grabbing the door handle. Inside the apartment, I shed my jacket and scarf before pointing to the living room. "Why don't you get comfortable? I'll be right back."

"You want me on the couch?" he asks, head tilted just a bit.

"Yeah. Make yourself at home."

"Okay," he says, leaning down to untie his shoes.

I watch him for a moment before turning and heading down the hall to grab Amadeus. Just bringing a guy I maybe, kinda, *definitely* like home to meet my scale-baby. Yeah, no big deal.

Amadeus is curled up at one end of his cage when I pop the lid. His tongue flicks out, but he doesn't move, sated as he is from his recent meal.

"Sorry, buddy," I tell him, scooping him into my palm. He's not very large—just under two feet long—and his tail wraps around my forearm as I lift him up. "This won't take long, and then you can go back to sleep, okay?"

He flicks his tongue again, and I blow out a breath as I head out of my room. *If he doesn't like your snake, it's okay,* I remind myself. Cas seemed eager enough to meet Amadeus, though, so maybe it'll be fine.

"So you don't have to touch him if you don't want," I say, rounding into the living room. "But he won't hurt you, so—" My words come to an abrupt halt when I set eyes on Cas, and I promptly choke on my tongue.

My date is spread out, hands behind his head, one leg bent up on the couch cushions, the other hanging off, foot flat on the floor. And he's *naked*. 100 percent, stark, buck-naked. He could not *be* more nude than he is in this moment. *All* of his goods are on display.

And my cock, my traitorous cock *twitches* because I've jerked off to this very buck-naked man before. It's not the first time I've seen him in this way, and my body reacts like muscle memory, primed, assuming release is on the horizon. But the idea of actually sleeping with this man is still as inconceivable to me as him being naked in my living room in the first place.

Which begs the goddamn *what the fuck* question...

"Where are your clothes?"

Chapter 7
CAS

Jason turns around almost as soon as he sees me, and I stare at his back in confusion as he asks me where my clothes are, his tone frantic.

"Did you...want to undress me yourself?" I ask.

He shakes his head, turning like he's about to look back at me, but then he faces firmly away again. "No? What? Why would I..." A long pause, and another head shake. "Why would you think I..."

Okay, clearly there's some sort of miscommunication going on here.

"You don't want to fuck me?" I ask.

He visibly startles. "What?" he all but screeches.

"You invited me in to see your snake," I say slowly. "And told me to get comfortable on your couch."

Jason holds out his arm, enough for me to see the small brown snake wrapped around it.

"You have...a real snake," I say in disbelief. "I thought—"

"Clearly," he says.

And *holy fuck*. Holy *fuck*. I really am an idiot.

"Jason," I say, hustling upright and grabbing my clothes off the floor. "I didn't mean to... I wouldn't have gotten naked if I..." I curse, the words getting all muddled in my mind.

Jason laughs a little harshly, and my gut sinks. I pull on my underwear and jeans quickly, followed by my shirt, and then I scrub my hands over my face.

"I'm sorry," I say, scooping my keys off the coffee table. "I'll go."

"No. Don't," he says staccato, and I pause. "Are you covered?"

"Yeah," I answer.

He spins back around, snake held near his chest. He holds it up a little. "Uh, this is Amadeus."

"Your snake."

He nods. "My snake."

Christ.

My shoulders slump. "Did I completely fuck this up?" I ask him, willing my eyes to stay dry.

Jason looks down at the snake on his arm for a long moment, his chest rising and falling. Finally, he shakes his head and meets my eye. "No. But I think we need to talk."

"Yeah, all right," I mumble.

"I'm gonna put Amadeus away, and then I'll be back out," he says. "Just, uh, wait here?"

"Of course."

Jason leaves without another word, and I fall back onto the couch, hiding my face under my palms. He wanted me to meet his snake. His *actual fucking snake.*

Char is right. I'm hopeless.

When Jason reappears, he walks briskly into the kitchen. "Do you want water? Cola?" he calls out.

"Water would be good, thanks."

He comes back with two bottled waters in hand and offers one. Once I accept it, he takes a seat next to me, tugging his beanie off and scrubbing his hair. It flies in every direction, the blonde a multitude of different hues.

"I'm sorry I freaked out," he says.

"Understandable," I counter, my glum tone matching my mood. "I just assumed you wanted to have sex with me. Most people..." That's what most people want from me.

"Yeah," he says, glancing my way before dropping his beanie onto the coffee table. "Everyone wants to fuck you. That's glaringly obvious."

He twists his hands together before slumping against the back of the couch, his leg bouncing.

"Does that make you mad?" I ask, curious about the strain in his body.

"I mean, they could be a little less obvious about it when you're on a date with me, you know?" he gripes.

And holy shit. He's jealous.

I can't help the smile that takes over my face, but as soon as I remember the reason we're even *having* this conversation, it slips away.

"But you don't want to have sex with me," I say. Because I'm pretty sure that's the truth. Most people who *do* wouldn't blanch and turn away the way Jason did when he caught me naked.

He blows out a breath. "It's complicated."

"Explain it to me?"

He nods immediately. "Yeah. So, I think I'm demi? Demi-sexual?"

I've heard that before. "That's where you're not attracted to someone unless you have feelings for them first?" I check.

He teeters his hand a little. "Sort of? There's not really a cut-and-dry manual for these things, but all I know is that I've only ever wanted to have sex with two people."

"Two people," I repeat.

"Yeah," he says, swallowing, meeting my gaze fully. "Do you want to hear about this?"

"Please," I tell him, eager to understand.

"Okay, so, the first time was in high school. There was this new guy at school my senior year, and after a while, I started to feel differently toward him. I'd see him in the hall, and..."

"You'd pop a boner?" I fill in.

He huffs a laugh, looking a little more at ease than he did before. "Yeah. And that had never happened for me before."

"You'd never had an erection before then?" I ask, trying and possibly failing to keep the shock out of my tone.

"No, I had," he says, rolling his eyes a little. "But it was always a matter of *right time*, not *right person*. It was only physical. Does that make sense?"

"Sure. Just good old-fashioned horniness."

"Exactly," he says, smiling a bit now. "But with this guy, it was the first time I *wanted* someone. Wanted to be *with* someone in that way."

"Okay," I say, nodding for him to go on.

He swallows down some water before continuing. "I never told him, and then I graduated and didn't see him again."

"That's..." *Sad.*

There are plenty of people I come across who I find attractive but never talk to. Never see again after a single meeting or fleeting glance. But for Jason, it's different. A missed connection for him, when he's only had that feeling *twice*, is... Well, it makes me ache a little.

"And the other time?" I prompt gently.

He nods. "A girl in my study group during my sophomore year of nursing school. We'd been meeting at the library for months before things started to change."

"Did you tell her?" I ask.

He nods again. "That time, I did. I asked her out. She wasn't interested."

"I'm sorry, Jason."

He shrugs a little, like it isn't a big deal. But it feels like one.

It takes me a good long moment to realize if he's only ever wanted to have sex with two people but he didn't get the chance with either, there's a possibility he's *never* had sex. But it's not my place to pry.

"So, I think I'm demi," he says again. "And probably pansexual. I lean towards guys, though," he adds, almost an afterthought. "I find men more appealing, even if I'm not, you know..." He makes a gesture I take to mean *popping wood*.

I nod, uncapping my water and swallowing a few gulps. I'm not ace, so Jason's experience isn't my own. But I do understand what he means about finding someone appealing even if you're not exactly attracted to them. Girls are pretty; I've always thought so, which is why I tried dating a few. But the chemistry? It was never really there the same way it is with guys. I'm attracted to men, Jason included. The guys I'm interested in? I *want* them in a way that's deep, a simmering in my gut. It's carnal and almost desperate at times. It's an urge beyond simple release.

It's different at the studio, I've found. Having sex with my coworkers is more like scratching an itch, similar to picking someone up at a club. It's not that all-encompassing desire for *more* of that person.

I have that with Jason. I do want to know more, and I'd be lying if I said I didn't want his body, too. But it's second to wanting *him*, the person.

But for Jason... It's different.

I set my water down. "So what does that mean for us?" I ask him. "I'd never pressure you. Despite the whole naked couch thing," I hasten to add, and he reaches over, giving my arm a reassuring squeeze.

"I didn't think you would," he says softly. "But that's the thing. I, uh... I might not *ever* want that. With you."

My breath whooshes out of me.

"I'm sorry, Cas," he says, hand tightening on my arm. "I know that's shitty, and if I could change the way I'm hardwired—"

I shake my head quickly. "No. It's *fine*. It's..."

Honestly?

It's pretty damn neat. The people Jason wants, they're special. They're lucky that someone is taking the time to get to know them first. That someone is looking past the surface and wanting them for what's inside.

It's kind of magical.

"I think you're one of a kind, Jason," I say. The words sound cheesy as soon as they leave my lips, but Jason sucks in a breath, those green-hazel eyes locking onto me in a way that makes me feel like I did something right.

"You... Really?" he asks.

I nod, reaching tentatively for Jason's hand. He grabs on easily, and I turn his palm in mine, thinking about all the ways Jason uses these hands. At the coffee shop, sure, but beyond that, he uses them to help people. I wish I could see him in action at the hospital. I bet he'd be beautiful.

"It doesn't bother me that you don't want to have sex," I tell him, and his breath catches all over again. "And I'd like to see you again."

"You really want that?" he asks, sounding as if he doesn't believe me.

I nod, trying to figure out how to explain it to him. "I told you about getting the job at Elite 8 Studios." He bobs his head slightly, and I go on. "There was this guy I was dating at the time—my brother's friend, actually. We were seeing each other in secret because he wasn't out yet."

Jason's face tightens slightly, and I give his hand a squeeze.

"It didn't upset me at the time," I explain. "But then, well... It took me a while to realize he didn't have a problem if people knew he liked guys. It was just that he didn't want to be seen with *me*."

"Cas," Jason says softly.

"He sent me an email to break up with me," I admit, swallowing. "It had a link inside to an open casting call for a himbo. The job at Elite 8. He said that maybe I could finally make use of my talent."

Jason's mouth drops open, his hand tightening in mine. "That's such fucking *bullshit*," he hisses. "How *dare* he?"

I shrug a little. "Yeah. He wasn't a nice guy, really."

Jason sets his jaw. "Understatement."

"But I ended up going to that casting call," I continue, wanting him to understand. "Maybe to show him that his barb didn't bother me. Maybe because I wanted a change. I don't know, but I got the job, like I told you." I take a breath. "My point is every relationship comes with risk. You never know if it's going to pan out in the long run. So *no*, it doesn't bother me that you look at me and don't want sex. Plenty of people want that from me, Jason. Simon did. People before him. People after. But none of my relationships have ended well for me, and I want something different. So if you'd like to try this dating thing, I'd really like that, too."

We're both silent for a long minute, and I give Jason the time to think things through. Finally, he says, "And if I never..."

"Want me?" I fill in before shrugging. "Then you don't. I'm willing to take that chance."

"Fuck, Cas," he says, the words all breath.

I huff a small laugh. "Is that a fuck *yes* or fuck *no*?"

"Yeah, damn it. Yes. I'd like to date you," he says, and my chest fills like a helium balloon.

"Yeah?"

"Yeah," he says firmly. "Just... If Brad says something to you about your nipples, ignore him, okay? He's a doof, but I'm stuck with him. That means you're stuck with him, too."

"Okay," I say, my grin stretching wide.

"Ugh, he's going to give me so much shit about tonight." He groans before startling. "Oh, my God. No. *Nooo*. I told you my snake wasn't big. Before, when I invited you in and you thought..."

I can't help but laugh, and Jason drops his head back, muttering words I can't quite make out.

"The size of your snake doesn't matter to me," I assure him.

He pins me with an almost hard look, and my cock jumps. I know it's not the time, and I know he doesn't mean to be looking at me like *that*. But that edge of steel in his expression is such a far cry from the shy, somewhat insecure guy he initially came off as that my body flushes hot in an instant.

"My snake isn't *small*," he says. "Not that it *does* matter, but..." He grumbles out a prolonged "*argh*" before huffing a breath through his nose. "We're going to pretend it never happened, okay? You kissed me at the door, and then you left, and there was no talk about *snakes* and no manspreading on the couch. We had a perfectly normal evening with all of our clothes on. No dicks were stamped."

"Jason," I say lightly.

"Yeah?"

"I had a really good time on our date," I tell him.

His shoulders soften. "Yeah. Me too."

"And I'm looking forward to the next one."

"Me too," he says again, eyes lingering on my lips. I bring his hand up to my mouth, kissing the back of it gently, and his breath leaves him in a little puff.

"So, um," I can't help but ask. "What's a dick stamp?"

Jason's groan has me breaking into another round of laughter.

Chapter 8

JASON

"Hey, Jason."

I look up from where I'm crouched in the storage room, grabbing a couple of bedpans for my evening patients. "Hey, Zeek."

Zeek leans against the doorjamb, arms crossed casually. "Haven't seen you in a while."

I snort a laugh. "Maybe because we're scheduled in different departments most of the time?"

"Fair enough," he says.

I stand up, grabbing a new box of gloves from the top shelf. When I glance over, Zeek's eyes are sitting low, like he's looking at—

"Oh my God. Are you checking out my stomach?" I squeak.

Zeek's eyes meet mine, and he grins a little sheepishly. "What can I say? You have a nice stomach."

"I..." *Fucking Brad*. "What do you want, Zeek?" I ask, skirting past the man.

He follows me down the hall, cocking his hip against the counter once we reach the nurses' station. "Just figured I'd see if you've had a change of heart since our last date."

My tension dissipates as I take in my coworker. He's in blue scrubs, a hopeful smile on his face, and despite the weird stomach fetish, I can't be mad at Zeek. He's a nice guy, always has been. It's not his fault my libido has no interest in him.

"Sorry, Zeek, but no," I tell him. "Besides, I'm seeing someone."

"Damn," he says sadly, and honestly, I'm surprised he's so disappointed. I didn't realize he liked me that much. "Can't blame a guy for tr—"

"Cas?" I ask in shock, cutting Zeek's words off. Because *what*? Why is Cas here?

The man is coming to a stop in front of the nurses' station, a smile on his face, a small box in his hand, and despite the fact that he looks unharmed, my brain kicks into trauma-mode, and I stride right over to him.

"Is everything all right?" I ask in alarm, feeling over his arms and then lifting the hem of his shirt, checking his stomach. No obvious cuts or contusions. I spin him around, checking his back.

"Jason," Cas says, my name rolling off his tongue like laughter.

"Where does it hurt?" I ask, tugging him to face me again and palpating his neck. *Lymph nodes aren't swollen.* I sweep my hands over his chest next, and Zeek makes a garbled sound from behind me.

"I'm fine," Cas says, eyes twinkling. Why the hell does he look so amused?

"You're not *fine*. If you were *fine*, you wouldn't be at the hospital," I tell him.

He cocks his head. "I came to give you this," he says, holding out the small box in his hand.

"The fuck?"

Cas laughs again. "Cream cheese pastries," he says. "You mentioned earlier that you lost part of your dinner to the floor, so I thought you might be hungry."

I gape. I did say that. Cas and I have been texting a lot the past few days, but I never expected him to show up here with an offering of cheese pastries because he thought I might be hungry. Who *does* that?

Before I can come up with a suitable response—*do you see babies as part of your ten-year plan?*—Cas notices Zeek.

"Hi," Cas says, holding out his hand. "I'm Cas."

Zeek practically trips over his feet in his haste to grab Cas's hand. "Zeek," he says, sounding out of breath.

Oh, fucking hell.

"Zeek is my coworker," I say, pushing his hand away when he starts to lick his lips. I grab Cas's hand in my own. "He was just *leaving.*"

"Okay, yeah," Zeek says, taking a step back. He runs into the counter and stutter-steps to the side. "Um, yep. Bye."

"Nice to meet you," Cas says cheerfully.

Zeek wheezes before turning around and hustling away. *Traitor.*

"You brought me pastries?" I ask, still not quite believing that part.

Cas nods. "It wasn't entirely unselfish," he says, setting the box down on the counter. "I wanted to see you."

Have you ever eaten a handful of Pop Rocks and then downed some cola? The way it crackles and fizzes and expands, and you wonder, vaguely, if you're about to pop because it's too much?

Yeah, that.

If I thought Cas's intentions had anything to do with getting into my pants, it'd be easier to brush aside his sweet words and kind gesture. But I *know* Cas isn't trying to get into my pants. Because he's aware, right now, that isn't an option.

No, this is all Cas. Just... *Cas*.

"You're..." I manage.

He cocks his head a little, waiting patiently. His dark, chestnut-brown hair is artfully windblown. He's wearing an olive-green Henley that wraps snug around his torso and arms. His jeans are faded in a way that speaks of wear, not money. And his lips are just...*there*. They're just right there.

I lean up and press my mouth to his lightly, and Cas lets out a happy little hum. It's short and dry, the kiss, but it floats down into my belly like those Pop Rocks I ate as a child, and I *like* it. I like it a lot, the way he makes me feel.

When I drop back onto the balls of my feet, Cas is grinning at me. His hand comes up to fidget with a piece of my hair—probably a flyaway—and he looks like he could easily settle in right here, leaned against the counter, watching me work. But then a few other nurses walk by, a phone starts to ring, and Cas straightens, letting his hand drop.

"You probably have stuff to do, huh?" he says.

And yeah. Yeah, I do.

"We still on for tomorrow?" I ask.

"You bet. See you then, Jason."

"Bye," I breathe.

Cas gives me a final smile before turning and walking off. A head pops out of a doorway down the hall when Cas passes, and I huff before spinning around and grabbing the bedpans that are awaiting me. My eyes catch on the box Cas left, and I tuck it under my arm.

Patients first. Cheese pastries from the cute porn star I'm dating—because apparently that's a thing now—second.

"Mom? Hey, what's up?" I ask, phone at my ear as I step out of my car.

I can practically hear the shrug in her voice. "Oh, nothing much. Just couldn't sleep, and I figured you'd be awake still. Your shift over?"

"Yeah, I'm just getting home," I tell her.

"I won't keep you long, then. Classes going okay this semester? Are you getting enough sleep?"

I chuckle a little, taking the stairs up to the second floor of my apartment building. "Not sure about that last one, but classes are good. Clinicals are good. Job at the coffee shop is good."

She hums. "I wish you'd let me help cover your schooling. Then you wouldn't have to work at the coffee shop on top of everything else you're doing."

"We've talked about this," I remind her. "You'd have to take out loans, and I don't want you doing that." My mom has enough debt after my dad's final years. "I'm fine. It's just one more year."

She sighs a little. "I love you, Jaybird. You're such a fighter, you know that?"

"You've told me enough," I say, unlocking my door and heading inside the apartment. The lights are off, which means Brad is probably already in bed, so I try to be quiet as I move around.

"Well it's true," she says. "I'll let you get some sleep. But next time you're available, let me take you out to lunch, all right?"

"Sure, Mom," I tell her softly. "Love you."

"Love you, too. Bye, honey."

With that, my mom clicks off the call, and I make my way into the bathroom. I'm bone tired after my shift, and in only seven short hours, I'll have to turn around and head back to the hospital for a long day of clinicals, followed by my date with Cas. So, with bed calling, I rush through my shower, brush my teeth, say goodnight to Amadeus, and crash onto my mattress.

Normally, this is the point where I'd be out like a light. But tonight, I can't fall asleep. My mind keeps whirring, and, for whatever reason, my dick is half-hard.

I look down at it. "Not now," I whisper-hiss. "I need my rest."

It doesn't listen, so I slam my head back against the pillow and think about bedpans and a million other gross things like draining abscesses. But try as I might, my chub won't abate.

"Ugh."

I slip a hand down under my waistband, and...yeah, okay. Maybe I could use a release. It only takes three strokes to work myself to full hardness, and the nice little *zing* that travels down my spine feels too good to ignore. I set a quick pace, wanting to get myself off and fall asleep, but my dick is not happy about that, in no mood to be rushed.

"You're demanding, you know that?" I say, rolling toward my nightstand. I grab the lube from inside and kick off my sheet, planting my legs wide. My curtains are drawn, but the streetlights shine softly against the thin material, giving the room the tiniest glow by which to see. As soon as I wrap my wet fist around my dick, it glistens under the lamplight.

I relax back, stroking myself slowly, every tug a measured, euphoric drag that spreads heat up and down my shaft. My skin feels tight, restlessness stirring beneath, but even so, every time I pick up the pace, my orgasm edges away.

So I slow down. Roll my palm over my crown. Flit my fingers along the sensitive ridges of my cockhead. I grip myself tight, a smooth, slick ring traveling achingly slow down my shaft. Not for the first time, I wonder what it would feel like being inside a person this way. Having their body hug me tight. Feeling the heat of them, their pulse.

I have a toy, a masturbation sleeve, and yeah, it feels good. But I'm sure a real person is different.

The thing is, my curiosity is only that. Curiosity. It's not an urge. It's not this feeling that I need to go out and experience the real thing. Brad and I have talked about it before because my friend, being the lovable, clingy asshole he is, wanted to understand.

It's like... In theory, sex sounds great. I know what my hands and my toys can do, and there are even more possibilities with a person. If I *wanted* to go punch my V-card, I could. I could wait until I'm horny or put on some porn, and then find a person to fuck around with.

But I don't *want* to. It's not about saving myself or waiting for *the one*. It's the fact that I have zero urge to get physical with another person. That's only happened twice, and those urges did fade over time, when our paths naturally drifted apart. Rachel was over a year and a half ago, and since then, there's been nobody my dick has been interested in.

If I try to imagine myself with someone random, it's hard. Even thinking of Rachel now is this blurry image in my mind's eye because my attraction to her *did* fade. If you don't nurture a thing, it dies, right? At least, that's the way I see it. Thinking of having sex for the sake of having sex, not because I *want* to, has never sat right with me. It's this blurry, faceless thing in my head. It's even more indistinct than watching porn.

So what's the point? Yeah, I like to fantasize about it. About sliding inside a nice, warm body. About feeling muscle dimple beneath my fingertips. Seeing a flush creep across skin or sweat beading along someone's back. I like to imagine them rasping my name, like to wonder if they'd moan loudly or clutch the sheets to rein in their sounds. I like to think that, someday, I'll experience that for myself in a way that doesn't feel empty. That I'll find someone who fills the picture in my mind with color and shape, who turns that hazy *what if* into something concrete and real. That I'll want *them*. Just them. And they'll want me back.

But until then, I have my hand, and that's good enough for me.

My breath stutters as I drag my fist a little faster, my orgasm building now. I chase the height of it, releasing the tension in my grip every few strokes and then tightening again to feel the spark of pleasure. I avoid my crown, waiting, letting the cool air rush over my slick skin, drawing that budding tension to the surface. My hips fuck up off the bed, pushing my cock through my fist. *Little more, little more.* My breath comes short.

I'm close, really close, and for just a moment, I let my mind wander. I think...maybe? And I picture Cas, spread out naked on top of my couch. I think about the way he wants me but has never pushed. I think about the long lines of his body and the arguably perfect cut of his abs. I think about the shape of his cheekbones and jaw, even his temple and the dark hair spilling over it. I think about the way he smiles—most of all, I think about that smile. The shape of it. The comfort in it. Those lips, so puffy and kind. I wonder what those lips could do to me.

I picture Cas here with me on the bed. Picture myself sinking into the tight heat of his body. *Real* heat. And I can see it. For just a moment, I can see it.

My eyes fly open in surprise, and my breath leaves me on a gasp. I redouble my efforts, toes curling against the bedsheets, lightning crackling down my spine. My back arches and...*now*. I curl my palm over my cockhead, squeezing, rubbing in a circle as my other fist works my base. My teeth clamp over my lip as all that pressure shoots downward. It's heat and the crashing of waves, and *fuck, fuck, fuck*.

My hips jerk as my cum starts to coat the inside of my palm. I stroke myself through it, teeth indenting my lip to the point of pain. And as blinding stars coat my vision and those waves crash inside my ears, I think of whiskey-colored eyes and the gentle press of a palm against my back.

Chapter 9
CAS

"Yeesh, little brother. What did that crab cake ever do to you?"

Charlotte's eyes are wrinkled in amusement as I lift my gaze to hers, and she raises her mimosa to her lips, taking a dainty sip.

"Sorry," I mutter, setting down my fork.

"No need to apologize to me," she says. "I'm not the one you're mutilating with your fork. Everything all right?"

I look at the notepad on the table between us, covered in Char's neat scrawl. Every item for my parents' fortieth anniversary party is carefully listed there, three pages' worth thus far. We've been working on it all morning.

"Is this just for canapés?" I ask, pointing down at a startlingly high number. Why does tiny food cost so much?

My brother frowns. "Looks right. Why? Would you rather go with the fondue bar instead?"

"No, I—" I huff out a breath. "Couldn't we do something simpler?"

My siblings blink at me in unison.

"Maybe have tacos or something?" I go on.

Leo's head snaps back as if I'd slapped him. "*Tacos*? At a black-tie event?"

"It doesn't have to be black-tie," I point out.

"We already planned around it," Char says, watching me with appraising eyes. "What's going on, Cassius?"

I let out a groan. "I hate spending all this money."

"Are you short on cash?" Leo asks in concern.

"No, that's not it."

"It wouldn't be your money, anyway," Char puts in. "We'll use the family funds."

"That's not the point," I say, getting a little frustrated. "Like, look." I point at the notepad again. "Why do we need to spend thousands of dollars on gold-foil invites?"

Charlotte exchanges a glance with Leo. "I suppose we could ditch the embossing, if you feel that strongly about it," my sister says. "Did you like the fleur design? I think that one was a little less expensive."

Char starts to flip through the samples of stationery, and I groan into my hands.

"No," I say, dropping my palms to find both of my siblings watching me with concern. "We have all this money." I wave at the interior of the posh restaurant we're in for emphasis. "More money than we'll ever need in our lifetimes. Don't you ever want to do *more* with it?"

Char and Leo watch me blankly.

"Never mind," I say, stabbing a piece of crab cake onto my fork. It tastes delicious, but it feels a little like lead going down.

"Okay," Char says carefully. "Why don't we talk about musical selection, then?"

I nod along, feeling defeated.

When the three of us finally leave the restaurant, breaking into our respective vehicles, it's almost noon. I idly wonder what Jason has been doing at the hospital while I brunched with my siblings. What he's doing right now. Probably helping people. Maybe even saving lives.

Maybe it makes me a hypocrite, but I pull my phone from my pocket and order a variety of baked goods to be delivered to the staff in his wing of the hospital. Then, I set off toward Neddy's.

"So, arc you going to tell me where we're going?" Jason asks from the passenger seat of my car.

I glance over at him. We've only been on the road for five minutes, me having picked Jason up around seven, but apart from letting him know there would be food where we're going, I haven't told him any other details.

"Do you really want to know?" I ask. "Or do you like surprises?"

He thinks my question over, and I'm curious how he's going to respond. "Surprise would be okay," he finally answers.

I give him a swift grin before throwing on my turn signal and taking a right. "How was your day?"

"Long," he says. "Tiring."

"I can't imagine," I admit. Working two jobs the way he is? Well, one paying job and then nursing school. But still, it's a lot.

"You said you work part-time, right?" Jason asks.

I nod. "Few days a week at the firm and no more than once a week at the studio. Maybe I should buck up already and accept a full-time job at my dad's company, but the truth is

I can't imagine being there every day doing something I don't enjoy and am not even good at. And the money isn't exactly something I need."

I wince a little after I say that. I didn't mean to include that last part, but maybe it's good to get it out there. Never mind the fact that I've barely touched my inheritance, the point stands, and I haven't yet gauged Jason's thoughts on my nest egg. I'm well aware I'm privileged—the kind of privilege that involved a literal silver spoon as a child—but I'm also trying to figure out how to make *good* with what I've been given. I think I'm on my way, but most people either see me as an opportunity, or they think I'm elitist.

It would hurt if Jason fell into either of those categories. It's probably best to know now, before I get in too deep.

"I envy that," Jason says after only a moment. "Money is tight for me. I do all right, but it'll be nice once I graduate and can focus full-time on being a nurse. I don't blame you for not wanting to jump into a job you have no passion for. If it were an option for me, I probably wouldn't be working at Hyped."

"You don't think it makes me lazy? Or spoiled?" I ask, heart thumping as I wait for an answer. I pull the car to a stop at a red light and chance a glance over at Jason. His lips purse slightly.

"I've never once thought you either of those things," he says, and it feels like something inside of me unshackles. Like there's an audible click and then the clattering of metal, and I can *breathe*. "Wanting to be happy doesn't make you a bad person, Cas."

"Thanks, Jason," I say softly, stepping on the gas again once the line of vehicles in front of me starts to move.

He squeezes my thigh before reclaiming his hand.

It only takes another ten minutes to arrive at our destination. Jason looks around before giving me a questioning glance. "What is this?"

"It's an outdoor theater," I tell him. "Like a drive-in, except you go in on foot. They have a bunch of local food trucks set up for snacks and drinks, and I brought a blanket to sit on. They even have heaters. I checked."

Jason is quiet for a moment, his mouth open.

"Is that all right?" I ask, worried about his lack of response. "Would you rather go to a restaurant?"

"No," he says quickly. "No, this is great. It's perfect."

I let out a relieved sigh, and Jason scoots quickly out of the vehicle. I follow him, chuckling. We check out the food trucks first, walking the line of them before picking our meals. Hands full, we head toward the expanse of manicured lawn in front of the massive hanging screen. There are a good many people here already, but there's still plenty of space, and we choose a spot about halfway down, near an unoccupied heater. Jason takes the food while I pull the blanket out of the backpack I brought, and then we settle side by side on the ground.

"This is really neat," Jason says, looking around. "I've never done anything like this before."

"Me neither," I admit. My family certainly didn't do stuff like this when I was young. We had our own theater room, so why bother? This hits differently. I inhale the fresh air before opening my box of bacon mac and cheese. I offer it Jason's way. "Want a bite?"

"Uh, yes," he says, like it's obvious. He spears a few noodles onto his fork and then moans happily around the mouthful. "Okay, I might be having regrets right about now. I should've gotten that. It's delicious."

I huff a laugh, happy to see him enjoying himself. "I can go grab another."

I'm halfway off the ground when Jason tugs my arm, pulling me back down. "No, it's fine," he says, chuckling. "Let me work my way through what I have first. If I'm still hungry after, I'll go get some."

"Okay," I say, resettling. "You can have another bite of mine, though, if you want."

Jason eyes the mac and cheese I not-so-subtly waft under his nose, lips quirking up at one end. "Fine. One more bite."

I grin, and as Jason and I eat our food, I notice a couple with a dog nearby. "Do you ever bring Amadeus out with you?"

His eyebrows pop up. "What, like for a walk?"

I shrug. "Yeah, why not? He could probably go out in a carrier, couldn't he?"

"Huh," Jason says, taking a sip of his drink. "I've honestly never thought about it. Maybe? Probably not somewhere this crowded, though. And not when it's cold."

I nod. "Do you think you could show me how to handle him sometime?"

Jason's lips twitch at the corner. "You want to learn how to handle my snake?"

"Well, yeah."

He shakes his head a little, looking at me almost fondly. "Yeah, Cas. I'll show you how to handle my snake."

My grin is back in full force, but as Jason's face draws suddenly into a scowl, I look around in concern. "What? What is it?"

"Nothing," he says dismissively, but then he goes on, almost in a rush. "Just a couple women over there checking you out."

"Are there?" I ask, twisting around. A woman with short blonde hair gives me a big smile and a wave while her friend tries to tug her arm down. I hold my hand up in a friendly hello before refocusing on Jason.

He huffs before stuffing a few fries in his mouth. He looks...distressed.

"What's wrong?" I ask. "You know I'm not interested in them, right?"

"I know," he says, the words tossed out quickly. "It's just—" He makes a frustrated sound and an aborted gesture with his hand, and I don't know what to make of the sudden ire rolling off him. "Everywhere we go, people fucking *stare* at you, Cas. And I get it 'cause you're... You're *unreal*. But this isn't like your job at the studio, you know? People are supposed to look at you then. It's a given. But out here, you're just trying to live your life, and everyone treats you like...like it's all that matters, and I don't *like* it. I don't like them objectifying you, okay?"

My heart thumps heavily in my chest as Jason pushes a fry against the bottom of his to-go container hard enough for it to snap in half. I open my mouth, but with a flick of his head, Jason glances up and huffs again.

"They're coming over here," he mutters.

I barely have time to turn around before the blonde woman is standing beside our blanket.

"Hi," she says, cocking her hip a little and giving us a beaming smile. Her friend, the brunette, is hiding halfway behind her. "Beautiful night, isn't it?"

"Sure," I say, doing my best to be polite, even though I want nothing more than to continue my conversation with Jason.

"Are you two here alone?" she asks, shifting her weight in a way that draws attention to the sway of her hips.

Jason scoffs lightly from behind me, the sound quiet enough that I doubt either of the newcomers heard. It takes me a long moment to understand what, exactly, she's asking.

"Oh, no," I tell her, reaching back and giving Jason's hand a squeeze. "We're here together."

"Oh," she says, eyes flaring in understanding. "*Oh*."

"Jess, I told you," the brunette whispers, trying to tug her friend away.

Jess waves off her friend. "Okay. Well, have a good night. *Casablanca* is super romantic. Great choice." She winks and turns away, and the brunette mouths a quick *I'm sorry* before following.

"Jason," I say softly.

"Mm?" he says, looking resolutely down at where our hands are connected.

"Thank you."

That gets his attention. He lifts his gaze, eyes looking more brown than green in the waning evening light. "For what?"

"For caring," I tell him, tugging his hand atop my leg and just...holding on. I've never had someone act so...*protective* over me before, like they're genuinely concerned about my feelings. "Thank you for caring about me."

Jason doesn't seem to know what to say to that, but the crackle of the speakers drags our attention to the screen, where the opening credits of *Casablanca* are rolling. After a moment, Jason settles at my side, his leg pressed close to my own as we watch the movie.

Jason doesn't see me the way others do. And admittedly, I like that. But it does make me wonder... What *does* Jason see when he looks at me? What made him say yes to that first date? To the second? What made him agree to be here with me now?

Before long, as the night draws darker and the air cools, Jason shivers.

"Cold?" I ask him.

"Little," he admits.

I figured. Reaching for my backpack, I pull out the extra sweatshirt I brought. Jason looks at me in surprise when I hand it over. It's nothing fancy: just a light gray, hoodless sweater that's fleece-lined and big, even on me. But Jason takes it into his hands as if it's precious.

"Thank you," he says, tugging off his lightweight jacket and pulling the sweatshirt over his head. It disrupts his beanie, so he straightens that once the sweatshirt is in place, but then he simply tucks his hands inside the sleeves and tugs the hemline down over his drawn-up knees. He doesn't bother putting his jacket back on, so the fleece must be enough.

He looks incredibly endearing tucked inside my sweatshirt like that, and I wrap my arm around him, hoping he doesn't mind. He doesn't. In fact, he wriggles closer, looking up at my face for a long moment. His eyes travel from my eyes to my mouth, and then he settles his head against my shoulder. Feeling warm, I watch him and—sometimes—the show.

It's fully dark when Jason and I leave the outdoor theater. The hour isn't terribly late, but it was clear by the way Jason's head kept listing against my shoulder that he's beat. So instead of suggesting prolonging our date, I drive him straight home. I catch him looking over at me once, his eyes on my mouth again, and when I give him a smile, he looks away quickly.

Jason is quiet on the way up to his door, but as soon as we stop in front of his apartment, he spins to face me.

"Cas, I, uh…" He trips over his words a little. "Thank you for tonight."

"My pleasure," I tell him sincerely. "Can I see you again?"

"Yeah," he huffs, almost a laugh. "Unless I say otherwise, just assume my answer to that will be yes."

My smile widens, can't help it, and there goes Jason's gaze, dropping again.

"I'm gonna," he says, and then he's tipping forward. He snags my lips with his own, and I lean into it, breathing through my nose and catching a whiff of coffee and vanilla. Jason kisses me harder, more forcefully, and for a moment, I'm caught off-guard. But my surprise quickly makes way for elation as Jason's hand tangles in the hair at the back of my head. He holds me tight, tongue catching my own for a drawn-out minute.

When he breaks the kiss and steps back, his cheeks are flushed and his mouth is wet. He takes a little stuttering breath as fizzing warmth lingers in my veins.

"Um. Goodnight, Cas," he says, reaching back and grabbing the doorknob.

"Night, Jason."

He turns and walks inside, giving me one last glance before shutting the door, and I head toward home, a smile on my face as I think about the soon-to-be nurse still tucked inside my sweatshirt.

Chapter 10

JASON

It could be a coincidence, I tell myself, looking down at my rather persistent erection. *Pure coincidence.*

Or it could be—

I stop that line of thought immediately, refusing to let myself entertain hope. Not yet. It's only been a few dates. I've only known Cas a couple weeks. It's not enough time, surely. I've never... Not so soon, at least.

Right, because your extensive prior experience is enough for you to extrapolate a trend.

I scoff at my brain. Sarcastic ass.

Even so, I strip out of my pants and underwear, grab the lube and my favorite toy from my nightstand drawer, and drop onto my bed. I slick myself quickly, and then I'm notching the sleeve against my crown and rolling onto my stomach. The motion has me sinking inside the toy with a muffled groan, and it only takes minutes before I'm shooting hard enough for my breath to catch.

"*Fuuuck*," I groan out, aftershocks making my hips twitch. "*Fucking fuck.*"

It's only after I've come that I realize I never took off Cas's sweatshirt.

"Morning, Jason," Marley says, greeting me as I walk through the back door of Hyped.

It's Monday morning and much too early for Marley's teasing smile, but I give her a mumbled *hello* and stalk toward the espresso machines to get my brain in order. I make the both of us our customary drinks while Marley unlocks the register.

"Functioning now?" she asks after I've had my first sip.

"Sorta," I mutter, rounding the counter to pull a chair down off a table. I take a seat, and Marley joins me. We have a good ten minutes before we'll need to open the doors.

"Sooo," she says slowly, the piercing in her eyebrow glinting as she raises it in a high arc. "Are you going to tell me what's going on with you and Himbo?"

I groan. Of course Marley knows about Cas's job. She knows about Dixon, too. She learned the hard way after Dixon made a comment about working in porn. She thought he was joking, but then I had to explain to her why I'd turned beet red, and, well, after she demanded proof, she could barely look Dixon in the eye for a week. *I know the feeling.*

Regardless, I'm not surprised she knows Cas works in the adult entertainment industry. But it does make the whole, you know, *avoiding talking about my virginity thing* more complex.

I sip my caffeine as I debate how to answer her. "I like him," I finally say, a feeble truth.

"He likes you, too," she replies, crossing her ankle at her knee. "He's been in here how many times to deliver little gifts?"

"Three," I mumble.

"Mhm," she hums, pleased. "He's like a housecat, bringing you dead mice." *Ew.* "Courting you." Okay, that's nicer. "Does he like the way you pet him?"

Marley laughs as I groan.

"I'm not answering that," I tell her. I haven't even given him pets. *Yet.* "Let's open up shop."

"Yeah, yeah," she says, standing with me. She helps turn all the chairs down, but before I can switch the lock at the door, she speaks up. "Hey, Jason? I'm glad for you. He seems like a real sweetheart."

"Yeah," I answer, flicking the lock. "He is."

Our first customers arrive within minutes, and Marley and I fall into our usual routine—she rings up orders and calls them out, and I make the drinks. It's easy to let my mind fall into the monotony of it. I don't *hate* this job by any means, but it's certainly not what I want to do with my life.

I try to imagine being here for another five, ten years, and it's hard to do. Especially because I know in less than one, I'll likely be gone. But it does make me think about Cas working at his father's company. About doing something he doesn't enjoy, just to try to make his dad proud. Because it's obvious to me that's what he's doing. Cas doesn't want to disappoint him. He wants to live up to the standards his siblings set, even though it's not his own dream.

What would he do if it were his own choice, devoid of guilt, however unconscious on his family's part?

The question, then, makes me think of my own dad. My choices were guided by my family, too, but not in the same way. My dad's declining health through most of my childhood was this ever-present push. I couldn't do *more* for him. I could only help so much. But it made me want to do better. It made me want to help other people, other families, who were struggling. Who were hurt.

So maybe that pressure was there in a way, but I love nursing. I wouldn't change that path even if I could. My dad is gone, but I can help others. I can make a difference.

Isn't that what Cas said he wants?

"Morning, Jason," a deep voice drawls.

I hiccup a breath, coming out of my head to find Dixon giving me a muted smile. I'm not sure the man smiles for real, but his lips are hitched ever so slightly on one side. Beside him stands Cas, his smile big and bright, and *ohh*. My gut swoops.

"Morning, Jason," Cas parrots. "How's it going?"

"Good," I answer, finishing up my current drink orders—a couple macchiatos—before starting on their lattes. "You, uh...come from the gym?"

Cas nods, his hair wet and tousled on his head. Vaguely, I wonder if that's sweat or if he already showered.

My brain does a complicated little stutter, and I nearly drop the jug of milk in my hand.

"That's, um. Nice," I finish.

Dixon peers at me critically, and I look away.

"You have labs tonight, right?" Cas asks, and I'm not remotely surprised he remembered. In fact, I'm fairly certain he has my schedule memorized. It would explain his ability to show up wherever I am to...drop off dead mice, as Marley would say.

"Yeah, I do. You?"

"Studio," he says simply, giving me a small smile.

I try not to frown. I'm not sure what it is I'm feeling. Not anger, exactly. Not disappointment. Jealousy?

"Um. Have a good scene," I say quietly.

"Oh, before I forget," Cas says, grabbing something from his loose gym shorts pocket. He slides it my way across the counter. "Here."

I pick it up. At first, I'm not sure what I'm seeing. But then I realize it's a small glass snowflake. It's relatively flat in shape, like a snowflake would be, but when I hold it up, it catches the light and reflects it, flashing a hundred different colors.

"Reminded me of you," Cas says with a shrug.

I swallow roughly, closing my palm around the smooth glass. "Thanks, Cas," I say, the words rasping a little on the way out. "I, uh..." I pocket the gift before shaking my head and capping their finished drinks with lids. "Here."

Dixon doesn't say a word, but I can feel his stare on my person. Cas, on the other hand, thanks me with his usual happy cheer.

"I'll see you tomorrow?" I ask Cas. It's kind of become our thing in the short time we've been dating. Going out Tuesday and Saturday nights, when I'm free.

"You bet," he says, sending me a casual wink that makes my pulse kick.

Cas and Dixon leave the coffee shop, chatting quietly, and I tug the snowflake from my pocket. What does it mean? Is it because we were talking about snow on our first date?

"I think you're one of a kind, Jason."

"Like a smitten housecat," Marley says, curling her hand into a claw when I glance her way.

I roll my eyes, stuffing the snowflake back into my pocket, and Marley laughs. I fall back into work-mode after that, until near noon, when my phone starts vibrating incessantly in my back pocket. The third time it goes off, I wipe my hand and fish it out. Brad is calling, which he wouldn't do during work hours unless it's urgent.

"Yeah?" I say, accepting the call and facing the back of the shop.

"I fucked up," Brad says.

"What happened?"

"I cut myself."

I pause as realization sinks in. Brad doesn't do all that well with blood. If it was a small nick, he'd be fine. But if it's bad...

"Do you need an ambulance?" I ask.

"No," he says quickly. "No, I just... I'm dizzy."

"Yeah, all right," I say, already pulling my apron strings free. I catch Marley's eye, and she must pick up enough from my expression and the fact that I'm getting out of my uniform because she picks up the phone near the register. "I'll be right there."

"God, I'm sorry, Jason."

"Don't worry about it," I tell him, putting the phone between my shoulder and ear as I wash my hands. "Just sit tight."

"Thank you," he says weakly.

As soon as I hang up, Marley turns to me. "You have to go?"

"Yeah, I do. Will you be okay?" The lunch hour rush is approaching, after all.

Marley simply nods. "Annabelle is on her way in early. Don't fret."

I huff a breath of relief. "Thanks, Marls."

"You bet. Get outta here."

I give her a quick, appreciative nod before hoofing it out the back door. Our apartment complex is less than ten minutes from Hyped, so it doesn't take me long to pull up and park. I make my way quickly inside and up the stairs, and when I unlock the front door and push my way into our apartment, I find Brad sitting on the floor of the kitchen.

"Oh, Bee," I say, walking over and crouching down in front of him. His hand is wrapped in a towel, the edges of it soaked in red.

Brad has always been bigger than me, ever since our kindergarten days. He's not a slight dude. In fact, he could easily pass as a jock type, not the total nerd he is. He's hella fit, but that's because he's an energetic guy who spends most of his days on the computer, working for a gaming company. He balances that by hitting the gym several times a week and going for runs around town.

He's always been my protector, for lack of a better word. Always looked out for me—the shy, small kid. He's been my big brother since the moment he called me Birdie. I love him, plain and simple. And to see him sitting with his head back, eyes closed, looking so *weak*, is like a kick to my gut.

He groans a little as I touch the cloth around his hand.

"You're going to have to let me see," I say gently, trying to peel his fingers off the towel.

He loosens his grip, eyes blinking open. He doesn't look down as I unfurl the cloth from around his hand, but I can see him wince out of the corner of my eye when I pull the wet towel away from his wound. I cringe internally.

"You're going to need stitches," I say, wrapping the towel back into place. "Stay here. I'll clean the wound, and then we'll go."

Brad doesn't argue with me. He just closes his eyes and makes a pitiful sound. Scrambling off the floor, I make my way quickly to the bathroom and grab supplies, including a little basin so he doesn't have to stand at the sink. Brad lets me clean the cut on his finger without fuss, and I bandage it quickly before grabbing his shoes.

"Thank you, Birdie," he says when I tug him up off the floor.

"No thanks necessary," I tell him, helping to support his weight as we make our way to my car. Luckily, I know a great hospital.

When we arrive in the ER, I get a few curious glances from the nurses at reception who recognize me, but when I explain what's going on, they sweep us through. One of the nurses, a really sweet lady named Fern, gets Brad some juice while we wait for him to get patched up. It isn't long before his color looks better, and even though I know his finger must be throbbing like a bitch, he eventually gives me a smile.

"So," he says. "This day is going well."

I huff a laugh from my spot sitting bedside. "I think your wellness meter needs adjustment."

He snorts.

"What happened, anyway?" I ask, now that he doesn't look so close to passing out.

He twists his lips, looking chagrined. "I was chatting with this girl..."

"Flirting," I supply.

"Flirting, yes," he answers with an eye roll. "I was reading her text and not paying very close attention to what I was doing, and yeah... I cut myself."

Brad got lucky, all things considered. The cut is deep, running the entire side of his index finger. A little further over, and he might have been looking at a reattachment, not a simple stitching.

But I keep that to myself. We don't need Brad fainting, and I can see he's embarrassed enough as is. He knows it was a careless mistake.

"I'm glad it wasn't worse," I say instead. "You'll be out of here in no time, back to your shameless flirting. Lord knows you need the practice."

Brad takes a swipe at me before remembering his hand. He freezes mid-air, hissing.

"You brought that one on yourself," I point out, patting his leg, even as my insides twinge sympathetically.

"Yeah, yeah," he grumbles, cradling his hand to his chest. "Distract me. What's going on with Cas?"

Brad looks over at me when I fail to respond, his expression going from curious to that of a dog with a bone.

"What is it?" he presses. "Tell me."

I huff a little breath, idly brushing over the snowflake inside my pocket. "I might be attracted to him, Bee."

Brad's face breaks into a grin. "Yeah?" he asks excitedly.

"I think so?" I say, weighing my words. "I'm not positive."

"How can't you be sure?" Brad asks a little incredulously. "Either you want to scrape his tonsils with your manhood or you don't."

"Scrape his... The *fuck*, Brad?"

He opens his mouth to respond, but the door swings in at that precise moment, putting an abrupt end to our conversation. The doctor who walks into the room gives Brad a small smile, looking at the chart in his hands before saying, "Well, I hear we almost lost a finger today."

Brad lets out a whimper, and I squeeze his leg in support. Honestly, though, that's what he gets for uttering the word *manhood* aloud.

Although... *Do* I want Cas's mouth wrapped around my cock? It doesn't sound like the worst thing.

Not by a long shot.

Chapter 11
CAS

As I wait for Jason to arrive for our date, I tidy up a bit. We went out for sushi earlier this week, followed by one of those paint-and-sip events. Jason spent most of the night trying not to laugh at my terrible artwork. Admittedly, what was supposed to be a dog frolicking in a wheat field did end up looking a lot like a bushy dick.

I hung the canvas above my bed.

Tonight, Jason is coming over to my apartment. It was his suggestion since I've met him at his place every other date thus far. Not that I've minded in the least, but I understand him wanting to keep things fair.

My place is simple—not big or flashy like my parents' or either of my siblings' houses—but it's clean and now neat, and hopefully, that will be enough.

Jason knocks just before seven, and I open the door with an excited grin I can't quite temper. He looks good, usual beanie in place, blonde hair curling around the edges. His hands are slipped in his pockets, his cheeks are a little bright from being outside where it's cooler, I assume, and there's a shy smile on his face.

"Hey," he breathes.

"Hi, Jason. Come on in."

He steps inside, looking around as he toes off his shoes. "I like your place."

"Thanks," I say warmly, holding out a hand for his jacket. He slips it off and passes it over, revealing the red shirt I like. "Want something to drink? I have water, beer, a sparkling lemon soda thing, or straight-up rum."

He snorts a laugh as I hang his jacket in the closet. "The lemon thing sounds good. Thanks."

"You got it," I say, heading into the kitchen to grab a couple cans from the fridge. My phone pings with a text while I'm in there.

Dixon: Need a raincheck for tomorrow. I'm going to a brunch thing with Niko's sisters.

I can just imagine him tacking on a *God help me* inside his head.

Dixon: Gym on Monday instead?

Smiling, I text Dixon back to let him know that's fine. Look at that. I think my grumpy coworker is finally warming up to me.

Drinks in hand, I head out to the living room, where Jason is waiting. He gives me a soft smile as I approach, and I sit next to him on the couch, popping the top on his lemon soda before passing it over. He takes a sip, hums, and then leans back into the cushions.

"Tired?" I ask.

He looks over at me apologetically, sitting up taller. "Yeah. Sorry, I'll rally."

"Hey, no. It wasn't a criticism," I tell him, giving his leg a squeeze. "Wanna stay in tonight? We could order food and just veg. Maybe watch a movie or something?"

"Really?" he asks, sounding relieved.

"Yeah, why not?" Spending time with Jason is the important part. "What kind of food sounds good?"

He thinks it over for a moment. "Do you have Thai around here?"

"Sure do," I tell him, pulling out my phone. Jason goes through the menu with me, picking out what he wants to eat, and I order it to be delivered.

"So, what'd you do today?" Jason asks, curling sideways on the couch to face me. He rests one arm along the top of the cushions, head in his hand.

I like this. The catching up. The way Jason looks at me like he actually cares about what I have to say.

"Worked at the office," I tell him. Although it was boring, like usual. Frustrating, too. Dorian pointed out a couple mistakes I made the other day, which didn't endear me to him further. "Played some basketball after," I add, significantly more excited about that. "There's this place I go to for local kids. I kind of just...hang out with them? It's a lot of fun."

I don't mention that I talked to Queenie about the type of donor support they receive at Neddy's. She put me in touch with a nonprofit that organizes fundraising for local youth programs, and I'm going to meet with them next week.

I'm not sure why I keep that part to myself, other than it feels a little vulnerable. And I don't want Jason to think I'm mentioning it for my own gain. It has nothing to do with me.

Jason cocks his head, the motion shifting his cheek along his palm. "You play basketball with kids?"

"Yes?" I answer slowly. Is that weird? "It's a volunteer program, technically, but it doesn't feel like it. It's just..." How do I even explain it? "It's just nice. Maybe that doesn't make sense."

"It does," he says quickly, reaching forward to touch my leg. "That's really sweet, Cas."

Jason's eyes drift down my body to where his hand is splayed, almost as if he's surprised to see it there. For a second, I swear I see something pass through his gaze, but then Jason blinks, and it's gone. He leans back against the couch, hand leaving my leg.

"Have you always played sports?" he asks.

"Um, yeah," I answer, thinking back. "I played basketball in high school, and then just for fun ever since then."

He nods, like he's not surprised.

"I actually thought about going into sports physiology in college, but—" I shake my head. It was only ever a thought. Nothing more. "Did you play any?"

He snorts. "No."

"Why's that so funny?" I ask, a smile curling my lips.

Jason raises an eyebrow, giving me a look. "Do I look sporty to you?"

I shrug. "Anyone can enjoy playing sports. There's no one right look for that."

He blinks at me. "Such a surprise," he mutters.

I'm about to ask him *what is* when the buzzer sounds.

"I'll get that," I say, popping off the couch. I let the delivery person inside the building and wait at the door. He arrives not a minute later, humming as he comes down the hall. When he looks up and spots me, his eyes widen, and then he grins.

"You Cassius?" he asks, checking the receipt.

"That's me," I say, holding out my hand. Instead of the food, he gives me his downturned palm.

"Charmed," he purrs.

"I, uh..."

"Oh, for fuck's sake," Jason says, pushing beside me in the doorway. He grabs the bag of food from the startled delivery person and hauls me back hard enough to dislodge our hands. "Thanks so much," he says in a saccharine sweet voice, shutting the door in the guy's face.

"Jason," I say around a laugh.

He tugs me back to the couch, pushing me down and sitting close enough that his knee is over my leg.

"Next time," he says, opening the bag of food noisily, "I'll get the door."

A slow smile curves my lips.

Marley called him a skittish kitten, but damn. I think he might be a lion.

"Whatever you want, Jason," I say, meaning it.

The two of us eat our Thai while we finish catching up on our days. Hearing Jason talk about his duties at the hospital leaves me in awe. He plays it off a little, I can tell, making sure to mention how he's still under supervision because he's not yet registered. But it's admirable, what he does—what he's *doing*—for people.

Not for the first time, I wonder how his dad passed away.

When our food is gone, we pick a movie, and Jason fidgets with his beanie a bit before tossing it aside. He brushes his hair into messy order, sneaking glances at me a few times.

"Would you want to, um..." he says, looking nervous. "Would you want to cuddle?"

My chest grows almost unbearably warm, and I'm sure my smile is ridiculously bright. "Yeah, Jason. I'd love to cuddle." I open my arm wide. "Here."

He looks at me like I'm a map he's having trouble reading, and it hits me that, despite suggesting it, maybe he's never done this before. I take a hold of his hand, and Jason lets me tug him close, pulling him beside me. Slouching down a bit, I make a more comfortable surface for him to lie against, and then I give his head a gentle push. He lays it on my chest, nestled in the crook of my arm, and, finally, his muscles go lax.

"Okay?" I ask.

"Yeah," he says quietly.

My mind tumbles over the man tucked in my arms as Jason and I watch the beginning of the movie, a newer Marvel release. I can't stop wondering about him. About the instincts that pushed him to be a nurse. About his mom and how she's doing after the loss of her husband. I wonder what his favorite color is and if he's ever been to the zoo.

There's so much I want to know. So much I have yet to learn.

It's a relief when Jason breaks the silence, seemingly as content to talk over the movie as me. "Did you have any pets as a kid?" he asks.

I grin, rubbing his arm. "No. My parents were never really animal people. Why a snake?"

He huffs a laugh. "I dunno. I just like them, I guess? They're misunderstood."

"How so?"

He shifts a little, hand landing on my stomach. "So many people are scared of them, but they're really sweet. Well, maybe not *sweet*," he amends. "They're not the most cuddly. But they're nice. I've had Amadeus for a year, and he's never once tried to eat me."

"I think he'd need to be a little bigger for that," I point out.

Jason chuckles. "Still, I feel bad when people look at snakes and only see a monster. That's not what I see."

I like the way you see things.

"Amadeus is lucky to have you," I say.

He lifts his head off my chest and looks up at me, still nestled in the crook of my arm. For a moment, his hand passes unintentionally over my nipple, and I suck in a short breath, doing my best not to react. Jason watches me for a beat, not saying a word, and then he leans up and brushes his lips to my jaw.

I freeze, heart thumping as I wait for Jason's cue.

"Cas," he whispers, and then he tugs my face around.

The second our mouths slot together, sparks dance across my skin. They take off, skipping, hopping around like frantic, hopeful bunnies. His lips are warm and soft, and I'm careful to meet Jason's energy as he kisses me. Careful to let him set the pace. This kiss feels more exploratory than last time, like he's testing something. Like he's searching.

I wonder what he's looking for.

My dick goes hard, but I ignore it. It doesn't matter. Jason's tongue pushes into my mouth, greeting mine with a little flick, and he inhales sharply. Pauses. Does it again. His thumb passes over my nipple, harder this time, and I can't help it; I groan.

Jason pulls back, looking at my face. He seems...surprised. And then his gaze pans slowly down my body, landing on my lap.

"I don't expect anything, Jason," I tell him quickly, knowing he's getting an eyeful right about now.

He nods slowly, gaze dragging back up to my face. "I know."

I let out a breath of relief at that. "We can stop if you want."

Another pause. "Do you want to stop?" he asks quietly.

I answer honestly. "No."

His hand tenses slightly against my chest, fingers dimpling into shirt and skin. I wonder if I said the wrong thing. But then his lips meet mine again. It's softer this time. Gentler.

Jason kisses me like the fall wind blowing through trees. Like a breeze laying me bare. It's sweetly intense and makes me tremble, and just when I worry it's too much, that I may well be exposed if he keeps on much longer, he stops, his thumb moving across my pec like a tiny caress.

He draws back, looking between my eyes slowly. "Thank you," he says. "For the kiss. That was, uh. Yeah. Thanks."

I feel struck. "My pleasure," I reply a little hoarsely.

Jason nods, sliding down against my chest again, laying his head where it was before. His hair tickles my chin, and I close my eyes, feeling like I'm falling. Feeling like one of those leaves.

We're quiet this time as we watch the movie, and when Jason shivers, I pull a throw blanket over the two of us. It takes a while for me to realize he's fallen asleep. My heart beats fast beneath his ear, and I'm glad he can't hear it.

I don't want to let go. I don't want *him* to go.

When the end credits roll, I turn the TV off. Jason's breaths puff out evenly, and his back rises and falls against my arm. Even though I don't want to disturb him, I know, realistically, I need to give him the option of going home. I can't simply carry him to my bed for the night, no matter how appealing the notion.

"Jason," I say quietly, giving his arm a gentle squeeze. He stirs. "The movie is over."

"What, uh..." His voice comes out raspy, and he clears his throat. "What time is it?"

"Almost eleven."

He groans a little.

"Want to stay over?" I ask.

He goes still. "What?"

"If you don't want to drive home, you could spend the night here," I say. "My bed is big enough, and we could stuff pillows between us if it'd make you more comfortable."

He huffs a laugh at that, and it encourages me to go on.

"I have clothes you can borrow, and I'm almost positive there's an extra toothbrush in the bathroom. Plus, tomorrow is your day off, so you wouldn't need to rush home early. You're welcome to stay, but it's completely up to you."

Jason finally lifts his head, sitting upright next to me. There's a little crease on his cheek from my shirt, and the sight of it makes me long for things I have no right dreaming about just yet.

"You really wouldn't mind?" he asks.

"Not at all."

"Okay." His answer is so quiet I almost miss it.

"Yeah?"

He nods his head in a little jerk, biting his lip, and my insides tumble and soar.

"Come on, then," I say, standing up and holding out my hand. "I'll show you my room."

A blush spreads up Jason's neck, but before I can apologize for how that sounded, he grabs a hold of my hand, a smile on his face. The moment we reach the bedroom and I flick on the light, Jason starts to laugh loudly from beside me. I realize why when I follow his gaze.

"You hung up the painting?" he asks, letting go of my hand and stepping closer to the bed, where, yes, Dick Dog hangs.

I shrug, chuckling along with him. "I did. I know it's terrible, but it reminds me of *that*."

"Of what?" he asks, turning to me, that smile still on his face.

"Your laugh."

The humor leaves Jason in an instant. He blinks at me, mouth open in a little O.

"So, um, clothes?" I say, turning toward the dresser. I pull open a drawer, rooting around inside for something Jason would be comfortable sleeping in. I turn back with sweatpants and a t-shirt in my hands. "This okay?"

"Yeah," he says softly, coming over and taking them from my outstretched fingers. "Thanks, Cas."

"Mhm." I usually sleep nude, but I grab a pair of gym shorts for tonight. "You can change in here," I tell Jason. "I'll take the bathroom."

He gives me a little nod, and I leave him to it, closing the door behind me. The spare toothbrush is exactly where I thought it'd be, so I set it out on the counter before changing and taking care of business. Once I think enough time has passed, I head back to my bedroom and knock.

"Come in," Jason calls.

When I push open the door, my breath hitches just a little. Jason is standing inside the room, my t-shirt swamping his torso, sweatpants rolled up at the hem. He looks sleepy and soft and perfect, and something thrums under my skin. Something a little more possessive than I care to admit.

Jason, however... His eyes go wide when he sees me.

Ah, *shit*.

"I can put on a shirt," I assure him, kicking myself for being so careless. I didn't even *think*—

"No," he says, swallowing, shaking his head just a little. "No, uh. It's okay. It's fine. Good."

"You sure?" I check. The last thing I want to do is make him uncomfortable.

He nods quickly, eyes sinking down my torso before he tears his gaze away. "I'll just, uh...use the bathroom."

"Okay. The toothbrush is on the counter," I let him know.

He mutters something and pads from the room.

I decide to slip under the covers while I wait for Jason to be done, but it doesn't take him long. He returns within minutes, his face a little bright like he washed it.

"Do you have a side?" I ask him.

"Not really. It's fine how you are." He fidgets with the bottom of his shirt. "Should I get the light?"

"If you don't mind."

A second later, the room goes dark, and then the bed depresses.

"Do you want me to lay some pillows?" I ask softly.

Jason huffs a laugh, the sheets swishing as he gets settled. "No, Cas. I don't need a pillow divider. I trust you."

"Okay," I say, my smile wide.

"Thanks."

"For what?" I ask, shifting onto my side. My eyes aren't adjusted enough yet to make out Jason's features, but I can see his outline.

"For...tonight," he answers. "For this. I like this."

"Yeah, Jason," I reply, my heart thudding steadily inside my chest. "I like this, too."

Chapter 12

JASON

When I wake, it takes me a long, bleary moment to figure out what's going on. Apart from a handful of times with Brad, I've never slept with another person before. And Brad most certainly didn't cuddle.

But I'm not in my own bed, and there's a rather firm chest smushed under my cheek and an arm thrown over my hip.

Cas.

I inhale subtly, catching a whiff of man and spicy something-or-other. The sheet we'd been under is thrown down near my calf, and I can't say I'm surprised. Cas is a furnace, even better than a heated blanket. He's still sound asleep as far as I can tell, and... *Oh.*

I'm hard. I'm most definitely hard. And my stiffy is stamped right up against Cas's hip.

This is new. This is very new.

Cas shifts a little, and I hold my breath, unsure of what to do. But he resettles, letting out a soft sigh and tightening his arm around me briefly. My cock *throbs.*

God.

I've been in relationships before Cas, but they were different in two ways that are currently glaringly obvious to me, like little neon signs flashing inside my head. For one, I was never comfortable enough around the others to stay the night or let my kisses linger too long. I wasn't confident they wouldn't push for more. And two, I never—ever—got hard around anyone I dated.

Not until Cas.

It could be morning wood, sure. But I'm not usually horny in the mornings. Even though I'm not sexually active, I do consider myself to have a fairly active libido, and I practice self care several times a week. But first thing in the morning is not my usual go-to. I'm more *up and at 'em* at the end of the day, like all the stress and the constant *go, go, go* needs an outlet before my body and mind can settle.

Yet I'm hard now, curled up in Cas's arms. And I got hard last night when we kissed. It was unexpected and a little scary and a lot wonderful, and I couldn't help but doubt myself because *what if it was a fluke?* But now... I don't think I can chalk it up to coincidence any longer. This isn't a fluke. I want to *lick* him. I've never been so close to someone I wanted to lick before.

Cas shifts again, the change in his breathing indicating he's more awake. "Jason?" he says softly.

I tilt my head up and back, catching half-lidded whiskey eyes and a gentle smile. "Yeah. Hi."

Christ on a cracker. Hi?

Cas's smile only grows. "Morning. Is this okay?" he asks, nodding downwards. "You're not uncomfortable with this?"

This being the cuddle situation we found ourselves in, I assume.

"No," I answer, clearing my throat. "No. It's good. Fine. Yep. I like it."

He seems happy with that. "I do, too," he says, running his palm up and down my back, and *ungh*.

My eyes flutter closed, and I just... I want his hand on my skin, so I can feel the heat of him more solidly. I want him to slip it under my shirt or down my pants and *touch me*. I want...

I just *want*.

"I need to get up, though," Cas says, tone full of regret. "Bathroom."

"Of course," I say, easing back.

Cas gives me a warm smile before slipping off the end of the bed, and I watch him go, those shiny silver gym shorts he changed into last night clinging to his ass like flowing water with every step. They're riding up his crack, and *holy shit*, that shouldn't be as damn sexy as it is, but it gives me the most perfect view of each individual globe, and—

Oh. My. God.

I'm checking out Cas's ass. *I'm checking out his ass.*

Cas disappears around the corner, and my heart gallops inside my chest. I want him. I do. I *want* him. And I can have him, right? Cas wants me, too?

I've never been in this situation before. Never had my interest returned. What do I *do*? How does one initiate sex?

Is Cas's faucet broken? Can I offer my assistance with his plumbing?

This is not a damn porno, Jason. For fuck's sake.

Agh!

Okay, okay. Breathe. First things first—peeing. Because yes, I need to do that, too. So, okay. Um. Bathroom. Yes, that's a fine plan. A great plan. I'll brush my teeth while I'm at it, too.

Bathroom first. *Seduction* second.

Oh my God, this is going to be a disaster.

Eyes on the doorway, I scramble for my phone and shoot off a quick text to Brad. It's nearly ten, so he should be awake.

Me: How do I sex?!

That was...not my finest moment.

I hear the faucet come on in the bathroom, so I hop out of bed, changing quickly back into my jeans where my half-chub will be more hidden. For now, at least. I leave Cas's shirt on, though. And sniff the collar a little because, well, it smells nice.

Brad's response comes through as the bathroom door opens.

Brad: My baby boy! Don't overthink it. Just go with whatever feels good.

Cas pops his head into the room. He's still shirtless, those gym shorts sitting low on his hips, and I have to forcibly keep my eyes trained above the level of his nips. "Hungry?" he asks.

My lips smack apart, mouth pooling with saliva. "Yes?"

He gives me a nod before tapping the doorframe and heading off down the hall. I slump, grabbing my phone.

Me: No. How do I tell him I want to have sex?

Brad: You use...words? You know, those things that come out of your mouth?

Ugh. Fucking Brad, the reasonable asshole.

Brad: Or your stomach! Flash that sexy stomach, baby.

My fingers fly across the keyboard.

Me: I swear to God, Brad, I'm going to sacrifice your firstborn to a goat.

Brad: Whoa. Harsh, man.

My phone starts to ring, and I walk quickly to the door, peering down the hall. I can just make out Cas in the kitchen, pulling something from the fridge, so I ease the bedroom door closed and answer Brad's call.

"Birdie," he says.

I huff out a breath. "I know. I'm freaking out."

"If you don't want to have sex with him—"

"I *do*," I cut in. "I do want to, Brad. I've never... I've never been in this situation before. What if..."

God.

"What is it?" he asks gently.

"What if he says no?"

My gut sits heavy with the thought. I think it would crush me. It would hurt so much worse than Rachel's rejection or the regret of never pursuing my high school crush because I *know* Cas on a deeper level. He feels like mine already, and to have him turn me down now...

"You precious fool," Brad says fondly. "He's not going to say no."

"How do you know that?" I ask.

"Because I've seen the way he looks at you. He's *into* you, and he's allosexual. If you give that man even a hint you're ready for more, he's going to be on you like...well, *you* on that crispy baked cheese from that breakfast place you never shut up about."

"Oh my God," I moan. "The flaky pastry and the soft, gooey center and, *ungh*, the raspberry spread over top? So good, Brad. *So good.*"

"My point exactly," he says deadpan. "Now wipe your drool and go ask Cas if you can tug on his balls a little. He'll say yes."

"I want to be mad at you," I inform my friend. "Because the things that come out of your mouth are worrisome. But...thanks. Truly, thank you."

"Anytime, Birdie," he says. "Good luck. And when you get home, tell me every last detail, down to whether or not Cas's pubes are—"

I hang up the phone and toss it away like it's a live grenade. And then, I *breathe*.

When I get to the kitchen—after a visit to the bathroom—Cas is flipping pancakes on a long griddle. He shoots me a smile before refocusing on the task, and my eyes drag down the side of him. All smooth skin and lean muscle. The dips in his abdomen. The prominent V at his hips that I never quite noticed before. The swell of his ass and down further, to his thighs and calves. Since when are calves sexy?

My eyes make a return trip back up his body, giving his ass another glance because, I mean, c'mon. And then his chest, the little jut of his nipples, his cut jawline and *God*. The lips. *Those* lips.

"First batch is almost done," Cas says, turning around to grab two plates from the cupboard. "Do you like orange juice? Or I have water."

"Water would be good," I answer, throat definitely dry.

He nods and fills up a glass before handing it over. Then he checks the pancakes and slides them onto one of the plates. "Syrup is already on the coffee table. Go ahead and get started. I'll be there shortly."

I accept the plate without a word—not trusting my mouth at the moment—and tread into the living room, where forks and a bottle of syrup are waiting right where Cas said they'd be. As I work on my pancakes, my mind jumps back to when Cas was naked on my couch after our second date. I remember being startled, yes, and completely unsure of what to do. But I also remember my body reacting. And I thought, at the time, it was a purely physical response. A *right time* sort of moment because my body associated *his* body with good times.

But now, I'm wondering if that was the start. If that was the beginning of my attraction to Cas. Because there's not a doubt in my mind now that I *am* attracted to him. It's obvious.

It's not simply *right time*. It's *right person*.

I blow out a breath, rolling over this massive shift in my situation.

When Cas comes out of the kitchen, he has his own plate in hand, and he takes a seat beside me.

"Thank you," I tell him sincerely. "The pancakes were really good."

"It's just a box mix," he says with a little shrug, brushing off the praise. "I'm not much of a cook. But I'm glad you liked them."

"Yeah," I say, watching Cas lift a syrup-covered bite of pancake to his mouth and chew. *Chewing is sexy now?*

I force myself to give Cas time to finish his breakfast while we chat a little about insignificant things—the weather getting cooler, the movie we semi-watched last night, whether we'd rather see space firsthand or the Mariana Trench. But all the while, my eyes rake over every inch of Cas, and I feel like there's a very real possibility I'm going to crawl out of my skin. My heartbeat is throbbing in time to my cock, my fingers won't stop tapping, and I can't recall a single other instance where I was this hard up. Where I wanted someone so singularly.

Where I thought if I didn't have them, I might actually fall to the ground and wail.

"You okay?" Cas asks, setting down his fork and grabbing his glass of water. "You seem a little tense."

He watches me as he drinks, and I swallow once. Twice. My hands shake a little as he sets his glass down, and Cas eyes me curiously as I shift toward him on the couch.

"Can I..." I start. *Fuck.* "Can I just... Can I kiss you?"

Cas nods after only a beat, even as he looks concerned by whatever he sees written across my face. But I swing my leg over his lap, too keyed up to attempt any more words, too consumed with *want* to hold back any longer. I settle over Cas's legs, and, with one more glance at *those lips*, I bring my mouth to his.

Cas tastes like syrup, sweet and rich and all-consuming, and he makes a small noise of surprise as I dive into his mouth. His hands settle at my hips, palms smoothing along my jeans, his thumbs dipping just under the hem of my shirt and gracing my skin. And *yes*. *Yes, yes, yes*. That. More. I want...

Cas's breath hitches as I drag myself forward, rubbing against him, and he jolts his head back, breaking the connection between our lips. His gaze pings downwards before landing back on my face, and he looks between my eyes with a clear question.

"Jason?" he says, hopeful.

I don't have words, so I just urge, "Yes. Yes, yes, please. Yes."

His eyes *light*. Cas dives back in, snagging my lips and tugging me to him, no longer tentative, no longer holding back. His tongue sweeps into my mouth, and I make an embarrassingly needy sound, my dick leaking precum like mad inside my briefs. I'm so hard it actually *hurts*. His mouth makes its way to my jaw, to my neck, and, *oh God*, I'm going to die. This is how I go.

He sucks gently against the skin near my jugular, wet, open-mouthed kisses one after the other. "Is this too fast?" he asks before finding a sensitive spot near my clavicle. "Do we need to slow—"

"Don't you fucking dare," I say loudly, cupping his head to me. "Don't you stop. Don't stop. Don't you—" I groan as Cas licks up the column of my neck, my hips moving restlessly. He drags a hand down to my groin, and my entire body bursts to life, lights switched on, electricity licking through my veins. I gasp, and, "Do that," I encourage. "Do that, do—"

Cas, both hands between us now, opens my jeans, and then his hand is wrapping around my dick, and *fuuuck*. How, how... How?

"Jason," Cas groans, burying his face in my neck, smooth skin and soft lips brushing over my skin. "What do you want?" He pumps me. Sucks another kiss near my pulse. "Whatever you want."

"I..."

He swipes his thumb over my slit, and I momentarily lose the plot.

"Fuck, you taste good," he says, and *holy mother of God*, he licked his thumb.

"I want your mouth," I blurt, and Cas draws back, looking into my eyes.

"Yeah?" he asks.

"If you—"

"I do," he says, wrapping his arms around behind my back. In a fluid move, Cas stands, lifting me up with him. My jeans are open, my cock pressed against the heat of his stomach, and *his* cock is hard, the tip of it brushing my denim-covered ass through his gym shorts as he turns me around and lays me out on the couch. I don't even have time to contemplate next steps before Cas is sliding down my body, hooking my briefs and jeans, and then tugging them free.

In one moment, I'm half-naked on the couch, elbows propping myself up, cool air rushing across my skin, and in the next, Cas is sinking between my legs, flashing me a smile, and taking my cock into his mouth.

I shout, my elbows losing purchase, back hitting the cushions as Cas envelops my cockhead in heat and slick moisture. It's like nothing, *nothing*, I've experienced before. None of my toys compare. Not my hand. Not warming lube. *Nothing* has felt like this, and I don't even recognize my own voice or the half-words coming out of my mouth as Cas's tongue works the underside of my dick.

Fucking—

I hook my leg over Cas's shoulder, hips moving of their own accord. My hands are in his hair—*when did they get there?*—and Cas relaxes his throat, taking me deep, humming around the length of me as I shudder beneath him. It's like... It's...

"Cassius, holy fuck," I manage, looking down the length of him.

His *mouth* is on my dick. Those lips are wrapped around me. I'm getting a blowjob. Holy *fuck*, I'm getting my first blowjob.

"I can't..." I gasp out. "I'm gonna..."

I wriggle, my foot brushing up against Cas's cock through those obscene shiny shorts. I apply more pressure without a thought, and Cas jolts, his throat swallowing around me before he drags his lips up the length of my cock. The visual alone—my shaft emerging inch by inch, wet from his mouth—nearly has me blowing. But then he sinks back down, sucking and rolling his hips against my foot, and *oh my fuck*. His cock jerks, and then he *moans*.

I'm coming before I've even registered it. One moment, my entire body is a bundle of taut nerves, stretched thin and ready to snap. There's pressure. The incessant *tug* of Cas's mouth. The feel of his arousal matching mine. And then I'm splintering apart, my spine arching, my heel digging into Cas's back, my vision becoming littered with stars, and my cock throbbing out my release in great big pulses like a jackhammer.

I'm out of my body, floating, careening through space, and then I'm landing on soft cushions, in safe arms. I vaguely register Cas's mouth wrapped tenderly around my cockhead, his tongue soothing my slit. His cock sits soft now against the inside of my foot, and his fingers are running circles over my lower stomach.

And I just...

"Oh my God," I breathe, a whisper.

"You okay?" Cas asks, his head resting against my inner knee. His hair is mussed, his lips are puffy, and he looks like every wet dream I know I'll be having in the future, near and far.

"That was," I say slowly, "so very okay. So much better than okay. I'm very, definitely above okay."

Cas grins, slow and sweet, before placing a closed-mouth kiss against the end of my dick. My pulse spikes.

"Um," I say, trying to think of the most eloquent way to word what's on my mind. "We should definitely do that again, and I really want to tug on your balls."

Cas's soft laughter warms me through.

Chapter 13
CAS

Jason looks debauched and somewhat sheepish, his cheeks flushed bright red, but he's smiling at me in a way that has my heart trying to beat out of my chest.

He *wanted* me. He was hard for me. Which means he feels something for me, doesn't it? Does it?

I take one last look at Jason's cock, nestled against dark blonde curls, and sit back, unwrapping Jason's leg from around my shoulder. I don't go far, though, keeping a hand on him. I don't want him to think I'm pulling away.

"You...came, right?" he asks, sitting upright and glancing down at my crotch, as if looking for the evidence.

I snort. "Yeah, I came."

He shakes his head slightly, eyes wide. "I didn't even *do* anything. I barely touched you."

"Didn't need to," I tell him, smoothing my palm up his leg. He doesn't seem to have a problem sitting there cross-legged without pants, and I'm in no rush to remedy that. "That was really fucking hot, Jason."

"Yeah?" he asks, a hopeful lilt to his words.

I nod, swallowing. "Hearing the noises you made? Seeing you so clearly into it? That was enough."

The way he hooked my head and tugged me down on his cock? That alone nearly had me blowing.

He smiles, tugging the hem of his shirt slightly. He looks smug and happy.

"That was my first blowjob," he says, voice quiet. His eyes flash to mine only briefly before he looks back down at his shirt.

I had wondered.

"But you liked it?" I say, fairly sure of that. Jason's enthusiasm was raw in the way I experienced sex as a teen. He was unapologetic, unabashed in a manner that many adults aren't, too hardened or apathetic as they are. Jason was...pure.

"Yes, I liked it," he mutters, lips twitching. But then he blows out a breath. "I'm sorry I didn't tell you beforehand. That...I'm a virgin. *Was* a virgin. I should have."

I shake my head, adjusting myself to be closer to him and tugging his legs up onto mine. He shivers ever so slightly, so I grab a blanket and toss it over his exposed lap.

"No, that was up to you," I say. "You don't owe anyone that information, Jason. You're an adult who can make autonomous decisions over your own body without another's input."

Jason blinks at me, mouth falling open.

"But thank you for letting me know," I go on. "I'm glad it was a good first experience for you."

He huffs a little. "You, Cas."

"What?" I ask, rubbing his legs through the blanket.

"You're just... I'm glad it's you."

My insides *ache* with the force of my affection.

"Can we do that a lot?" Jason asks, picking at the blanket now. "I mean, not just that. Other things, too. But—*Christ*. I want to do that a lot."

My smile feels blinding. "Whenever you want."

"You might regret that," he says. "I have a *lot* of pent-up fantasies, and you're the only person in my sights."

You're the only person.

Wow.

"I mean," he goes on, "do you know how many years I've had to think about what sex might be like? Because it's a lot. And now you're here, and you want me back, and I *get* it, you know? I get the whole—" He waves his hand in front of me, shaking his head. "Like, whoa. Your nipples *are* sexy. Don't tell Brad. And I just—" He cocks his head. "What?"

I slink up Jason's body, settling over the blanket. He swallows. "I'm yours for any fantasy you want to try," I tell him.

Jason's lips part, and I snag his mouth, swallowing his breathy moan as something deep within me pulls. It's *this—this is what it's supposed to be* and *is he really mine, mine, mine?* Jason's cock stirs beneath the blanket, pressing against my stomach.

"Wanna take a shower with me?" I ask. The situation in my shorts is getting uncomfortable.

He nods against my lips.

Pulling back, I scoot off the couch and hold out a hand. The blanket falls away as Jason lets me drag him up, but he makes no move to cover himself, and the sight of his cock bobbing just beneath the hem of the shirt he's wearing—*my* shirt—has me wanting to invest in a bunch of space heaters just so Jason can walk around my apartment like this anytime he wants.

For now, I put the idea on the back burner and lead Jason down the hall. He sheds his shirt as the water heats, and I ditch my shorts. For what might be the first time ever, I catch his eyes raking over my body in an appraising way as I step into the shower. I start washing the drying cum off my skin, but before long, Jason joins me, his hand closing around my cock. I jerk in welcome surprise as he gives me a slow stroke. The sound he makes is part curious, part satisfied.

"Can I..." he says, giving my shoulder a little shove until I'm against the tile. "Let me just—" And then he's dropping carefully to the ground, and my breath is leaving me in a *whoosh*.

I don't know why I thought Jason might be timid when it came to sex, but he's quickly proving that assumption wrong.

He angles my erection out of the way, ducking his gaze. "You're waxed," he says, more statement than question.

"For work. At the studio."

"So pretty," he mutters, right before he drops his head and takes my ball into his mouth.

My head thunks against the tile, and I pull in a centering breath as his tongue explores. He gives my leg a push, so I widen my stance. Jason rolls his tongue along my sac before sucking the other side into his mouth, laving my nut gently as his hand keeps a firm grip on my cock. He squeezes a little, almost like he's testing the weight of my dick in his fist. The mere sight of him down there, resting so comfortably between my legs, leaves me dizzy.

Jason lets me go, giving my hip a tap. "Turn around."

My chuckle is more than a little throaty. "You're kind of bossy, aren't you?"

"Sorry, I—"

"No," I say quickly, turning as he asked and looking back over my shoulder. "I like it. Tell me what you want, Jason. You can have it."

His eyes hold mine for a moment, the green looking bright. The shower runs beside us, but neither of us are under the spray.

"I wanna see you," he finally says, spreading my cheeks.

Christ.

My pulse sprints, anticipation and something a little wild and scary curling tight in my gut as Jason palms my ass cheeks, his gaze focused. He runs a finger down my crack, slippery and wet, the motion a mere caress. Then there are two, traveling the same path. Softly. Reverently. He stands up, but he doesn't move his hand, simply rotates his palm, those same two fingers aimed downwards and rubbing more firmly against my asshole.

"I want to make you come," he rasps.

My insides light like a firework.

Reaching over, I grab the lube I keep in the shower and pass it his way. Jason snatches it out of my hand, his touch gone for five seconds at most before he's bringing wet fingers to my crack. He rubs against me with three digits before the fingertip of one presses in, and I brace my forearms against the wall, grateful for the support.

Jason curses as his finger slides deep, stroking, exploring. "I wondered, but *God*. That's..." He trails off, and then he's sinking in with two digits and dropping back to his haunches. He twists his fingers as he goes, a move that has my knees nearly giving out, and his other palm glides over my ass cheek. "You're just welcoming me in. Like it's so easy."

Jesus. Heat spreads over my body in waves, and I lick my lips as he fucks his digits in and out slowly. "Feels good," I manage to say, wondering if I might just have a budding power top on my hands.

Jason crooks his fingers towards my nuts as he grabs my cock, and I fly up to my tiptoes, my groan garbled and more than a little surprised. He huffs an excited laugh as he works me over in tandem, stroking inside and out, and *yeah*. Yep. Not timid in the least, this one.

"Fuck, that's hot," he says, motions quick now.

"I'm gonna come, Jason," I warn him.

"Do it," he says, tongue leaving a long trail along my ass cheek. He's practically wrapped around the side of my leg, his arm around my hip to jerk me off and his knee bumping my ankle. And when he focuses his fingers against my prostate in that *come hither* stroke, I lose it.

The orgasm feels sharper this time, the second in such quick succession. It's harsh and almost on the edge of painful. But as soon as all that sensation snaps from *almost* to *coming*, it's sweet, blissful relief. I pulse over Jason's fist, spurting against the shower wall again and again. He strokes me through it, fingers gentling as my orgasm runs its course. And then he slips slowly from my body, a wide-eyed look on his face as he gazes up at me. His cheeks are rosy, his cock is hard, and as soon as he lets go of my softening dick, I spin around and haul him to his feet.

I find his lips in an instant, and all of Jason's cool evaporates like the flip of a switch. He rubs himself against my hip, hands scrambling to find purchase on my wet body. I snake a hand down between us, wrapping him up tight, and he groans.

"God yes," he says, diving back into my mouth, words muffled. "Yes, please. More of that. More. Make me come."

It only takes a few strokes. Jason's breath hitches against my lips, and, with a stuttered moan, he comes against my stomach. He sucks in air afterwards, his hands gripping my arms tight, and for a moment, we simply stand, catching our collective breaths.

"A lot," he says. "We're going to do that a lot."

His lips curve into a smile as I laugh.

When we finish soaping off and get out of the shower, I wrap a towel around my waist before grabbing another for Jason from the hall closet. He accepts it with an almost shy smile, drying himself off before heading into the living room to grab his pants. I swing by my bedroom, getting into clean clothes and then snagging an extra sweatshirt for Jason. He laughs when I tug it over his head, but he doesn't protest in the least, instead pushing his arms through the sleeves, hands tucked away against the fleece interior.

Better.

"I have a question," I tell him as we settle on the couch with a plate of snacks between us. Jason goes for the dried apricots as I eat a chip.

"Shoot."

"You don't have to tell me if you don't want," I make sure to say. "It's completely up to you. I just... I'm curious if you've ever *tried* to have sex before."

Jason nods slowly as he finishes chewing. "Sort of? Well, not entirely. I made out with a boy in high school once, and there was a little over-the-clothes action, but I stopped it when I realized I wasn't really into it. And then another time in my freshman year of college, there was this guy I had a few dates with, and I thought maybe if I just *tried*, it'd be okay. But..." He shakes his head. "I was barely even hard, and I knew it would be some effort to go through with it, and I didn't want that. Not for me, and not for him. So I stopped it, and that was that."

Jason looks like there's more he wants to say, so I wait.

"I could have," he says, gaze meeting mine. "I know I could have if I'd waited until I was hard up and then met someone for that purpose. The idea of sex has never repulsed me. I just..." He sighs a little, toying with another apricot. "I guess I thought not having sex was better than meaningless sex. I didn't want it to be *just because*. I wanted to want it."

And he did want it. With me.

My throat feels tight, and I clear it, nodding. "I get that," I tell him. My own experience has been so vastly different, but I *do* understand what Jason is telling me. "The first time I had sex, I was fifteen."

"So young," he says.

I shrug a little. "It was a mess, to be honest. The guy was older than me, and I should've realized he only wanted me for one thing, but I was young and naive, and I thought I was something special to him."

"Cas," he says gently, reaching over and squeezing my hand.

I give him a small smile. "It's been like that a lot for me," I say, not wanting to hold that back from Jason, even though it makes me feel...well, foolish and naive still, in a way. "But after Simon, I didn't want to keep making that same mistake."

"Simon. The guy who broke up with you via email."

I nod. "Yeah. You're the first person I've been with since him. And I know he meant the porn suggestion as a joke, a cruel one, but Elite 8 Studios made me feel safe. Even though what I do for the cameras is meaningless for *me*, having partners who were considerate and kind felt better than what I'd had."

"Cas," Jason says, scooting into my lap. His hands bracket my neck, and I pull him to me, liking the weight of him, the evidence that he's solid and real. "I don't judge your choices if that's what you're thinking. Your decisions are your own. Your feelings are different from my own. I don't... I don't think less of you for working in porn, okay? I knew that going into this. I still wanted you. *Want* you."

I nod again, eyes stinging. I blink the ache away.

"I'm sorry you haven't had people appreciate you the way they should have," he adds.

And what do I possibly say to that?

"You don't feel like the rest," I tell him.

His smile is soft, but it's also sad. "You're unlike anyone I've ever known. It's not meaningless, what we have. I don't know what it is yet, but it... It's not that."

And that much I know. Jason doesn't give himself freely. But he's giving himself to me.

I've never so badly wanted to freeze time as I do in this moment. Because what if it doesn't last? What if we're only a season, and when it passes, Jason is gone?

I'm not sure I could stand it.

But relationships *always* come with risk. There's never a guarantee, no matter how much you want it. Permanence doesn't exist, not even for the toughest materials, the strongest glass. Time, pressure, outside forces—they erode. My dad taught me that.

There's no way to know if Jason and I will last. But for as long as my heart beats, I will hang onto hope that my person exists. That there's someone out there who will grow to love me. Who will grow *with* me.

Maybe that person is Jason. It could be.

It's scary how much I *want* it to be.

"Hey," Jason says, fingers drifting through my hair. "What's wrong?"

"Nothing," I tell him, tucking my face against his neck and just *breathing.*

He hums, a curious sound, but then he rubs his hands over my head. Along my shoulders. Down my back.

"Do you think we should get out of the house today?" he asks, voice soft. "*Or...*"

There's a lot of weight in that *or*, and I grin against his skin. "What'd you have in mind?"

"What are your thoughts on being rimmed?"

My chuckle starts somewhere deep, but before long, I'm shaking hard enough to jostle Jason in my lap.

"Hey," he grumbles without any heat, laughing with me. "It's your own damn fault. Have you seen your ass?"

Oh God. I think I've unintentionally created a monster. *My monster.*

Mm. Yeah. I'm okay with that.

Chapter 14

Jason

"Ugh, this is the literal worst," I complain, slumping into a seat across from Brad.

My friend is in the coffee shop today, working from his laptop and drinking his weight in caffeinated beverages. Most days, he works from the apartment where he has a more complete setup: three computer monitors, a bunch of RAM or some such to run his gaming simulations, and a boatload of gadgets I don't understand. But about once a week, he comes to Hyped to be around people. Not that he ever bothers to talk to anyone but me.

"Yeah?" he replies, clearly distracted. His face is in his laptop, and he's typing in a somewhat disjointed manner with one hand while the other, injured finger included, sits around his coffee mug.

"Bee," I say, snapping my fingers in front of his face. "Focus."

He blinks at me. "Huh?"

"I need you to listen. This is important."

Brad gives me his serious face and sits taller in his seat. "What is it?"

"How do you *do* this?" I whisper-hiss. "How do allosexuals get anything done? Like, ever?"

Brad blinks at me for a moment before tucking his lips between his teeth. He pops them free before saying, "You horny, Birdie?"

"Don't laugh at me," I groan out as Brad laughs at me.

He waves his hand in front of his face. "No, no, it's just... I've been there, Jason. I went through this at thirteen. Well, not the actual sex part, but the thinking of sex part. Many a sock was sacrificed during those days."

And *ew*.

"I can't... *Fuck*, I can't stop thinking about him," I admit quietly. "We had sex three times yesterday. *Three times*. And I jerked off again this morning, and... God, I want him again. Have you *seen* his jawline?"

Brad grins. "You're fantasizing about his jawline?"

"I want to paint it," I mumble, covering my face when Brad's booming laugh catches the attention of a few customers in the shop.

"You're a dirty little fuck, aren't you?" Brad says quietly, sounding so damn proud. "And if I recall correctly, you did that very thing the first time you met. You know, with the whole—" He makes a *pshh* sound and squeezes his hand, demonstrating the *whipped cream incident*.

"Yeah, yeah, I remember," I mutter, but then I groan because thinking about that? Yeah, not helping. Those *lips*.

Brad snorts as I squirm in my seat. "Dude, just call him up. Watching this is painful."

I raise a brow. "What, just tell him I need some relief if he has time, please and thank you?"

"Uh, yeah."

"Can I...do that?" I ask a little incredulously.

"You precious baby fawn," he says, shaking his head slowly. "He's your beau. He's going to want to take care of you during this...very *hard* time. Trust me."

"Well, it's going to have to wait, one way or another," I say. "I'm meeting my mom for a late lunch, and then I have lecture."

"Say hi to your mom for me," Brad says. "And Birdie? It'll get better."

"What will?"

"The way you're feeling," he answers seriously. "The frantic edge. I'm not saying the desire will go away, but you and Cas will marathon fuck for a few weeks, one or both of you will probably pull a muscle, there might be chafing in places, and you'll *definitely* want to watch out for dehydration, but then things will settle down. It won't be so busy up in here"—he points to his head before pausing and pointing at his lap—"or down there."

I huff a laugh. "Thanks, I think? That kind of sounded like decent advice."

Brad shrugs. "Sometimes I'm a decent guy."

"More than sometimes, Bee," I tell him, getting out of my seat. "More coffee before I go?"

"Please," he says, passing me his mug.

I get Brad a refill, give the top of his head a kiss, and then I'm out the door.

My mom and I agreed on a casual diner for our late lunch, and when I arrive at nearly three o'clock, she's already seated. She waves me over with a smile on her face, and then I'm being tucked into a warm embrace that smells lightly of my mom's favorite freesia perfume.

"Hi, Jaybird," she says happily.

"Hey, Mom."

She gives me a kiss on the cheek before letting go, and I slip around to the other side of the booth, sliding into the seat across from her. The red vinyl is cracked so wide the white batting shows through, but the table is clean, and the air smells perfectly of bitter coffee and bacon.

"How've you been?" I ask.

The last time I saw my mom was a good five or six weeks ago, but she looks as she always does. Her blonde hair is in a loose ponytail, pieces falling out around her face, and a few wrinkles sit at the corners of her eyes. My mom is in her late forties—she had me at twenty-three—but she doesn't look it. She's always seemed younger than her years. Maybe it's that smile she wears—the one that never seems to dim, at least not for long.

"I'm just fine," she answers. "I joined a book club."

"Did you really?"

"Mhm. Marjory convinced me. We're meeting next week, and I'm bringing muffins."

"That's great, Mom. What are you reading?"

She hums. "Smut."

I jolt and cover my ears, then my eyes, then my ears again. "Oh God. Nope. No. I don't need to hear about that."

My mom laughs, tugging down my arms. "Your mother is perfectly familiar with sex, Jaybird. She had *you*, after all."

"Bleach," I mumble, shutting my eyes tight. "I need bleach."

She continues to laugh, but thankfully, the waitress arrives just in time to save me from further embarrassment. She fills our waters before taking our order. I get grilled cheese.

Once we're alone again, my mom sits back in her seat. "How've you been, honey?" she asks seriously. "What's new?"

A smile flits across my lips, and I can't help but sigh as I think about Cas. "I'm seeing someone."

"You are?" she asks, happily surprised. "Tell me about them. Did you meet at the hospital?"

I shake my head. "No, we met at the coffee shop. He was a customer."

"What does he do?"

"He works at an architecture firm?" I tell her. There's no way I'm mentioning the porn. She'll have to pry that information from my cold, dead fingers. "But he doesn't really like it there, so I don't know. Maybe he'll find something else."

"And his name?" she asks, a smile playing across her face.

"Cassius. Cas."

"Cassius," she parrots, humming a little. "A warrior."

Or hollow.

I don't say that either. Cas is *not* hollow.

"That's fitting for you," she says before taking a sip of water. "You're both fighters."

I huff. "Mkay, Mom."

She *tsks* at me. "You're a champion, Jaybird, and you'll never convince me otherwise. Now c'mon, tell me what you like about this Cassius."

"He's...patient," I say. "And kind. So kind. He thinks about things differently than I do, and I like that. He's constantly surprising me. And, uh..." I clear my throat a little. "He's pretty cute."

Understatement. I literally saw someone walk into a glass door at the hospital last week when Cas stopped by to drop off a sandwich and say hello. It would have been hilarious if it didn't make me want to claw their eyes out.

My mom is quiet for a moment before she asks, "Does he know?"

The smile slips right off my face. "No. It's too soon for that."

My mom hesitates. "Maybe so. But, honey, if you're getting serious with this boy, don't you think he deserves to know? It would affect him, too."

And that's... It's not fair. She's right, but it's *not fair*.

"I'm not ready yet," I tell her, the words scraping like glass on the way out. "I just want..."

I just want to enjoy this—finally having someone to call my own. Someone I want, who wants me back. I want weeks of sex marathoning, like Brad said, and being so stupid in lust that Cas and I end up at the hospital with intravenous fluid drips because we couldn't be bothered to stop and drink water.

I want to enjoy the first *real* relationship I've ever had—the first one that has the potential to go somewhere—before telling the guy I'm dating that there's a fifty percent chance I'll die young from the same degenerative nerve disease my father had.

How the hell do you bring something like that up?

Who would stick with someone who did?

"Honey," my mom says softly, squeezing my arm. "Have you put any more thought into getting the test?"

"What's the point?" I say, voice cracking.

She makes a pained sound. "It might give you peace of mind. There's every chance you don't have the Huntingtin mutation."

Huntington's disease. A rare, inherited mutation in the HTT—*Huntingtin*—gene that causes the progressive breakdown of nerve cells in the brain. It can be slow, the loss of voluntary movement and cognition. But it's always complete. By the end, in the late stages, professional care is required in order to cope with the inability to walk. To speak. To *breathe*.

My dad died at the age of forty-six after having lived with symptoms for sixteen years. Not that long, all things considered. Sometimes progression of the disease can take thirty years.

I still can't decide if that was a blessing in his case or not.

"It's a fifty percent chance," I correct my mom, swallowing around the lump in my throat. "Fifty percent I don't have it. Fifty percent I do."

"And right now, you're 100 percent uncertain. If you get the gene test," she says, tone soft, "at least you'd know."

"If I have it, I don't *want* to know," I get out. "I don't want to wait for that. I don't want to..."

"Prepare?" she suggests gently, and I can't even be mad at her because she *knows* what it's like to go through this. She experienced it the same way I did. She lost someone she loved the same way I did. "If you have it, you can prepare. You and your partner *both*."

I rub my eyes, looking away. Fuck. *Fuck.*

It takes a long moment before my throat loosens enough to talk. "Do you regret it? Marrying Dad?"

"Never," she says immediately. "I loved your dad, and his disease didn't change that."

"But if..." I clear my throat. "If you'd known ahead of time, would you have done things differently?"

"No," she answers, again right away. "If I knew your dad had Huntington's, I still would have married him. We still would have had you."

"How can you know that?" I ask. "How can you be so sure?"

"I feel it," she says, touching her chest. "I feel it in here. A life can be lived fully even if it's not for long. Your dad had a full life, Jaybird, albeit a short one. I would've wanted to offer the same to my child, even knowing the chances. A full life, lived with love? I think that's enough. I hope you're not upset with me for that."

"No," I say, grabbing my mom's hand and squeezing. "I'm glad you would have given me life, one way or another. And I wouldn't blame you if...if I have it."

"And you wouldn't blame your father, either," she says assuredly.

I shake my head. I wouldn't.

"Sometimes life is messy," my mom says, her tone airy, like her perfume. "It's beautiful and messy and far from perfect. It's also fleeting, no matter which way you look at it. But, honey, what happened with me and your dad is different from your situation."

Because my dad never knew about the Huntingtin gene. He never knew his own father, and his symptoms were a surprise when they developed. It was a surprise to him and my mom both.

But I *do* know. I know about the disease, that there's a chance I have it, and keeping that information from Cas for much longer would be akin to lying.

If I got the test, though. If I got the test and I don't have the mutation...

"Ultimately, it's your choice," my mom says, as if she can read my mind. "But wouldn't it be better to know, one way or another?"

"I'm afraid to hope," I admit.

Her face softens. "Hope can be a wonderful thing, Jason." And if she's using my real name, I know she wants me to listen. "I have hope for you. Hope that this disease isn't something you'll have to face again. Hope that you'll find someone to live a full life with. Maybe even this Cassius, hm? I hope for your happiness every single day."

I nod, not knowing what else to say.

"Maybe Cassius could help you with this," she says. "Maybe it'd be good to talk about it."

Or maybe he'd leave me.

"Brad says hi," I say, belatedly remembering the message from my friend. My mom doesn't call out my deflection.

"That sweet boy," she replies. "Give him a hug for me."

"I will," I tell her, sitting back as the waitress shows up with our food. Conversation switches gears after that, and we stick to lighter topics. And even though I know my mom is right—that I can't keep burying my head in the sand—I'm not ready to face it all.

Not ready to face my possible diagnosis. Not ready to tell Cas. Not ready for any of it. So I push it from my mind, at least for the time being.

Right now, I just want to hang onto what I have while I still can.

Chapter 15

CAS

Jason: Can I see you tonight?

Me: You bet. Stay in or go out?

Jason: In. My lecture just got over. I can come to you.

Me: Nah, I'll meet you at your place. You have work in the morning.

Jason: Thanks, Cas. See you soon.

"Everything okay?" my mom asks, taking a sip of her Cosmopolitan. Her blouse blows gently in the breeze as we sit poolside, her enjoying a post-dinner drink. Dad took a work call and is up in his office, and Charlotte, who joined us for dinner, already left for home.

"Everything's fine," I tell her, pocketing my phone. "Just making plans for tonight."

"Ah, to be young," she says wistfully.

I huff a laugh. "You're not that old, Mom."

"Retired is old," she says, taking another sip of her drink.

I don't bother mentioning that Dad is older than her and still working. I doubt he'll ever quit.

"Mom, do you..." I stop myself.

"What is it, Cassius?" she asks, giving me her full attention. Her hair, dark like mine, Leo's, and Char's, is cut short in a smart bob. There's a little silver in it that I didn't notice until recently.

"When you worked at Kinsley Richman, did you...*enjoy* it?"

She watches me silently for a moment, just long enough to make me feel like I'm being inspected, and then she sets down her drink and swings her legs to the side of the lounge chair she's in. She leans toward me before speaking.

"I enjoyed working there very much. You know that's how I met your father."

I nod. I do.

Dad wasn't Mom's direct boss when she started working at the company. In fact, she'd been there a good year before they met at an office holiday party. The rest was history, as they say.

I always wondered if my mom had plans—dreams—that she didn't follow because she ended up marrying into the business. But I never asked. Because if I did, I might have had to face the fact that I'm not following *my* dreams, whatever they might be.

"Cassius," my mom says gently. "Are you unhappy at work?"

I don't have time to answer her before Dad is stepping onto the patio, letting out a great, big sigh. "Sorry, dearest," he tells my mom, placing a kiss on her cheek before taking a seat beside her.

I hop up. "I need to get going," I tell them.

My mom's face draws down slightly, but she nods. I'm guessing we'll be coming back to this conversation another time. "Have a good evening, darling," she says.

My dad gives his own goodbye, and then I'm walking back through their multimillion-dollar home, wondering why

I don't *want* this more. Wondering if there's something wrong with me.

When I get to Jason's apartment, my mood lifts so quickly it leaves me a little lightheaded. It reminds me of how I feel at Neddy's, when I'm on the court. Of how it feels to exercise a dormant muscle. Like my body is breathing again.

Like *I'm* breathing again.

It only takes a moment for Jason to open the door when I knock, and once he does, he tugs me inside so swiftly I'm left lightheaded once more.

"Hey," he says, shutting the door, looking at me with big eyes. His hand is on my arm, and his chest is rising and falling like he's slightly out of breath.

"Hi, Jason."

"Hey, Cas," Brad calls out from the kitchen. He waves my way, and I raise my own hand, but Jason tugs me from the entryway before I can utter a hello.

"Buh-bye, Brad," Jason says, leading me down the hall, my shoes still on. Brad's amused grin follows me.

"Everything okay?" I ask in concern.

Jason nods, dragging me into his bedroom and then letting go to shut the door.

"I—" He cuts off, palms flat against the wood, chest heaving. He looks like...

Oh.

He looks like he's two seconds away from mauling me.

"Jason?"

"I need you," he practically whispers. "Is that okay to say? Can I say I need you?"

My cock kicks up so fast it's staggering. "Yeah, Jason," I respond. *Want me. Please. Need me.* "That's definitely okay."

"Okay. Yeah. Good," he says in a relieved rush, and then he's pushing off the door and stalking toward me. He grabs the back of my neck as soon as he's within reach, hauling me down to meet his lips.

It's like a tiny detonation goes off between us.

Jason walks me backwards, hands slipping beneath my shirt as we kiss. "How was your day?" he mumbles against my mouth.

"Good," I answer breathlessly, still not entirely used to this side of Jason but not about to complain about it. "Better now."

His teeth catch my lip, and I shiver.

"Good," he mutters, giving me a little shove as soon as my legs hit the bed. I sit down, and Jason climbs onto my lap. He's hard, his pants straining with it, and he grinds down on me in an unpracticed move that's hot as hell. It's desperate and wanton, and if yesterday hadn't demolished any reservation I might have had about whether or not Jason was into me, the way he shudders and moans against my mouth right now would.

He tugs at my shirt quickly, groaning this sharp little *ungh* once it clears my head. His eyes rake over my bare chest, and then he's pushing me back.

I land flat on the bed, pulse racing as Jason's blunt nails drag down my pecs and abdomen. This confidence he has, this surety, is a massive turn-on. Jason may have been a virgin up until a day ago, but he's certainly no wallflower. He's fierce.

My little lion.

Jason leans forward, his weight pressing me firmly to the mattress. "Too many options," he says roughly, lips skimming my jaw. The corner of my mouth.

"We have time," I remind him, blood pumping hot. "Plenty of time."

He blows out a little breath before capturing my lips. He kisses me hard, palms flat on my chest as I hold tight to his thighs. He moves down my jaw, my throat, mouth replacing his hand on my pec. His tongue swipes over my skin, tasting, exploring, and then he closes his mouth around my nipple. I grunt, my hips jolting as he sucks and teases the bud.

"Fuck," I mutter.

"Good?"

I nod repeatedly. "Yeah."

He hums, lips drifting feather-light across my chest until he reaches the other nipple. He licks it, the barest swipe of his tongue, like a cat, before sucking it into his mouth.

I squirm. "Fuck, babe."

He looks up at my words, eyes endlessly bright. His tongue rasps against me one more time before he releases my nipple with a pop. Cool air rushes over the wet bud as he trails his lips inward, feathering kisses and little licks down the center of my chest and stomach. My legs are still dangling off the bed, and Jason steps down onto the ground between them as his lips journey over my body. He presses one last kiss to my hipbone before grabbing at my jeans.

"Naked please," he says quickly, pinging the button free.

I huff a laugh and lift my hips as he tugs my jeans down without unzipping them. He makes a frustrated sound when he sees me still in my shoes. With zero finesse, he shucks them off, followed by my socks, tossing all items aside. Then he tugs down my jeans and briefs, and—

"*God*," he breathes, dropping my clothes lightly at his feet. His eyes rake over my body, taking me in. My legs. My cock. My stomach and my face. There's not a single inch of me he doesn't cover.

I've been the center of attention plenty. Had people look at me like they want me. I may not know much, but I do know that. I know desire. Lust. I've seen it shine in the eyes of my partners before. I've been coveted and fucked and urged to fuck.

But I have never before seen someone look at me as if I'm a treasure. As if I'm the oxygen they need to breathe.

There's no doubt in my mind Jason finds me attractive, that he desires my body. But it's layered on top of the almost nervous affection we started with. It's wrapped over the core of whatever it was that drew Jason to me, the same way I was drawn to him. Lust isn't our foundation.

The way Jason wants me? I've never felt anything like it.

"I thought I might have imagined it," he says, tugging off his shirt.

"What's that?" I ask, licking my lips, my heart thudding a steady beat.

He unzips his jeans, pushing them down his hips and stepping out of the material. His underwear goes next, and then he strokes himself slowly as he looks at me.

"You," he says simply.

I lose my breath.

"Would you touch yourself for me?" he asks.

"Fuck, Jason," I groan out, squeezing my dick.

His eyes widen, and his hand stops. "What?"

I shake my head quickly, not wanting him to feel remotely self-conscious about the bossiness I apparently find irresistible. *And wasn't prepared for.*

"Where do you want me to touch myself?"

He sucks in air, as if he hadn't considered more than one option. Finally, he says, "Stroke your cock."

My pleasure. Tucking one arm under my head, I widen my legs and loosen the tension on the base of my dick. I give myself a slow stroke. Two. Twist my hand over my crown. Jason's eyes stay glued to my actions, watching my fist move up and down.

"Can you..." He trails off.

"Can I what?" I encourage, jerking myself lazily. "Unless we're talking hard kinks, I'm into most things. Just ask."

He huffs a laugh at that. "Can you flip over?"

I raise a brow but let my cock go to heft myself higher up the bed. Once in the middle, I roll onto my stomach, cross my legs at the ankle, and then look back at Jason, flexing my ass cheeks. He groans.

"Hands and knees," he rasps.

Fucking hell.

Blowing out a breath, I shift onto all fours, cock hanging hard and heavy below me.

Jason swallows roughly. "Can you..." He swallows again, eyes flicking to mine. "Can you do that arch? You know, that thing you do sometimes in your videos?"

I bite my lip. "You've watched me, Jason?"

He rolls his eyes. "You know I have."

Honestly, I wasn't sure. He knew Himbo, but that doesn't mean he actually watched me perform. Apparently, he has.

Keeping my head turned, I widen my stance until my legs are far enough apart that I know Jason is getting an eyeful, and then I lower my chest to the mattress, creating that deep arch Jason is asking for. Prostrating myself.

He groans again, and before I can even blink, he's striding forward and joining me on the bed. I jolt in surprise when his hands land on my ass cheeks, and my breath leaves me in a rush when his tongue swipes across my hole.

"Jesus, Jason," I groan out, voice hitching. Face against the mattress, I clutch handfuls of Jason's sheets as he licks me for all he's worth. His palms roam over my body, touching whatever skin he can reach, and his tongue relentlessly flattens and circles and *prods* until my cock starts to leak.

"God," he says between licks. "I never thought... it could be... this good."

I huff, moaning when his hand cups my balls, tugging gently.

"You're like... everything I thought... I could want," he says before leaning back. His hand moves up my taint, one finger sinking inside of my ass. "*Christ.*"

"Jason," I moan, hardly able to keep my hips still. He didn't fuck me yesterday, just ate me out until I came across his sheets, but—

"Can I have you, Cas?" he asks. "I wanna be inside you. Wanna fuck you."

God yes.

"I was waiting for you to ask," I admit. Ever since he practically put me in a headlock and rammed his cock down my throat.

"Really?" he says. "You're not...surprised?"

I huff a breath. Why? Because he's smaller than me? Or less experienced? "I'm not surprised, Jason. You're pretty toppy."

"Huh," he says, removing his finger. I make to ease up, but Jason presses his palm flat against my back. "Not yet. There's no way I'm going to last long, so I need you as close to coming as possible."

Oh, Jesus. What is he...

That tongue passes over my hole again as his hand wraps around my dick, and I can't stay down. I just can't. I get my elbows under me, forehead on my closed fists, and rock back against Jason's face. He makes a happy sound, flitting the tip of his tongue back and forth across my entrance like he did to my nipple, and I nearly sob.

Screw power top. I may just have a pleasure Dom-awakening on my hands.

"You like it, right?" he asks before licking me broadly. "You like being fucked?"

"Yeah," I breathe out, hips jerking as his fist focuses on my crown. He spreads the precum, jerking me swiftly. "You, *ah*... should probably get inside me now."

"You're close?" he asks, nuzzling my ass cheek.

"Ah-hah-hah," I answer, entire body jolting when he rubs my hole. He slips his finger back inside, not very far, and then retreats.

The loss of sensation is jarring, all touch gone in an instant and cool air wafting over my skin. Jason slides off the bed, walking over to his nightstand. He grabs lube and condoms before looking back at me, gaze hot and proprietary all in one.

"Cas," he says roughly, climbing up next to me and nudging my hip until I roll to my back. He settles his weight on top of my body, our cocks pressing together and his hands beside my head. He's only a little shorter than me, two inches at most, so he kisses me easily, a soft, gentle touch. "I'm going to be honest."

"Okay?" I say, swallowing tightly, my hands running along his smooth back.

"I'm not going to last long," he says, peppering me with another kiss. "I'm just not. I'm probably going to lose myself, and I might not get you off before that happens. But I'll do better next time, okay?"

"Jason," I say with a chuckle. "Sex isn't this perfect thing. I don't expect us to come in tandem, and I'm not worried about you getting *better*. Everything between us has been pretty fucking awesome as is."

"Yeah?" he asks, a curl to his lips.

"Yeah. So c'mon," I say, sliding my hands up his back until I can sink my fingers into his hair. His eyes flutter closed, and he rests his lips against mine. "Suit up and fuck me, babe. You know you want to."

"*Fu-u-uck*," he hisses, opening his eyes. The hazel is dark. "You can't say shit like that, Cas. I'll come."

I snag his mouth, a smile on my lips, a lightness in my chest. "That's kind of the point."

"Not until I'm inside you," he retorts, nipping my bottom lip before he draws back. "All right, here we go. Ready?"

I nod, biting my lip. "Yeah. Ready."

He blows out a breath, grabbing the bottle of lube. "Hold on to your socks."

Chapter 16

JASON

Holy fuck. Holy *motherfucking* fuck.

One finger slides inside Cas easily. His body doesn't put up any resistance, and he watches me with a steady sort of calm.

Me, on the other hand—I feel like I'm about to burst out of my skin. My cock is rock-hard and begging for some sort of friction—for *release*—but I haven't dared touch it since we started, knowing it would take no effort at all to fall over that edge.

Part of me can't believe I'm about to fuck Cas. To find out, once and for all, what it feels like to sink into someone real. Someone I care about.

And yet, the funny thing is...even with how keyed up I am, I know I'd be perfectly happy with the alternative of getting Cas off in spectacular fashion and then humping myself to orgasm against the mattress. Just being here with this man—making him feel good—is a high unlike any other.

I didn't know it could be like this. I didn't know I could want his pleasure more than my own.

Focusing on what Cas's body is telling me, I slip the tips of two fingers into his hole. There's more pressure this time, but only for a moment. Cas breathes out, and I slide in to the first knuckle. I fuck him with my fingers slowly, easing them in further, spreading them, stretching him. He's laid out on his back, one foot planted on the bed, leg angled wide, and his other drawn up toward his chest.

"Yeah," he says, licking his lips. "Another."

Ungh.

"No dirty talk," I remind him, slipping out and pressing in with three fingers.

He huffs a laugh, holding his drawn leg tight. A little sweat beads his brow, and I get a strange sense of pride seeing that. Like I got him there. *I* did that to him.

I jerk his cock a few times, and Cas curses. *Ooh*, yes. This is fun.

"If you don't get your cock in me soon," Cas says, chest heaving, "I'm gonna milk your fingers instead."

"*Jesus*," I hiss, my own dick throbbing. *Rinsing bedpans, sick puppies, that gross end piece on a banana.*

"Come on, Jason," Cas says soothingly. "You're ready."

Me, not him. Because we both know he's ready. He's assuring me I am, too.

I give his knee a kiss, closing my eyes for a moment and then drawing out my fingers. I grab a condom, my hand only shaking slightly as I tear it open and roll it down my cock. *Yes, I've practiced.* I add lube, keeping my mind off the feeling of my fist briefly working my length, and then I scoot forward, settling between Cas's outstretched legs.

"Don't worry about going slow," Cas tells me, whiskey eyes soft. "Just fucking *fly.*"

I nod—not trusting my brain to produce words—and notch against his entrance. Cas grabs his other leg, holding himself open, and as I press forward, he pushes against me. It's so easy, how quickly my crown slips in. My mouth parts, and I watch, rapt, as I sink slowly inside Cas's body.

Holy fuck.

I'm shaking. My hands. My arms. My legs. My *everything*.

"Go, babe," Cas says. "It's okay. Go."

So I do.

It's almost a blur. I pull my hips back. Sink in. *Sob* with relief. Cas's body welcomes my own as I drape myself over him. He's all hard muscle and tanned skin. Cut abs, long cock, perfect fucking pecs and perfect fucking nipples. I bend down and latch on to one, drawing it into my mouth as my hips move of their own accord. Everything at my core is drawn tight—my cock, my balls, my gut—as if inside a vise, but I block it out. I block it out, and I *move*.

My lips at Cas's pec. He smells like man. Like spicy Heaven. I lap him up.

My body dragging against his. Over his. *Inside* his, so silky smooth.

His cock at my stomach, a steel length. The tightness of his legs wrapped around my waist like he doesn't want to let me go.

His mouth under my own now. Tongue against mine as I drink him down. As I taste him. Trying to get closer.

It starts as a distant ache, so far back in my mind it's like the roaring of waves. It's coming—I know it is—but I'm not ready. I'm not ready.

I sink my face into the crook of Cas's neck, and he grunts against me.

"Jason," he breathes.

Not ready. Not ready.

His inhales are sharp little bursts, his hips meeting my movements, timed with me. His leg drops from around my waist, and I grab it, holding him to my side, shifting with the weight of it. He *groans*, the sound breaking into pieces.

"There," he says. And, "There. There."

It's too much. I can't—

"Coming," he says, his voice a gasp.

And *fuck*, I can't...

Cas draws in a breath, and I feel it against my stomach first, the swelling of his cock. His fingers tighten in my hair and on my shoulder blade, his ass starts to spasm, and I'm gone. I cry out against his neck as I crack over the edge so harshly it feels like I might pass out. I don't recognize the sounds coming from my mouth. Barely even register the distant thump of the headboard against the wall. I can't feel a thing other than the implosion of my universe into a singular second so bright and so beautifully painful that, for a moment, I wonder if I'm even still conscious.

I knew it would be different. I knew it might even be special.

But I didn't know it could be *this*.

My cock is still throbbing when the height of it passes. Still pulsing weakly into the condom. Cas's ass is still tightening around the base of me rhythmically in a way that reminds me of a kneading cat. His breath is rushing past my ear, heavy and interspersed with little reactionary moans. And I don't know how I'm ever going to get my brain in working order again to speak, so I kiss his neck instead. I kiss him over and over, every spot I can reach. And when that's not enough, I lift myself up and find first his eyes, catching them for a moment, reading...I don't know what. And then I find his lips.

He's pillow-soft beneath me, his mouth pliant and sated, but moving against my own like a slow, gentle song. It's sweet and sincere, and Cas's words about snowflakes float into my mind. I think I get it. I think I understand how something can be so short-lived but brilliant. How it can feel like a gift just to be a part of the moment.

My dad passes into my mind, too, but I can't think about that. Not right now.

"Jason," Cas says softly, sighing against my lips. "Anytime you wanna rail me into your mattress, you just let me know."

I let out a laugh, I can't help it, and my cock gives a little jerk. Cas moans, shifting under me, and I ease back, lifting my weight.

"Okay?" I ask.

The smile he gives me is all satisfied smirk. "More than."

A beat passes where we simply look at each other, both of us grinning like fools, and then, from the other side of the wall comes, "*Duuudes*."

I jolt. "What the fuck, Brad!" I squeak. "Were you listening to us?"

"Uh," he calls back, sounding unrepentant. "It was literally impossible not to. You two are *loud*."

"Oh my God," I grumble, dropping my face to Cas's chest.

He shakes against me in laughter.

"I didn't know you could sound like that, Birdie," Brad says, sounding more than a little surprised. "I mean, *damn*, boy."

I shoot upright. "I swear to God, Brad, if you don't shut your mouth right this instant, I'm buying you a cock cage and putting it on when you're *asleep*."

There's a long beat of silence.

"Dude," he says. "Kinky."

Brad laughs when I pound a fist against the wall, but then he falls silent.

"I'm so sorry," I say to Cas, sinking back down against his chest. "Next time, I'll lock him outside the apartment."

Cas is biting his lip. "It's fine. But, uh, Birdie?"

I groan, and it's then I realize I'm still inside Cas. "I'm gonna..." I say, pointing downwards, and Cas gives me a nod. I hold the base of the condom as I pull out, and *holy shit*, that's just a whole new experience, isn't it?

Realizing I don't even have a trash can in here, I toss the condom to the foot of the bed. Cas is spread out without a care in the world when I turn back, one arm up behind his head, the other resting on the mattress between us. There's cum spread across his stomach and chest, lube between his thighs, and, uh... I go offline for a moment.

"Come here," Cas says, urging me forward.

I blow out a breath, easing down beside him as he opens his arm.

"Birdie is Brad's nickname for me," I explain. "My parents called me Jaybird, so it's a diminutive of that."

"Why'd your parents call you Jaybird?" he asks, hand running along my shoulder.

"Um. I guess because my name starts with the letter J? You know, like when a parent calls their kid Buddy, which morphs into Butters, and then, all of a sudden, they're cooing to their Butterbean?"

"Uh, no," Cas says, eyes twinkling. "I don't. I was always just Cassius."

I hum a little sadly at that. "Well, I think that's why. Jason was Jay was Jaybird."

"And then Birdie," he says.

"Mhm. He's Bee. B for Brad."

"You two are sweet," he says, kissing my forehead.

"Ugh, don't let Brad hear you say that. He'll gloat."

Cas chuckles.

"You're okay, right?" I check, drifting my fingers along his side. "I didn't hurt you?"

"No, you didn't hurt me," he says calmly. "That was really fucking spectacular, Jason."

"Really?" I ask, more than a little surprised. "It didn't last long."

He huffs a laugh. "Didn't need to. I like being with you. It feels good. Feels right."

"Yeah," I say, throat closing up a little. "It does, doesn't it?"

"Mm."

"So, uh... Do you want to clean up?" I ask, eyeing Cas's torso.

He chuckles. "Probably not a bad idea."

"And then, um... You could stay the night if you want?" I offer. "I have to be at the coffee shop at six, so it'd be an early start. But if you don't want to go home?"

Please don't go home.

He gives me a smile, tugging me in for another kiss against my forehead. "I'd love to stay."

"Okay," I breathe out. "Good. Yeah, that's..."

"Good?" he supplies.

I swat his chest, and he laughs.

And *damn*. I could get used to nights just like this.

"*Fuuuck*," I groan in dismay, immediately regretting everything. I swipe my phone alarm off and peel myself off the hunk of hot flesh under me before realizing, *holy shit*, there's a hunk of hot flesh under me.

My regrets disappear.

"Did you just call me flesh?" Cas mumbles, shifting and rubbing his eyes.

And *ohh*.

Cas is spread out beside me on the bed, his long upper body on display. The sheets are hanging over his hips, low enough that the base of his dick is visible, and I must make some sort of hungry-ass sound because Cas chuckles.

"Morning," I manage.

"Morning to you, too," he says. "Although are we sure it's morning? Feels like the middle of the night."

"Yeah, sorry about that," I say apologetically. "I know it sucks."

"'S'fine," he mumbles around a yawn. "I'll just get a jumpstart on work today."

I hum, watching Cas's hand smooth down his chest and abdomen. *Keep going*, I urge it. *Little further.*

It stops on his stomach, and I nearly groan.

Christ, since when am I such a horndog? *Since you lost your virginity and found out how amazeballs sex is, you dummy.*

Right.

"Do you want me to make some breakfast?" Cas asks, pulling my focus. "I don't know how to cook anything fancy, but I could probably scramble eggs or something."

Jesus, this man.

"I don't think we have eggs, but there's cereal, oatmeal, fruit..." I mentally comb through the pantry. "Bagels, probably. I need to visit the bathroom, but help yourself. I'll be there shortly."

"You sure?" he asks.

"Yeah, absolutely," I tell him, easing out of bed. I turn around as Cas steps to the floor, and *ho, my God*.

Back to me, Cas reaches up toward the ceiling, stretching out his muscles. The room is still mostly dark, illuminated only slightly by the lamp on the nightstand that's programmed to turn on at the same time as my alarm. His muscles bunch, the line of him catching the light in a way that makes him look like a carefully drawn work of art. Like every piece of his body was meticulously sketched out to highlight the masculine form. His ass is round. His waist trim. His thighs and calves weighted with lean muscle. His back arches in a way that has me flashing to last night. And his hands touch for just a moment above his head as he turns his face to the side, gifting me with a view of his crisp jaw, plump lips, dark eyebrows, and mussed hair. And then, as quickly and smoothly as he started stretching, he drops his arms to his sides, and the moment of stillness is shattered.

Cas turns and grabs his briefs off the floor, glancing over at me. "All right?" he asks, a crooked smile on his face.

I swallow audibly. "Toilet," I mutter before walking from the room, clipping the doorway in the process.

Holy shit. Ho-ly *shit*.

Cas is *hot*. Like, really fucking hot. *The guy I'm dating—and fucking—is really fucking hot.*

I knew this, in theory. I always thought he was pretty. But it didn't really hit me how much of a smokeshow Cas is until right this moment, when I became the asshat walking into a wall because I couldn't take my eyes off the man.

Ugh, those fucking lips.

I close the bathroom door lightly, glaring down at my much-too-excited dick. "*Not now*," I hiss. "There's no *time*. Go away so I can pee."

It doesn't listen.

"You're going to have to get used to this, buddy," I tell it. Although I might be speaking to myself. "We can't stay home and fuck all day." No matter how appealing *that* sounds now that Cas is in the picture.

I groan, erasing his lovely face from my mind with a mental image of foot fungi while I splash cold water on my cheeks. Finally, after reciting every intestinal parasite I can think of and brushing my teeth, I'm able to take a piss.

When I get back to my room, it's empty, and I make quick work of dressing for the day, beanie atop my head. Cas is in the kitchen when I reach the end of the hall, standing in briefs and rooting around in the cupboards. He pulls a box of cereal free before seeing me in the doorway and smiling.

"Found it," he says, brandishing the box.

My heart skips. Literally skips, the jaunty fucker.

"Yeah," I breathe because *words*.

"Everything okay?" he asks, head cocked a little.

"More than," I answer, stepping close. And palpitations be damned, I lean against that broad, naked chest and kiss him. He hums happily, arm coming around my waist in a loose hold.

I debate telling him exactly how okay I am. That I haven't been this excited about a person *ever*. That I'm already dreaming of nights ahead and days where I can see Cas's smile. That I want to hear more about snowflakes and all the things he finds important in life.

I could tell him this, but I can't quite find the words. So, instead, I lock my lips with his.

And based on the curve of his smile, it's enough.

Chapter 17

CAS

"Hey, sugar pop. How's it hanging?" Alex asks as the door to the break room swings shut behind him. He drops into a seat across from me. "I feel like I've barely seen you in *weeks*."

"Yeah, the last time was..."

"The hospital scene where Nurse Tink helped Himbo with his urgent and uncontrollable erection?" Alex supplies.

I snort. "Yeah. That."

Alex snickers, and I dig into my sandwich. I'm always a little hungry post-scene, but today, I needed more than a bag of chips or a granola bar. Niko and I had to reset several times while shooting because they kept having an issue with the lights flickering in and out. Let me tell you, holding a man's weight up against the wall for that long is a trying task.

I had no clue porn could be such a workout.

"*Sooo...*" Alex says, catching my attention. His tone isn't casual in the least. "Are you still seeing a certain favorite barista of ours?"

My lips curve into a smile. "I am."

He squeaks, clapping his hands together once. "And how *is* Jason?"

"Did you know he's an actual nurse?" I say. "Well, just about. He should be registered in a few months."

Alex's brows pop up. "No shit?"

"That's a tough job," Teddy puts in. He's lounging on a couch in the back of the room. I thought he was asleep, but I guess not.

"It sure is," Alex says. "I'm impressed."

"Me, too," I add, more to myself than anything. It's especially impressive considering Jason has a full-time job to put himself through nursing school. I never had to worry about that. My parents paid for my education. Jason, on the other hand, is working hard to achieve his dreams. It's admirable.

Alex's smile is soft. "Look at you, boo. All smitten." At a louder volume, he adds, "Need any help in that department, Teddy? If you haven't heard, I'm an expert matchmaker."

Teddy doesn't even open his eyes. "I'm good."

Alex hums, a thoughtful sound. "Does that, *perhaps*, mean you already have your sights set on someone?"

"You're nosy," Teddy states.

"It's called caring," Alex says, huffing once. "You might as well give up the goods, Teddy Bear. You know I'll get it out of you one way or another."

"Don't you have your own bears' goods to worry about?" Teddy retorts.

Alex's grin is immediate. "And what goods they are," he says with a sigh. "I'm telling you, if you haven't been smushed between two hunks of beefy men, you haven't lived."

"I'm pretty sure most of us here *have* been in that situation, Alex," I point out.

He snorts a laugh. "Too true. Hey, we should hit up Sublime this week," he says, bouncing excitedly in his seat.

There's a standing tradition for the Elite 8 cast and crew to meet up at a club in town, Sublime, on Friday nights. I've been a handful of times, and it's good fun. An easy way to pick someone up for the night, if that's what you're looking for. I haven't gone in a while—not since I started seeing Jason.

"I'll bring my bears," Alex goes on. "You bring your Jason. And Teddy, anyone we should invite for you? *Hmm?*"

"Nope," the man says.

Alex rolls his eyes. "Fine. But I'll see you there?" he asks me.

"Assuming Jason wants to go," I answer. "He has a shift at the hospital on Saturday, so we probably wouldn't stay out late."

"Oh, honey," Alex says, a wicked grin lighting his face. "Neither would I. Watching my two men grind up on one another gets me horny as all get-out."

I huff a laugh at that. I'm pretty sure my coworker has his hands full with those two boyfriends of his, and I'm even more sure he enjoys every second of it.

Alex hops out of his seat. "Okay, gotta go. Yes, home to my men. Isn't love *grand?*"

"Subtle," Teddy mutters.

Alex shoots me a wink. "Night, boys. See you Friday."

With that, Alex flounces out of the room, and Teddy chuckles, sitting upright and rubbing his eyes.

"Such a little shit," he says.

I cough around my last bite of sandwich. "Does it bother you, him pressing about your private life?"

I'm fairly certain Alex would stop if Teddy asked him to. When I first started working here, Alex dragged me aside and told me that my feelings inside these walls were important and that I shouldn't ever do anything I didn't want to do. He told me everyone here would respect my boundaries and if anyone didn't, I should let him know right away so he could kick their ass.

It was an impassioned repeat of what Jerome himself told me. Alex may be small, but he's mighty. And he has a good heart.

Teddy shakes his head. "No, the little sprite doesn't bother me. I just like making him work for it. He has more fun that way."

I chuckle. "Everyone here is kind of a family, huh?"

Teddy nods, rubbing his hand through his short brown hair. Even sleep-rumpled, there's a soft smile on his face. "Yeah. We look out for each other."

It's pretty great. I hadn't planned on working in porn, and I can't say I see it as my future. But I *am* glad I met the people within these walls. They accepted me without question, they're the reason I met my barista-slash-nurse, and now, I know I have a little more family of my own.

I wouldn't change that for the world.

"Tell me your wildest story," I request of Jason, smiling as he hooks his foot around mine under the table. I've lost count of what date this is, but we're back at the Italian place near his apartment. He likes it here, which means I like bringing him here.

"Okay, so there was this one guy," he says, snorting at whatever he's remembering. "He comes in complaining about rectal pain."

"Never a good start," I note.

Jason laughs. "No. He's acting really weird the entire time we get him set up in a room. Squirming a lot. And being vague when answering questions."

"Oh boy."

"Oh boy indeed," Jason says, pressing his lips together to hold in his laughter. It bleeds through in his tone, however. "So it takes a while, but we finally get the truth out of him. There's a small cucumber lodged up his ass."

"No," I breathe before barking a laugh.

"*Yes*. He lost his grip on it while he was, you know," Jason says, eyes twinkling. "And he couldn't get it back out."

"Holy crap. How mortifying."

"For him, yes," Jason agrees. "For the rest of us? The nurses had a field day. For a solid week after that, pictures of cucumbers would randomly pop up all over the hospital. And every day, at least one person brought in cucumber salad."

I can't help but laugh. "You really like it there, huh?" I ask him.

He cocks his head. "I do, yeah. It's hard at times but worth it. My clinical rotations have me moving around a lot, but I like the nurses and the doctors I've worked with. I like the patients I see. I like what I'm doing."

"That's really great, Jason," I tell him sincerely. "I'm so glad you have that."

He looks at me almost sadly. "If you had gone into sports physio, what would you be doing?"

The question catches me off-guard, in part because I didn't realize he remembered my one mention of sports physiology, and in part because I have no clue how to answer the question. I'm quiet as I figure it out. As I sift through those dreams I once had—and dismissed. Jason waits patiently, taking a sip of his water as I collect my thoughts.

What *would* I be doing if I weren't at Kinsley Richman?

"Maybe I'd have been an athletic trainer," I finally answer. "Or gone into physical therapy."

"Have you ever thought of going back to school?" he asks gently. "You could still do that, you know."

Could I, though? I made my decision a long time ago. I chose my path. The same one my parents traveled. The same one my siblings went down.

But I don't want the same things as them.

"I don't..."

"Cas," Jason says, squeezing my hand. "I didn't mean to make you sad. I just... You can do whatever you want to. I don't know if anyone has told you that, but you can."

"I don't want to let them down," I admit.

"I know," Jason practically whispers. "But what about you? Are you letting yourself down?"

And fuck. I'd never thought of it like that.

As the waitress arrives with our food, Jason lets my hand go. He doesn't bring up my job again. Instead, once we start eating, we chat about simpler things. Easier things. I find out Jason's favorite color is blue, and he learns about the time I was fourteen and decided to jump from the roof into the pool just to see if I could make it. Thankfully, I did.

When we go, Jason grabs my hand before I even have a chance to reach for his. I give him a smile, insides feeling light. When he starts tugging me down the sidewalk swiftly, I laugh.

"All right?" I ask him.

"Yeah, c'mon," he says, pulling out his phone to check the time and then shoving it back in his pocket. "I want to show you something."

"Okay," I mutter, perplexed. Jason leads me to his car instead of inside his building, and then he gets into the driver's side while I take the front passenger seat. "Where are we going?"

He buckles his belt before looking over at me, hands on the wheel. "Do you want to know, or do you like surprises?"

My grin spreads swiftly. "Surprise me."

He nods, turns on his car, and backs us out of the parking spot. It only takes fifteen minutes to get to where Jason is taking me. He pulls off into a manned parking lot, stopping to pay the fee to get inside.

"The park is closing in thirty minutes," the attendant tells us.

Jason gives her a nod. "I know. We'll be out soon."

With that, she lets us through, and Jason parks in the empty lot. I'm dying to ask what we're doing, but I keep my mouth shut and follow Jason out of the car.

It looks like there are hiking trails nearby, and signs point toward a campground. But Jason leads me over to a lookout with a metal guard rail. Curious, I join him at the high point overlooking the small valley below, and my breath catches.

"You said you like the flowers in the spring and summer," Jason says, arms resting against the rail. "And this isn't that, but I thought you might enjoy it."

I ease out a breath. The terrain below is grassy, interspersed with rocks jutting from the earth. A small pond or lake sits in the middle, and all around it are trees. Yellow trees and orange trees. Red trees. Some green still, and a few bare. Fall colors, all earthy and bright.

It's beautiful.

Before I can utter a word, Jason says, "My dad died when I was twenty. He was sick for a long time. My entire childhood, really."

"Jason," I say quietly, my chest clenching. I rest my hand on his arm, and Jason leans into the touch, but he doesn't look over at me.

"When I graduated high school," he goes on, "my parents wanted me to go off to college. That was the plan. But my dad... He was getting so much worse, and I couldn't. I couldn't leave him like that. I couldn't leave my mom to deal with it alone."

"So you stayed."

"I stayed," he says. "And I don't regret that. I never will. My dad died two years later. It...sucked. It sucked really bad. But at least I had two more years with him."

I don't know what to say. I've been fortunate in that I haven't had to deal all that closely with death. I can't imagine losing a parent the way Jason did.

"How did he die?" I ask softly.

Jason is quiet for a long time. Long enough that I start to wonder whether or not he's going to answer me. Finally, he says, "He had Huntington's disease."

"I'm not familiar with that," I admit.

Jason nods, swallowing a little. His eyes ping to mine for a brief moment before he looks back out at the color-changing trees. "Have you heard of Alzheimer's or Parkinson's?"

I nod slowly. "Yes."

"They're not all the same thing, but, uh, they're all degenerative nerve disorders. That's what my dad had."

I want to ask more. I want to ask what it was like for his dad; if he remembered his family or had trouble getting around. I want to ask what it was like for Jason, growing up with a parent who was ill. I want to ask how he and his mother coped. But it feels like too much. Too big of a wound to spread open in front of these sunshine-and-rust-stained trees.

"You've been a nurse your whole life, haven't you?" I ask instead.

Jason swallows. "In a way, yeah. I guess I have."

I run my fingers through the hair at the side of his head, over the shell of his ear, along the back of his neck. Jason closes his eyes, breathing deeply. When he opens them again, he turns to me, so much strength there in his gaze. Strength and compassion.

"Cas, it's never too late. That's what I wanted to tell you. I put off nursing school to be with my family, but then I went once I was ready. You can change your mind. Just because you went one direction, that doesn't mean you can't change course."

My heart thuds dully inside my chest. Could it be that easy?

"Plenty of people have jobs they don't love," I point out.

"That's true," he says, gripping my hand. "And I'll drop it if you want me to. But every time you talk about working for your dad, your eyes go dim, and you lose your smile, and I *hate* that. I fucking hate it. You have a *whole life* ahead of you," he says, voice cracking over the words. "Do you really want to spend it wishing you were somewhere else?"

I don't know what to say. Don't know how to explain that ever since I was a child, I knew my path in life. I was a Kinsley. *Am* a Kinsley. And like my dad and my mom, my brother, and my sister, I have a name—a reputation—to live up to.

But I never have, have I? I've never lived up to the Kinsley name.

And I'm getting tired of trying.

"Have you ever been terrified of going after what you want?" I ask him. "Ever been scared to hope because... Because if you try and you don't get it, then you'll be right back where you started from except *worse*? So much worse because you'll know exactly what you're missing?"

Jason swallows hard and nods once.

"What if I fail at that, too?" I ask him, voice quiet. What if I let everyone *and* myself down?

"Cas." His voice breaks. "What if you don't?"

Chapter 18

Jason

On the drive back to my place, we're silent. My knuckles hurt with how hard I'm gripping the steering wheel, and I keep telling myself, *say it. Say it, say it, say it. Tell him you might have it, too.*

I can't.

Cas's troubled face enters my mind.

"Have you ever been terrified of going after what you want? Ever been scared to hope because... Because if you try and you don't get it, then you'll be right back where you started from except worse? So much worse because you'll know exactly what you're missing?"

I glance over at Cas in the passenger seat and swallow roughly.

What if he leaves me?

What if I take the test and I have the gene mutation?

The silence is heavy.

"Do you want to go home tonight?" I ask Cas, taking the turn onto my street.

He shifts, and I can feel him watching me. "Do you want me to go?"

I shake my head slowly.

"Then I'll stay."

Relieved, I park my car, and Cas follows me up into my apartment. The door is unlocked, and Brad looks up when we enter.

"Hey," he says, his happy expression falling when he sees my face.

"Evening," Cas replies, toeing off his shoes.

I remove my jacket and beanie, giving Brad a little shake of my head when he raises his eyebrows in question. It's early still, not even eight-thirty, but when I incline my head down the hall, Cas gives me a nod.

The moment we're inside my bedroom, Cas tugs me around.

"Come here," he says, pulling me into his arms.

Much to my mortification, a sob breaks free, but Cas just wraps me up tight, his lips near my ear as he says my name—"*Jason*"—so softly, so calmly. My hand bunches in his shirt, and I breathe through it. The memories of my dad. The fear that I'll go through the same. That terrifying ache I get any time I think of my loved ones being on the opposite end.

I don't want to put my mom through that again. I don't want Cas to go through it.

Tell him now. Before it's too late. Before he doesn't have a choice.

"Jason," Cas breathes, kissing the side of my head. "It's okay."

It's not.

"Do you want to lie down?" he asks.

I nod.

Cas leads me to the bed, pulling back the covers before guiding me down in front of him. He wraps his arm around me, our knees brushing together, and for a long moment, I stare. I stare at his whiskey eyes and the smooth lines of his dark eyebrows. I stare at the hair curling gently against his forehead and the tiny freckle at the edge of his nose. I stare at his lips, so soft and sweet and sincere.

Cas doesn't seem the least bit surprised when I kiss him. His arm tightens around me, and he rolls onto his back as I slot my leg between his own and push. His breath hitches as I rub my thigh against his crotch, and he thickens beneath me.

"Want you," I mumble, tasting those lips. Taking those lips.

"Yours," Cas replies, and God. *God.*

Maybe I'm avoiding my problems—burying my head in the sand—but I don't care. I tear his shirt off and toss it aside. Cas helps me undo his pants, and he kicks out of them while I lift up and tug off my own top. His hands glide up my stomach, and I hastily unzip my jeans. I have to move off Cas to tear them free, and I grab supplies while I'm at it. Cas waits, slowly stroking his cock, and when I get back on the bed and give him a gentle shove, he rolls easily onto his stomach.

I hitch his leg up.

Lube.

Cas moans as I slip a finger inside his body. I kiss his back as I stretch him, anywhere I can reach. His shoulder. The notches of his spine. The little scar he told me was from when he had chicken pox as a kid. All the while, he stays splayed out for me, his arm up near his face, his leg bent high and wide. The other leg points straight down, his toes occasionally curling.

When I remove my fingers and roll on a condom, Cas looks back at me. He doesn't say a word, but he licks his lips. I wrap my arm around his chest, tugging him partway onto his side, and my lips graze his jaw before I reach down, steadying my cock.

When I push inside Cas, he makes this sound. This *ah* that hits me deep. It tugs at me, some part of me unseen, and I worry it's too late for me. That I've already made my choice. That whether or not this man stays, a part of me will always be his.

I thread my fingers through Cas's when my hips meet his ass. I hold him tight, arm around his chest, our hands near his heart, and I *push*. I push into him, giving him with my body what I can't say with words. I fuck him steadily, my heart hammering, my lips at his shoulder, my body behind and over his, curled around his.

When I can't hold off any longer, I let his hand go and reach for his cock. His palm hits the mattress, and he slips forward before pushing back against me. His leg is still bent up, holding himself open. His cheek is pressed against the bed.

"Jason," he rasps, panting.

I stroke him harder.

I don't get him there before I come. It's sudden, and I sob when it happens, pain and relief flowing through me all at once, crashing, splintering apart. I think I call out his name, but I can't be certain. It's too much, too...

Don't cry.

As soon as my vision clears, I stroke Cas's cock again. My dick is oversensitive, the tightening of Cas's body more pain than pleasure, but I don't move. Not yet.

"C'mon," I tell him, teeth skimming his shoulder. I twist my fist the way he seems to like it. "Come for me, Cassius. Come *on*."

His breath leaves him on a gasp, and his body bows against me before he jerks, ass clamping tight and cum coating my fingertips. Relief hits hard, and I stroke him through it, forehead against the back of his neck as he milks my dick.

He pants when he's done, his arm falling flat against the bed. I slide my hand up his chest, holding tight to his heart, glad he can't see my face.

And if a single tear runs free the moment I slip from his body, no one has to know about it.

"Well, that's something," Brad says.

"What?" I ask, setting his coffee down in front of him. Black, like his soul.

"That, uh... You know." He points to his own neck. "Lose a fight against a vacuum cleaner, Birdie?"

I clamp a hand over my neck, gasping. "I have a hickey?"

"Uh, very much so," he says flatly.

"Why didn't you tell me sooner?" I hiss, trying to tug my shirt up to cover it. I'd been feeling steadier on my feet since last night, a little calmer, but that was before finding out Cas apparently gave me a *hickey*. When did he even manage that? This morning while we were making out?

Brad's eyes are wide as he watches me trying to cover the mark. It looks like he's *laughing* at me, the asshole. "I just got here," he says. "Like...two minutes ago. When would I have told you?"

"That's beside the point," I mutter, slinking down into a chair next to him. *Far* down. "What do I *do*?"

"Well, first off, you can't hide under the table all day," he points out.

"I can *try*."

"And secondly," he goes on. "So what? You have proof that a hot dude is snacking on your neck. Own it, my man."

I groan. "He is hot, though, isn't he?"

Brad laughs.

"Ugh, I need to get back to work," I tell him, glancing around the blessedly empty coffee shop before getting out of my seat. *God*, I have a hickey. How embarrassing. How wonderfully, horribly embarrassing. "If you happen upon a scarf or a collar or something, send it my way."

Brad's eyebrow goes high up. "A collar?" He drops his voice, leaning close. "Needa get owned, Birdie?"

"Oh my *God*," I exclaim, smacking Brad on the shoulder as he dissolves into laughter. "I meant like a *Victorian* collar. You know, one of those ruffly things?"

Brad wheezes. "I can't... That's even worse... Good *God*."

"I have the worst friends," I bemoan. Seriously, is it too late to trade Brad in? "Besides, if anyone were to wear a collar, it'd be—"

I promptly clamp my mouth shut, but Brad sits up taller in his seat.

"Tell me," he says, a harsh whisper. "Tell me, tell me."

"Byeee," I say, hoofing it back behind the counter, ignoring Brad's answering call. Marley gives me a pointed look as I come around the corner, her eyebrow arched. I wonder if she realizes she and Dixon look the same when they do that.

"Do I even want to know?" she asks.

"Probably not," I mumble, setting to work getting rid of the empty milk cartons.

Marley follows me to the back of the shop. "I don't suppose it has anything to do with that planet-sized love bite on your neck."

"For fuck's—" I cut off, heaving a sigh. "*Why-y-y* did no one tell me?"

"I thought you knew," she counters, eyes round and amused.

I groan, dropping the cartons in the trash and pulling at the collar of my shirt again. "Is it really that bad? Has everyone seen it?"

"Jason," she says, laughing now. "It's *huge*. Anyone in a two-block radius could see that thing."

"I'd like to disappear now," I inform her. "Just, like...be raptured. Poof. Gone."

Marley shakes her head, following me back out front. "I'm going to miss working with you, you know that?"

And *ugh*.

"Marls," I moan, bringing a few carafes to the sink to wash. "No feelings right now, okay? I can't do feelings."

I've had too many of them lately.

Marley sighs, patting me on the head like a child. Or a dog. "In that case, tell me how things are going with Himbo."

She waggles her eyebrows, but I bristle a little bit. I can't help it.

"Can we not call him that?" I say, drying my hands on a towel.

Marley cocks her head, looking surprised by my clipped tone and a little concerned. "Of course," she says. "Does the porn bother you?"

"No, it's not that," I say quickly. "I just..."

God, how do I explain it to her? I hate that word. I hate that Cas himself is okay being called a himbo, like he's heard it so much it doesn't even bother him anymore.

Like he believes it.

"Hey, it's okay," Marley says, giving my arm a squeeze. "Say no more. I won't call him that again. You know I like Cas. He's a total sweetie pie."

"Yeah, he really is," I agree. Too sweet sometimes. Too good.

"Things are good between you two, though?" she asks.

"Yeah," I huff. "Really good."

"Good, 'cause he's here."

"What?" I say, spinning around. Sure enough, Cas is walking through the door, a wide smile on his face when he sees me. He's wearing a button-down today, as well as gray slacks, so he must be going into the office. He waves before being sidetracked by Brad, who calls him over.

"You're drooling," Marley says, tapping the bottom of my chin.

I walk away as she laughs at me. By the time I reach Brad's table, he has Cas chuckling about something. Cas turns to me right away, pulling me close.

"Hi," he says, kissing my temple.

I melt. This man makes me melt.

"Heyo. 'Sup," I say. Then cringe. Because that's my life.

Brad chokes on his coffee.

"What are you doing here?" I ask Cas.

He steps away enough to reach for a flat box on the table. "Brought you something," he says, handing it over. He shrugs before adding, "It's getting colder."

I open the box, setting eyes on a striped scarf. There are six repeating colors, all shades of blue. Because I told him it's my favorite?

Cas lifts the scarf out of the box, winding it smoothly around my neck as my heart hammers. He adjusts it just so and then smiles. "There."

"I..." *Words.*

"Look at that, Birdie," Brad says. "A scarf just like you wanted. Now you can't see the hickey anymore."

Cas's eyes shoot to mine, and he tugs at the scarf, fingers brushing my neck as he looks for said hickey. How he missed it in the first place, I'm not sure, considering it's apparently the size of Texas. When Cas sees it, his eyes widen, and then he grins, looking *smug*.

"Oops," he says.

I smack him on the chest, laughing. "You're not sorry."

He shrugs a little, biting his lip. Ugh, *I* want to bite that lip. "Not really," he admits. "In fact, why don't I just take this back for later and—"

I snatch the scarf out of his grip, holding tight. "Not a chance." I give it a rub. *So soft.* "Thank you, Cas."

He smiles at me. "I have to get to work, but see you soon?"

"Mm," I agree rather coherently.

Cas gives me another peck before turning and heading off. He stops on his way to the door, picking up a couple items that slipped out of a woman's purse. A tube of lipstick, a tissue, a compact mirror.

I sigh a little because, well, chivalry, but also that ass. That wonderful, plump—

"Huh," Brad says.

I look his way, finding him watching Cas, too. Finding his head cocked and his eyes low, like...

"No," I say in dawning horror. "No, no, *no.*"

"What—" Brad starts to say, but I step between him and Cas, blocking my friend's view and cutting off his words.

"You stop that right now," I hiss, glancing over my shoulder to make sure Cas is gone before rounding on a surprised Brad. "Not you, too, Brad. I swear on everything that is holy, I'll disown you if you start staring at Cas like all the others. That man? Mine. His perfect fucking face and the painfully sexy dimples on his lower back? Mine. Nipple left and nipple right? Mine."

"Jason," Brad says, laughing.

"Nuh-uh. That ass you were just staring at? It's mine, Brad. *Mine*."

I gasp as soon as my own words sink in.

"What's wrong?" Brad asks quickly, his expression going from amused to worried.

"Oh my God, I... I'm objectifying him, aren't I?" I realize aloud. "Am I objectifying my boyfriend?" I might've squeaked that last part.

"Your boyfriend?" Brad asks, a smile spreading over his face.

"Not the point," I groan, waving my hand through the air. "You know what I mean."

Fuck this day. Fuck it so hard.

"First off," Brad says calmly, the absolute douche, "I'm not after your beau's ass, Birdie. You know I'm straight. And I'd never do that to you."

"Then why were you staring?" I moan, plopping down into a seat next to him. I feel a little woozy.

He shrugs. "An ass is an ass."

"*You're* an ass," I mutter, rubbing my forehead.

He rolls his eyes before giving my shoulder a reassuring squeeze. "Secondly, you're not objectifying him. You have feelings for him, Jason. You're not treating him like an object to get off on. There's a difference."

And yeah, okay. Maybe he has a point.

Still. "I can't have you doing it, too, Brad. I can't. Please don't look at him like that."

Brad lets out a small breath. "I promise. I won't do it again. And I'm sorry. I didn't realize you were so...protective of him."

"You can call it jealousy," I point out. "I know that's what it is."

"Then why doesn't the porn bother you?" he asks, giving me pause. "Aaaand... Can we talk about that whole 'boyfriend' thing? Are you two, like, a real item now?"

I thump my head on the table. I can't deny that's exactly what I want. Something real with Cas. To be his boyfriend and for him to be mine.

Brad's right. I have feelings.

Big ones.

Chapter 19
CAS

"Cassius," my dad says warmly. "I'm glad you stopped in. Take a seat."

I sit in one of the big burgundy wingback chairs in front of my dad's desk inside his opulent, glass-walled office. A large water fountain is visible in the courtyard outside, a small oasis amongst the sprawling infrastructure of the city.

"How've you been since we last spoke?" he asks.

A smile slips onto my face, despite what I came here to do. "I've been good. I'm seeing someone, actually." *I think it's getting serious.*

"That so?" my dad says, folding his hands atop his desk. His own lips curve up in a gentle smile. "Do I know the man?"

I shake my head. "No. I met him at a coffee shop. He's...sweet," I settle on. Feisty, too, but I'm not about to tell my dad that. "I like him a lot."

"That's wonderful, Cassius. I'm happy for you. It's been, what, a good year since you last dated?"

I almost correct him that it's only been six months, but then I remember my last relationship was in secret. With Simon. Neither my dad nor Leo know about it.

"It has been a while," I say instead.

"Well, hopefully your mother and I can meet this young man soon," he says. "Now, how are things going in the Human Resources department?"

I blow out a breath. Here goes. "Not well."

My dad's brows furrow. "I haven't heard anything more from Dorian."

Right. Because Dorian has chalked me up as a lost cause. He's relegated me to the most basic of grunt work and takes to ignoring me if at all possible.

"Dad," I say slowly, trying to figure out how to voice what it is I need to say. He's going to argue it, one way or another, for my own benefit. "My being there is a waste." My dad opens his mouth, but I hold up my hand. "Please, let me finish."

He nods, settling back in his chair, and I go on.

"I know you want me to work at your company, but I'm not cut out for this. I'm not like Leo or Mom. Or *you*. I don't have the skill set for architectural design. And Char is a whiz with computers, but they're like a foreign language to me. I'm never going to move up in the ranks here, and sticking me in a support job that a more qualified person could do in half the time doesn't make sense. It's a waste."

"Cassius," my dad says evenly but firmly. "You are not a waste. Not *ever*."

I puff out a breath. "That's not what I mean."

"Has someone made you feel unwelcome?" he asks, voice deceptively calm, and I groan just a little. Of course my dad's first instinct is to rise to my defense. Never mind that his intuition is correct, I'm not telling him about what Dorian said because it doesn't matter. It's not the point.

And I need to stop skirting the real problem.

"I don't want to do this," I tell him quietly, putting voice to the truth that has been all but screaming inside my head ever since Jason brought me to that overlook. I can't pretend I don't hear it anymore. I can't pretend I don't want something *more* for myself. "I don't want to be here, Dad. It's not... It's not what *I* want. It never was."

My dad is quiet for a long moment, and I turn my gaze away, looking out at the water fountain, watching the gentle spray of water mist into the air. It's such a serene scene, and I wish I could take comfort in it, but my insides are curled tight like a fist, waiting to hear what my dad will say. Waiting to hear how I've disappointed him.

"Cassius," he finally says, tone soft. I turn to him warily. "I'm sorry if I haven't listened to you."

"What?" I ask in surprise.

He lets out a small sigh. "This isn't new, is it? This sounds like something you've been hanging onto for a while."

I work my jaw for a moment, feeling the inexplicable prickling of tears.

"All I want," he says, "is for my children to be happy. I love you, Cassius. I want what's best for you. If that's you being elsewhere, I'll support that."

Shit.

"I'm sorry," I manage to croak out.

My dad shakes his head quickly. "Don't be. I'm the one who's sorry. The fact that you didn't feel like you could come to me about this sooner—" He clears his throat, shaking his head again. "I didn't realize you were so unhappy here."

I couldn't bear to tell you.

"You're not upset?" I ask him.

"Son, no," he answers. "I'm proud of you. I'll always be proud of you in whatever it is you decide to do. You've worked so hard. And I know you'll continue to do so. I just wish I knew sooner. I've made a lot of assumptions, I'm afraid."

"It's not your fault," I tell him, throat tight. "You didn't know."

"Yes, well, maybe I should have. I'm your father, after all."

And what do I say to that? It's easy to keep secrets from the ones you love. I debate, ever so briefly, telling my dad about the porn. But in the end, I keep it as my own.

"I'll give Dorian my two weeks' notice," I say.

My dad nods. "Of course. And Cassius? I'll miss having you here, but I won't be sad to see you go. Not if it's what you want."

"Thanks, Dad," I utter, voice nearly lost.

The smile my dad gives me is sad, resigned. But it's also full of understanding, and it hits me like a ton of bricks that we could have had this conversation a year ago. Two. Three, even, if only I'd had the nerve. I'm still scared. Scared that I might not succeed. Scared that I'll never amount to the sort of success the rest of my family has achieved—the success my dad was pushing me toward because all he wanted was what he thought was best for me.

But my idea of success isn't the same as theirs. I never cared about the money or the prestige. I don't need a fancy house or car or clothes. All I want is a simple life. One of my own choosing. One that makes me happy.

And I think, just maybe, I might be on my way.

"So, I'm not really sure how to do this," I tell Celeste, the woman I'm meeting with from the youth support nonprofit Queenie directed me to. As I've learned, they have a base here in Las Vegas, but they also have a sister location up in Reno. Both have the same mission: fundraising for programs that benefit underprivileged children and teens.

Like Neddy's.

"That's okay," Celeste says. We're sitting in her small office downtown, and she's wearing a bright yellow sundress, despite the fall temperatures, with a magenta shawl over top. The outfit is bold and sunny, just like the woman herself. "Why don't you tell me what you're hoping to accomplish here...volunteering, fundraising, a one-time donation...and we'll go from there."

I nod, swallowing. "Okay, so, I'd like to help out somehow. I have time to give." Especially since I'm about to be down a job, and I'll have months before starting a physio program. *If* I apply. Even then, I'd have free time around classes.

Christ, am I really going back to college?

"I'd also like to donate," I tell her. "Maybe I could set something up annually?"

"Sure," she says, jotting a couple notes down on the pad in front of her. "How much are you thinking?"

"A quarter million?"

She looks up at me, blinking.

"I don't want it," I tell her softly. "I don't *need* it. I just want to do good."

Celeste sets down her pen. "Queenie said you were a bleeding heart. I see that now. I'm going to be honest about something, Cassius."

I give her a nod.

"Don't go around telling people what you just told me. They'll want to take advantage of you, and I'd hate to see a sweet, young man like yourself fall prey to other people's greed."

"I know," I say. "I'm not..." Despite what people think, I'm not *completely* clueless. "I looked you up. I researched you and your foundation. I know where your money goes, and I know that you do it because it's personal to you. Because you grew up in a district with a sixty-three percent graduation rate, nearly twenty percent lower than the state average. I read about how you single-handedly raised enough money to offer free breakfast for kids at over a dozen schools in the city. How you funded a traveling library. How you restored six different run-down parks."

"You did your homework," she says.

"I did. You just want to help people. And that's what I want, too." I let out a breath, rubbing a hand through my hair. "I've been really fortunate in life. Maybe more so than I deserve. I have more than I need, but there are others who don't have nearly enough. I'll donate anonymously, and I won't tell people about it. I just... I need to do *something*, you know?"

She nods gently. "I do. But I'll just say this one thing."

"Okay?"

"You're worth more than your money. It's not the only valuable thing you have to give. If at any point, you decide you need to stop donating, I won't hold that against you, you hear?"

I nod, throat tight.

"But heck, I'm not about to turn down what you're offering," she adds, shaking her head as she scrawls something on her paper.

"And my time?" I ask. "What can I do to help?"

The smile she gives me is as bright as her sunshine dress. "So much, dear boy. So very much."

When I get home, my mood is lighter than it's been in quite some time. I feel buoyant, like a raft floating at sea. I grab a quick dinner—a microwavable meal—and vow to take up cooking so I can make myself and Jason something that doesn't come from a box, a can, or the freezer. I never did learn when I was young. We had staff to handle the cooking.

As I'm finishing my food, I check the time on my phone. I laugh when I see a text from my coworker.

Alex: Look, sugarplum! You could wear it on your next date.

Attached is a picture of a shirt that says, "I consent to mouth-to-mouth resuscitation." I'm sure Jason would love it, and I thank Alex, telling him so, before messaging Jason. He should be getting out of his lab right about now.

Me: Hope you had a good class. Can't wait to see you again.

Then, I call my mom, knowing I should talk to her about what happened today. She deserves to hear it from me, too, even if she's already gotten the news from Dad.

She picks up on the third ring. "Darling."

"Hi, Mom. Have you heard?"

She hums. "You mean have I heard about you forsaking the business?" Her tone is light and teasing, and I'm instantly set at ease. She's not upset. "I wondered the last time we talked, Cassius, but I didn't realize you wanted out. Or perhaps you never wanted in?"

"No," I tell her softly. "I didn't."

"Oh, my boy. We wouldn't have pushed you so hard."

"I know," I tell her. Because despite what I told myself—that I needed to follow their footsteps to make them proud, that I needed to be good enough for *them*—I knew the truth. They love me. They support me. My family always has.

I was only trying to prove something to myself.

"I also hear you have a special someone?" she asks.

"Yeah," I breathe out. "His name is Jason. Maybe you could meet him soon?"

"I'd love nothing more," she tells me. "Now, what are your plans, my darling? What are you going to do?"

So I tell her. For the first time, I speak it all aloud. Going back to school. Maybe, eventually, having a career that feels like *breathing*. I tell her about Neddy's and volunteering some of my time to the community. I even tell her a bit more about Jason. How he's a nurse. How proud I am of what he's accomplished.

By the time I'm done, I feel wide open, but not in a scary way. I feel seen. Understood. Accepted, even.

When I hang up with my mom, I check my phone for messages. Nothing from Jason yet, but I know he'll respond when he has a chance. In the meantime, I pull up my internet browser and do a search on Huntington's disease.

That smile I'd be harboring all evening slips quickly away, and with every word I read, the lightness in my chest dims to black.

Chapter 20

JASON

"Green or blue?" I ask Cas, holding up two shirts.

He slips off my bed, coming over and taking the green shirt from my hand. He holds it in front of me, pondering, before doing the same with the blue. Then he goes to my closet, rummages around for a minute, and pulls out a deep-cut burgundy shirt I forgot I owned.

"This one," he says. "The color suits you. Makes your eyes pop."

"Oh," I say, swallowing a little roughly as Cas brushes my bangs aside, looking into my eyes like...

Like I don't know what. But it makes me feel hot.

"Or you could go naked," he says casually, handing off the shirt. "That suits you, too."

I cough. "Yeah, um... No thanks. Dancing in a club full of strangers naked sounds like my literal nightmare."

Cas chuckles. "I can guarantee at least somebody there will be naked. Or nearly as good as."

"Even so, I'll stick to wearing a shirt, thanks," I mumble, tugging the red one over my head. It does look nice, even if it shows off more chest than I'm used to. "At least my bruise is mostly gone," I note, rubbing at the faint mark on my neck.

"I could always give you another," Cas says, winking as he falls against my bed.

And *ungh*. Those two actions should not be allowed in tandem. Cas winking. Cas on my bed. *Cas winking and talking about hickeys on my bed.*

Focus.

Club. Dancing. Clothes. Right.

Cas himself is wearing a simple black t-shirt for our outing with his coworkers tonight, along with torn-up jeans. He has *no right* looking as hot as he does in them. It's criminal.

"I think I'm ready," I tell him, flashing my eyes to his in the mirror. I catch a hint of something on his face I'm not expecting. Something pensive and...sad?

When I turn around, Cas jumps up, giving me a smile. "Let's go."

"Hey," I say, grabbing his arm and looking for whatever it was I noticed a moment ago. But it's gone. "Everything okay?"

He cocks his head. "Of course. What do you mean?"

"Nothing," I mutter. Must be losing it. "C'mon."

When Cas and I get to the club, he grabs my hand and leads me past the line of guests waiting to get in. After a quick exchange with the bouncer, we're let through.

I've only been to Sublime once before, at Dixon's behest, actually. But I didn't see the VIP loft where Cas is leading me now. It's set up above the dance floor with a balcony looking out over the club, and it's *full* of porn stars. At least a dozen of them. Men I've seen naked. Men I've jerked off to.

I'm pretty sure my face is as red as my shirt.

"Want a drink?" Cas asks, mouth at my ear. He smells like that spicy cologne he wears, and I find myself leaning toward him before his question seeps into my brain.

"Uh, yeah. Anything is fine."

Cas gives me a nod, tugging me along to where a server is standing beside a high-top table, dropping off drinks from his tray. He's wearing nothing but booty shorts, and *holy crap*. Cas was right. The guy might as well be naked.

The server gives Cas a swift grin when we approach. He says something I can't quite hear, but Cas chuckles and nods, and the server leans close, presumably to hear our drink orders. But then he touches Cas's arm, stroking, lingering, and yeah, no. *Nope*.

I step forward and plaster myself to Cas's side, grinning a little ferally. The server's eyes widen, and he pulls his hand back before I have a chance to bite it. "I'll be right back with those," the guy says before walking off.

Cas wraps his arm around me. I think he says, "So cute," before kissing the side of my head, but I'm not positive.

If he thinks my growling is cute, that probably bodes well for me.

"So," Cas says, "do you want to meet—"

"Jason, hi!" a beaming blonde interrupts, stopping in front of us with a bounce. I recognize him immediately.

"Oh Lord," I mumble. "Um, hi, Tink. Uh, Alex. Hey." I wave a little awkwardly because of course I do.

The performer known as Tink—real name Alex—grins. "It's so good to see you again, cutie. Come on, let's show you around."

My "*ah*" is lost to the noise of the bar, and before I know what's happening, Alex is tugging me toward a couch of his costars.

"You know Dixon, of course," Alex says, pointing to my regular. Dixon up-nods. "And his boyfriend, Niko." *Aka Adonis.*

"Um, yeah," I manage, sure my eyes are wide. "Nice to see you again."

"Next to Niko is Emil," Alex goes on. "He's a crab daddy now. Isn't that the cutest?"

"Alex," Emil groans. Like in his videos as Felix, Emil is wearing glasses. "You can't just say it like that. I have a hermit crab," he explains before sighing, eyes closed. "You know what? No, that's not better."

As Emil bemoans his life choices, Alex spins me around.

"And look!" he says. "Bears, *oh my.* The two on the left are mine. Say hi, Grizzly Bear."

"Um, hi?" the big bearded man says shyly. He looks to the man next to him, a redhead with tattoos down his arms, who squeezes the first man's thigh.

"And I'm Finn," the redhead says.

"My Ginger Bear," Alex adds, audibly sighing. "And the teddy on the right is Teddy. Neat, huh? This is Jason, Cas's beau."

"Hi," I say a little weakly. "I like your, um, shirt?"

Teddy, who's wearing a tank top so low I can almost see his nipples, snorts a gentle laugh.

Am I sweating? I feel like I'm sweating. You think I'd be used to this by now—being in the presence of porn stars, considering I bone one on the regular—but apparently not. What do I say? What do I do with my *hands?*

Alex gives me a squeeze around the middle while I squeak. "Welcome to the family, boo."

"I, uh... *Ho.* Um."

Luckily, a pair of familiar arms curl around me from behind, and I breathe a sigh of relief, spinning to face Cas.

"Save me," I mumble into his chest.

"Any time," he says, lips at my temple. "But what am I saving you from?"

"My own mouth."

Cas chuckles. "I like your mouth," he replies, and *oh fuck*. Shivers. "Dance with me?"

I swallow. Hard.

When I lean back, Cas's lips are pressed into a smile. His hair looks nearly black in the dim interior of the club, and his eyes sparkle like sin and the promise of filthy things to come.

"Uh-huh," I answer.

Cas grins just as the server shows back up, holding a lowball out to Cas. Cas takes it and hands it to me, keeping the second for himself. He thanks the server before turning to me.

"To your mouth," he whispers before downing half of his drink in one go.

"Fuckballs," I mutter, drinking my own.

The music thumps around us as Cas leads me down the stairs. It's heavy, like liquid sex and dirty secrets. It reeks of indiscretion and hormones and *want*.

This isn't a place you come to show off your dance moves. It's a place you come to fuck.

Cas keeps my hand in his own as we move out onto the dance floor. I can't hear a thing other than the throbbing beat of EDM. Lights shift back and forth over the crowd, painting it in hues of neon pink and green. There are bodies *everywhere*, jostling and bumping. Grabbing. Grinding.

Cas stops somewhere in the middle of the dance floor, turning to me. He slides close, his hands on my hips, his crotch against my own. He moves like water, all flowing beauty and confidence that I can't take my eyes off of. For only a moment, I think, *What is he doing here with me?* But I dismiss it just as quickly. I know Cas wants me. That he likes me...maybe quite a lot. I won't diminish that just because he's quite possibly the most gorgeous person I've ever set eyes on.

It's what's underneath that makes Cas who he is. That's the part of him that wants me. And that's the part of him that leaves me breathless.

I've barely moved a muscle, too caught up in the man before me, and maybe Cas takes that as nervousness because he leans close, guiding my hips with his hands, moving me with him. "It's just like sex, Jason," he says, lips brushing my ear. His leg is between my own, hip against my cock. "Just like when you fuck me."

I close my eyes, hands tightening on Cas's shirt. I grab his side, his ass, my breathing heavy.

"Yeah, babe," he says. "Like that."

Fuck.

How I want this man. *Always.*

Cas's eyes are half-lidded when I tug his head back. His mouth pops open, and I take it, pulling him down to me and sliding my tongue between his lips. I can feel the vibration of his moan, taste the cherry from his drink.

When someone's hand drifts over the one I have on Cas's ass, the touch a feather-light question, I nearly snarl. I break from Cas's mouth, finding the man behind him who's sporting a raised brow.

"No," I tell him loudly enough to be heard over the music.

He holds his hands up and backs away, turning to find another dance partner.

"Jason," Cas says against my ear, a reassurance.

Brad said it's not jealousy, but what else do you call it when someone looking at Cas, someone touching him without his permission, makes me *rage?* They have no right. They don't *see* him. They don't know him like I do.

It's different from his job at the studio. I don't know why; it just is. Porn is a show. It's not real life, and what Cas does with those men up in the VIP lounge doesn't extend out of the walls of his workplace. It's Himbo, not Cas, and I refuse to be jealous over something Cas himself told me is meaningless.

But out here, when it comes to this man, to *Cas?* No one else gets to touch him. They don't get the chance to *hurt* him.

I lose track of time as my tongue tangles with Cas's. As we grind together, an imitation of sex. As his hands roam my skin, under my shirt, and as mine guard him from those men at his back.

It's too busy in here. I want... I need...

"C'mon," I tell Cas, grabbing his hand and leading him off the dance floor.

The sound cuts nearly off when we enter the bathroom, only the thump of bass remaining. It's jarring, and for a moment, my ears ring.

"Jason," Cas says, "what are you..."

I tug him past the men using the urinals and into the only open stall. When I slam the lock down, it sounds like a gunshot.

"I wanna blow you," I say.

Cas blinks at me.

"Yas, honey," someone in the bathroom calls. "Do it."

I ignore them.

"Can I?" I ask, fumbling for the front of Cas's pants. He doesn't stop me, not when I rub him through his jeans and not when I open his zipper.

"They'll listen," he says. The people in the bathroom.

"I don't care." I slip my hand into his pants, and he groans. "They can't see you. Do you care?"

"No," he says, practically a breath.

"Good," I answer. "Then they can hear how you're *mine*."

Cas's breath hitches, dissolving into a reedy moan as I palm his dick. He doesn't say another word as I drop to my knees and tug his pants down to his thighs. I slip his briefs down, too, tucking them beneath his balls, and then I swipe my tongue over his crown.

Maybe this is reckless. Stupid. Maybe I'll even regret it later—I doubt it. But all I could think about out on that dance floor was how much Cas has shown me of himself. How vulnerable he's been, sharing his insecurities and dreams. I want to protect that. I want to show him he's safe with me. That those soft spots are safe with me. I want him to trust me to take care of him.

I *want* to take care of him.

Is he safe with you, though? Really?

I tell my brain to fuck off as I suck Cas's cock into my mouth. I never claimed to be a pro at giving head—hell, I'm still learning—but by Cas's curse, I must be doing something right.

"Babe," he says, and *fuck*, I love that. I love being *babe*.

Cas's fingers thread through my hair as I suck the end of his cock. He doesn't push or pull, just holds, and I do my damndest to take him apart. To make him feel a fraction of how wild and wonderful he makes me feel.

His dick is silky smooth, and a burst of precum hits my tongue when I stroke him in time to the suction of my mouth. He spreads his legs just a little, grunting, his hand flexing against my head, and I reach for his balls, rolling them, pressing two fingers under the waistband of his briefs and back against his taint. There's a clunk against the metal stall as Cas groans and shifts, his weight making the wall shudder. He sounds close, so I grab the base of his shaft and milk him, sucking and kneading. It's sloppy and uncoordinated, but Cas moans again. He likes it.

"Jason," he says.

I look up, and for a moment, I'm trapped. Drowned in those damn whiskey eyes of his. Drunk off of them. His chest heaves as he holds my gaze, his cock swells, and then, with a cry, he comes inside my mouth. I swallow him down, watching his panting breaths, the pleasure-crease of his eyes. He looks disheveled and utterly perfect, and even when clapping starts up outside of our stall, I can't find it in me to be embarrassed or regret a single moment of this night.

"Fuck," Cas mutters, closing his eyes and thunking his head back against the stall.

I give him one last lick before tucking him away inside his briefs. "How many more times do you think I can make you come tonight?" I ask, far from done.

He huffs out a breath before muttering, "*Pleasure Dom. Called it.*"

"If he can't go again," someone in the bathroom yells, "I volunteer."

Aaand okay. Maybe I'm a little embarrassed. *Ugh*, they're going to see Cas when we leave. I didn't think this through.

"I don't suppose you'd let me cover your face with my shirt when we walk out of here, would you?" I ask Cas.

He laughs, hauling me to my feet. "Jason," he says, rolling his lip between his teeth before giving me a swift kiss. "You really are one of a kind."

I'll take that as a compliment.

"Come on," I tell him, grabbing his hand and preparing myself for what is bound to be a walk of shame that haunts me the rest of my life. "Let's go home and wreck the bed."

Chapter 21
CAS

Jason wasn't kidding. The moment we get back to his apartment, he pushes me up against the door, kisses me, and then drags me down the hall. I catch a glimpse of Brad in the living room as we pass. The man is putting on his new noise-canceling headphones.

"Jason," I say a little breathily.

He shuts his bedroom door, backing me against it. I don't know what's gotten into Jason tonight, but his presence in this moment is big, and I feel caged. Caged and secure.

"How many more times can you come?" he asks, just like before.

I groan, licking my lips as he strokes me through my jeans. "Once?"

He hums. "Think I can make you come twice?"

Fuck.

"I don't know," I admit.

"What would get you there?" Jason asks, tugging me toward the bed. He pushes me down, stripping off my pants.

My heart thunders. "Gag me."

He pauses, hazel eyes sharp.

"Put me on my back," I say slowly, "sit on my face, and gag me with your cock."

He closes his eyes, dropping his head forward. "Jesus fucking Christ, Cas," he says, voice wrecked. He shakes his head once before setting to work, pulling my shirt free. He has me naked and on my back within half a minute, and another minute after that, he's climbing over me, nude. His movements are urgent, as if he needs this. As if he *needs* to make me feel good. "Tap my leg if it's too much?"

"Yeah," I breathe.

Jason straddles my head in reverse, his face aimed away from me. He looks down and strokes my lip slowly before giving me a tap. I open up, and *God, fuck. This.*

Jason feeds his cock into my mouth, his balls above my face. My head is arched back, making it all too easy for him to slip inside, and he doesn't hesitate. He fucks my face in shallow thrusts until I gag, his hand stroking over my abdomen as mine spasms against his thigh. My cock jerks, too, and he grabs a hold of it, pumping me as spit slips out of the corner of my mouth.

"God, Cassius, you..." Jason thrusts his hips a few times before pulling back. "Your mouth is fucking magic."

I don't say anything. I can't.

Jason strokes my cock again. "You're going to come," he says confidently, "while I'm choking you. Because apparently that's a thing that happens in my life now."

My hands flex against his legs again, and he holds himself still, his cock hanging shallowly in my mouth, enough that I can breathe. Everything in me feels tight, like a rubber band that's about to snap.

"And then," he goes on, continuing to work my cock, "once your cum is on my fingers, I'm going to flip you over, push it back into your body, and then eat it out of your ass until you scream. Sound good?"

My moan is lost as Jason starts fucking my face again. This time, when I gag, he doesn't retreat. He holds his cock deep in my throat, his balls at my nose, and he strokes me furiously, chanting my name like a command.

"Cassius, Cassius, *Cassius.*"

I come. My hips jerk, my vision spots, and Jason pulls out of my mouth immediately.

"That's it," he says, stroking me through my release, the tip of his cock bumping into my lips and chin as I moan so damn loud I'm not sure Brad's headphones will be able to block the noise.

As soon as my dick stops pulsing and I go lax against the bed, Jason lifts his leg and swings around to face me. His eyes case my face, pinging between my own, lower, as he brushes his fingers tenderly against my lips.

"Okay?" he asks.

I nod, my breathing still labored. My neck is sore from holding my head back at such an awkward angle, and I'm pretty sure my voice is going to be hoarse later, but I don't give a damn.

Jason leans down, brushing his lips over my own. "My warrior," he mutters. "Turn over."

"*Fuck.* Jason, I—"

"I think you can," he says. "Unless you want to stop?"

My heart pounds, and every part of my body feels sensitive. Too much so. My cock, my stomach as Jason drifts his fingers over my skin, my head, and my heart. But I flip over, canting my hips up, waiting...

Jason coos my name, and then slick fingers stroke over my hole. It's intense, but as Jason presses his cum-drenched fingers inside my body, touching the one place he hasn't yet tonight, I have a feeling he's going to get his wish. It's not quick. Not in the least. But Jason strokes his fingers inside me slowly, patiently, until my body starts to react. And only once my dick is hard again does he replace his fingers with his tongue. He eats me like his life depends on it, like his one goal is to make me feel good. It's excruciatingly exquisite, and I'm practically sobbing by the time he finally clasps his hand around my dick.

My nerves are drawn tight. It's prickly in the best way. The *scariest* way. But Jason's touch on my dick is light even as his mouth is demanding. There are a few times I think I'm there; I think I'm going to come. But then I keep rising higher, keep climbing that scary fucking precipice. I don't know if I can do it. I don't know if I can—

Jason replaces his tongue with his fingers as he pulls my cock back, his mouth engulfing my crown, and I fucking soar.

I'm crying when I come to, my entire body electric and raw. I feel like I've been dunked in a tank with eels, but Jason's palm smooths over my back, and his lips press soothing kisses at my cheek. He's wrapped around the front of me, holding me tight.

"So gorgeous, Cas," he whispers, a kiss at my cheekbone. "You're beautiful."

I have never believed those words more than I do now.

Thoughts race through my head. Words like *love* and *forever* and *yes, yes, see me. Do you see me? Want me. Stay with me.* Questions, too. So many questions about my job, the future, Jason, and his dad's disease.

But my brain is quieting, and my body is going lax. And as Jason tugs his comforter over the two of us, I drift into the inky dark.

"Okay, so I think that's everything," Charlotte says, setting down her pad of paper. "Invites have been sent. Catering ordered. Flowers arranged. Am I missing anything?"

"An ice sculpture of Mom and Dad on their wedding night?" I joke.

"An ice sculpture?" Leo repeats. "I'm not sure that's the best choice for Nevada, brother, even in the winter."

"I..." I shake my head. "Jesus, I was joking. We're good, though? Can I go now?"

Leonidas purses his lips. "Where are you off to in such a hurry? Certainly not the office on a Saturday."

"You know he quit," Char puts in.

"I'm finishing out my two weeks," I amend. "But no, not the office. I just have somewhere to be."

Jason and I didn't get a chance to talk this morning before he had to go to the hospital. And after last night, well... We really need to talk.

Char hums. "Must be the new boyfriend."

"Oh?" Leo says, kicking his leg over his knee. "You're dating someone?"

I don't even bother to ask how Charlotte knows. She must have talked to Mom.

"Yes, I am," I say, impatient to see said man. "His name is Jason, he's a barista and a nurse, and he fucks like a freight train. May I go now?"

Leo chokes as Charlotte laughs loudly.

"Go. Get out of here," my sister says.

I give her a kiss on the cheek before clapping Leo on the shoulder. Then I'm out the door.

I text Jason on the way to the hospital to see where he's stationed since he mentioned he'd be rotating to a new department soon. When he messages back, he says he's on his break and that I can find him in the cafeteria. It only takes a minute to navigate there via signs inside the hospital, and only a minute after that to find Jason amongst the occupants of the room.

His head lifts when I get close to his table, and a blush crawls up his neck above his scrubs.

"Hey," I say, swooping in to kiss his temple before I drop into a seat next to him.

"Hey, Cas."

It astounds me that this man who can give me shy smiles is the same one who forced three orgasms out of me yesterday. The same one who blew me inside a club bathroom, uncaring about our audience—so long as they couldn't see. The same one who used my own cum as lube, even when, an hour before, he was stammering in front of a room full of porn stars.

I think Jason could put half of them to shame.

"I have something for you," I say, tugging the card from my jacket pocket.

Jason snorts. "Of course you do." When I hand over the invite, his eyes widen. "Oh."

"Would you come with me to my parents' anniversary party?" I ask. "It's next month."

He swallows, looking from the card to me. "You want me to meet your parents?"

"Yeah, Jason," I say softly. "I really do. I'd love to introduce them to my boyfriend, if that's something you want."

"Oh," he says again. "Oh, wow. Yeah, um." He blows out a breath. "Yeah, that's good. I'd really like that. Being your boyfriend, I mean. Uh, does that mean…"

"What?" I ask, chuckling a little, even as my insides fizz.

Jason seems to calm when I cover his hand with mine. "Does that mean we'll be exclusive? Just you and me?"

"Jason, it's been you and me since the night you invited me in to meet your snake."

He lets out a laugh, but it's the truth. Since the moment he turned me down, only to tell me he didn't see me like that—that he needed to get to know me first before sex was an option—I was his.

I've been treated carelessly so often in my life. Seen as someone to fuck around with but not someone to build a life with. Like Alex said, I've been used. And maybe that's partly on me for not seeing the signs ahead of time. For not guarding myself better. I don't know.

But not many people have cared about my feelings the way Jason does. Not a single one saw me for who I am and still wanted me.

When Jason told me he's demisexual, it was like this lightbulb going on inside of me. I thought, *Here, this is my chance.* Because if Jason liked me, it meant something. If he saw me and *wanted* me, that meant something.

And he did. He does.

"I'm in this," I tell him. "Unless you tell me to go away, I'm in this. So yeah, I'd like to be yours, exclusively. And yeah, I'd like you to meet my parents."

Jason barks a short laugh. "Cas," he says, shaking his head. "You're the only person I want. Why would I possibly tell you to go away?"

I stutter a breath, my chest so light I could float away. "Can I kiss you?"

I don't know how Jason feels about PDA at his workplace, but he shakes his head again and—

"C'mere," he says, tugging me forward.

His lips are lemony-sweet and warm, and it briefly reminds me of the palo verde tree I used to play under in front of my parents' house, of the bright yellow flowers that would drop to the grass in the spring. But then his tongue curls between my lips, and all childhood memories disappear like smoke, leaving only this man and the way he makes me feel wanted and safe.

He doesn't linger—we *are* inside a hospital cafeteria, after all—but his smile, when he sits back, tells me he'd be happy to pick this up later. He won't hear any complaints from me.

I'm about to bring up the subject of my working at the porn studio when Jason's phone chimes, and he looks down at the display.

"I need to get back to work," he sighs out.

I nod. "Of course. Still on for tonight?"

Jason smiles. "Why? Want a repeat of yesterday?"

I cough out a laugh. "Uh, I think another night like that might kill me." I lower my voice before adding, "Pretty sure you drained me dry."

"Well, I'll just have to fill you back up, then, won't I?" he whispers.

"Jesus," I say, shaking my head, a smile on my lips. "What happened to that shy barista I knew who kept hiding behind the espresso machines?"

He bites his tongue before leaning close. "He met this guy who told him he was toppy. And he found out how much he likes *being in charge*."

With that, Jason stands, running his hand through my hair in a way that has my head arching back. Then he sends me a wink and walks off while I stare.

"Holy fuck," I mutter to myself. "Definitely created a monster. Oh, hi, Zeek."

The man I recognize from my first time visiting Jason here at the hospital stutters a step and waves as he passes the table. "Hngh," he says, and then he's gone.

And me? Well, I'm pretty sure I'm going to get railed by a monster tonight.

Can't wait.

Chapter 22

JASON

"On my back. Behind me! Yeah, right there."

I pause, front door cracked open as Brad's voice reaches my ears.

"Take it. C'mon, take it!" he says.

A new voice adds to the mix. "I don't know what I'm doing." *Cas*.

"You just...thrust," Brad says. "Hard as you can."

My eyes widen.

"Yes! Look at that hole," my friend says. "Beautiful."

I push the door wide, taking in the sight before me. Brad and Cas on the couch. Looking cozy. They don't see me yet.

Cas tenses. "Brad?"

"I know, I know. I'm coming. I'm coming! *Urgh*."

"Uh, guys?" I call out.

Cas's head whips my way, and he gives me a big, beaming smile. "Hi, Jason."

Brad shouts, fingers mashing his controller. "*Nooo*. Toss another grenade, Cat. They're overrunning us. Fuck! *Aaand* we're dead." He slumps against the couch, groaning.

"What are you guys doing?" I ask, kicking off my shoes.

"Killing zombies," Cas answers.

"Being *killed* by zombies," Brad corrects.

I don't know whether to be amused or highly concerned.

Cas jumps up off the couch, jogging over. He brushes a kiss against my lips that has my breath coming short in no time.

"Sorry I'm late," I mumble against his mouth.

"No problem," he says, hands at the sides of my face. "Brad's kept me company."

"Did he call you Cat?" I ask, swaying forward just a little. It's been a long day, and Cas, well, he smells and feels so damn good. I could just curl up against him and sleep for days.

Cas leans back enough to catch my gaze. He swipes a finger under my eye, probably over the dark circle that's undoubtedly there. "Guess he wanted me to have an animal name, too," he says. "Think it fits?"

I immediately flash back to Marley making a claw and calling Cas a housecat. He gives me a funny look when I start laughing.

"You sound a little drunk," he says, guiding me toward the couch.

"I feel it," I admit. After the late night with Cas and then a full day of clinicals, I'm beat.

Brad scoots over as I all but fall onto the couch. He gives my knee a squeeze. "Okay, Birdie?"

"Yeah," I tell him, waving off his concern and then slumping back against Cas as soon he sits beside me. "Just tired."

Cas wraps his arms around me, and I twist, laying my cheek on his chest.

"Good pillow," I tell his pec, giving it a little pat. Cas clears his throat when my hand lingers.

Yes, he likes my pets.

I hear Brad chuckling, and then a blanket is being laid over me.

"Just gonna..." I mumble.

"Mhm," Cas says, and then there's a kiss against the top of my head. "Sweet dreams, my little lion."

I'm in my bed when I wake. Cas is lounging on his side next to me, Amadeus curled around his palm and up his arm. I blink a few times, just to make sure I'm not seeing things.

Cas notices me stir and gives me a smile. "Hey."

"Um," I say, clearing my throat. "Are you petting my snake?"

He huffs a laugh. "He seemed lonely."

Good grief. There goes my heart.

I rub my eyes. "You look like an underwear ad," I note. Except for the clothes. "Yeah, clothes could definitely go."

"Huh?" he says, cocking his head.

Christ. Sleepy Jason has no filter.

"How long was I out?" I ask.

"Just an hour and a half," Cas answers.

Good. That shouldn't throw off my sleep schedule too badly.

"Hungry?" he asks.

"Yeah," I admit, sitting upright, trying to clear the fuzz from my brain.

"I'll order something. What sounds good?"

"Anything edible," I tell him.

Cas chuckles, shifting off the bed to return Amadeus to his tank. He's so gentle about it, handling my snake with care—*snort*—and I can't help but watch him fondly.

Once he secures the top of the cage, he hops back onto the bed and pulls out his phone. "One of these days," he says with a swift grin, "I'm going to learn how to cook a real meal. Then I can feed you."

So many palpitations.

Reaching over, I squeeze his leg. "You don't have to do that for me."

He shrugs. "I want to. For me, too," he says, tapping away at his phone. "I never got the chance when I was younger because we had a cook prepare all our food"—he winces a little at that, like he's embarrassed by the fact—"but I'd like to learn."

That's so sweet. And a little sad.

"There," he says, dropping his phone on the bed. "Twenty minutes."

"Mkay," I mutter, shivering a little.

Cas hums when I grab his sweatshirt off the floor, tugging it over my head. His lips twist into a smile. "You look good in...or out of...my clothes," he comments, leaning back on his elbows.

I fight my smile, fidgeting with the cuff of the sweatshirt. "You look good with my tongue in your ass."

Cas booms a laugh, and I chuckle with him. But then he turns pensive.

"Hey, there's something I wanted to talk to you about," he says.

And *shit*. That's not good, is it?

"Uh, okay?"

Cas rolls closer to me on the bed, looking up at me like a puppy. An adorable, sexy puppy.

Was I petting him earlier?

"Before, you said you were okay with the porn," he starts, and my focus immediately shifts, "but it's been a while since we talked about it, and we just agreed to be exclusive. So I guess I was wondering how you see my job fitting in. If you want us to be fully monogamous."

"Oh," I say, realizing I hadn't even considered that. As far as I'm concerned, Cas's job rests outside the bounds of our relationship. Him quitting porn hadn't even crossed my mind, and yet...

I take a moment to choose my words carefully as the caveman part of me screams, *Yes! Be mine! Only mine!*

"I *am* okay with the porn," I tell him slowly. "You told me it's a safe space for you, and I wouldn't... I wouldn't want to take that away."

"You make me feel safe, Jason."

And *oh*. Oh, God.

"I would miss my coworkers at the studio," he goes on as my heart beats furiously. "But I don't think I need that anymore. It was never my dream, you know? And now..." He grabs my hand, rolling it over in his grip, looking uncharacteristically demure. "Now I have this guy who treats me better than anyone else I've ever been with, and I like *that*. I want that. I don't need the rest."

All the fucks.

"So if you quit..." I say a little weakly.

He shrugs again. "I could still keep up with the guys. Would you..." He twists his lips a little. "Would you be okay with that? I know you liked the videos. Would it bother you if I quit?"

His question makes me realize I haven't even watched porn since before our first date. I haven't needed to. And maybe a part of it was out of sight, out of mind when it came to my now-boyfriend being involved in said activity; I don't know. But my enjoyment of those videos was never personal. It had nothing to do with anyone specific, Cas included. And the idea of having this man all to myself? That he wants that, too?

Blowing out a breath, I roll over Cas's body. He lies flat, catching my hips as I settle on top of him, my hands in his hair, face inches from his. "I liked watching porn because it got me off when I didn't have anyone to call my own. But I like *you* better than any porn. So if you don't need it anymore, if you don't want it, then I will take care of you. I will be kind"—I kiss his cheek—"and considerate"—I kiss the other—"and absolutely filthy when you need it. I will do whatever I can to make you feel safe, Cas."

Safe. And loved.

Don't make promises you can't keep.

I will, I practically shout at my brain. I'll get the test. I'll find out if I have the HTT mutation. And if I do, I'll prepare. I'll figure it out. I'll make sure Cas will be taken care of, *somehow*. And I'll love him for as long as I possibly can.

"Jason," he says, eyes closed, his air and mine one and the same.

The buzzer is like a shot, jolting me and Cas apart.

"I'll get it," Brad calls.

Cas opens his eyes.

"Food?" I say, voice a little shaky.

He gives me a nod.

Brad is in the kitchen when Cas and I walk down the hall. "Dudes, that's a lot of grub," he says.

Cas huffs a laugh. "Ordered enough for you, too."

Brad beams. "Cat-man, my *man*," he crows, and I can see the precise moment my friend falls a little bit in love with my boyfriend.

I'm not even sure I can blame him.

I grab plates as my mind cycles over that conversation in my bedroom, and Brad pulls the to-go containers out of the bag. After dishing up our food, the three of us sit at the couch, meals in front of us on the coffee table.

"Do you have a specific place you go to work out?" Brad asks Cas, apropos of nothing.

Cas shakes his head, chewing his food before answering. "Not really. I've been going once a week or so with my coworker to his gym near Hyped, and sometimes I use the gym at the studio or one near my place."

Brad nods. "Cool. If you ever wanna check out the place I go to, let me know. They've got some great classes."

What...is happening right now?

"Yeah? I'll take you up on that," Cas says.

"Cool, cool," Brad replies.

"Oh my God..." I realize aloud. "Are you two... Is this a budding gym bro thing? Should I be worried?"

Brad snorts. "Two buddies can practice their pelvic thrusts together without it being sexual, Birdie."

I slow pan over to Brad.

"Or, ooh, groiners?" my ex-friend suggests. "Get a good flex going before really going to town, y'know?"

"How..." I question, "are you straight?"

Brad's nose wrinkles. "Huh?"

I shake my head, turning back to my food. "Bee, I would not be the least bit surprised to learn you fell on a cock one day, rode it to orgasm, came so hard you saw *rainbows*, and then decided, 'Huh, yeah, jizz tastes great. I think I'll have a daily dose of it before my morning coffee.'"

It's quiet when I finish speaking, and I look over at Cas, who's biting his lip. Brad's eyes are wide when I turn his way.

"That," Brad says reverently, "was *graphic*. I'm impressed."

I sigh. "Learned it from you."

Brad squeezes me around the middle. "Aw, Birdie," he says as my insides squeak. "I love you, too."

"Hate this," I mumble. Brad rocks me back and forth while Cas laughs. "Hate this all."

I don't. I really don't.

As Brad releases me, he says, "What *does* jizz taste like?"

"*Oh my God*," I groan, dropping my fork onto my food. "No, nope. We're not doing this. Change of topic. *Please*."

Cas clears his throat. "I have one. I put in my notice at Kinsley Richman."

It's silent again for just a moment as Cas's words saturate my brain.

"You did?" I ask quietly, turning to him. I know we were just talking about him possibly being done with porn, but I didn't realize he'd quit his job at his dad's firm, too.

He shrugs a little. "Yeah."

"Because of what I said?" I ask, not sure what I want his answer to be.

"In part," he admits. "It made me think about things I'd been burying for a while. But mostly because I wasn't happy there. You were right about that. I don't... I don't want to waste my life. I don't want to turn around ten years down the road and regret the choices I've made."

I nod, throat tight. When I squeeze Cas's thigh, he places his hand on mine.

"If you need any help," I say, "I'm here for you. I don't know what I'll do, but... I'll try."

Cas grabs my chin, smacking a kiss against my lips. "You've already helped me more than you know."

My heart beats like a drum.

"So what are you going to do?" Brad asks.

"Go back to school," Cas says. "Maybe do physical therapy? I've always been good at bodies. Activity, you know? I think I could be good at that."

"You'll be great," I tell him, sure of it.

Brad bobs his head. "Next time I pull a hammy, I'll come to you."

"My boyfriend isn't touching your hams," I inform Brad.

"Whoa," Brad says. "I didn't know you could growl, Birdie."

"Hot, isn't it?" Cas says.

Brad laughs loudly as I blush, just a little, and even though I'm more than a smidge worried about my best friend and my boyfriend being in cahoots, I'm not sure I've been as happy as I am in this moment.

Everything feels right. Like it's falling into place.

Like nothing could possibly go wrong.

Chapter 23

CAS

"Cas? You good?"

Crap, am I zoning?

"Fine. Sorry," I tell Niko, realizing he's already wearing a robe. Our scene just wrapped up, and here I am, thoughts drifting to a certain sandy blonde who has the ability to make me come about a hundred times harder than Niko did a few minutes ago. Nothing against Niko and his...talent. But *Christ*. All Jason needs to do is utter *Cassius* in that way he does when he's turned on, and I'm done for.

I'm surer than ever that I'm ready to be done with porn. I'm just not looking forward to telling my boss. And everyone else here at the studio. I'll miss them.

But, I realize, *I won't miss this*. Not now that I have Jason.

I push off the bed, grabbing the spare robe sitting at the corner, and an assistant begins stripping the sheets. The cameramen are in the process of rolling their equipment away, and the rest of the crew is in post-production mode, clearing the set.

"Coming?" Niko asks, canting his head toward the door.

"Yeah, just give me a minute," I tell him, searching for Jerome. I find my boss talking to Marco, one of the boom operators, and head his way.

Jerome sees me approaching and turns. "What can I do for you, Himbo?"

I try not to fidget as I stand in front of him in nothing but a robe. He just saw me naked and having sex a moment ago, so I don't know why it feels odd. "Could I talk to you at some point today?" I ask.

My boss raises an eyebrow. Jerome is known as a bit of a hardass—he's gruff and to the point—but he's a good guy beneath it, and he accepts my request without question, aside from his curious brow. "Yeah. Meet me in my office in thirty?"

"Sounds good. Thanks, Jerome."

He gives me a nod before turning back to Marco, and I jog off, catching up to Niko near the exit of Studio 3.

"All good?" Niko checks.

"Yeah," I answer, letting out a breath.

"So how's Jason?" my coworker asks, brushing his tangled hair out of his face as we leave the studio and head toward the locker room. Trevor, another performer, passes us with a nod, a book tucked under his arm.

"He's good," I tell Niko. "Thanks for asking."

He hums. "You know, I've known the guy for over a year, ever since Dixon and I started dating. But I've never seen him so..."

"What?" I ask.

Niko opens the door to the locker room, waving me in. Teddy is inside, toweling his hair dry. Unlike us, he's dressed.

"Confident?" Niko finishes, stepping with me toward our lockers. "I saw you guys dancing some the other week, and he was... I don't know. Different."

I think the word he's looking for is *fierce*. Jason has a protective streak a mile wide, as I'm learning, and I like it a lot. Most of the people I've dated liked showing me off. At least, that's how it felt. Like I was a fancy new accessory they wanted to flaunt. I felt like a prop. A toy. Disposable.

But Jason doesn't care about showing me off. He'd rather show me how much I mean to him, and that...that is something I've never had before.

"He's really great," I say, at a loss for how to explain how wonderful Jason is. "Does, uh..." I huff a laugh. "Does Dixon know he'll be done at the coffee shop after the spring?"

Niko goes stock still, his robe hanging open around his body. "He what?"

"He'll be working full-time as a nurse," I explain. That bit of news must not have made it around the grapevine. "He won't be at Hyped anymore."

Niko drops his head back, groaning up at the ceiling. "Dixon is going to be *such* a grump about that. You have no idea." He shakes his head, giving me a smirk. "Do you know how much he complains on the weekends when Jason isn't the one to make his latte? He'll be insufferable for months."

Based on Niko's face, I don't think he minds his boyfriend's grumpiness one bit.

"Maybe I shouldn't have mentioned anything," I say around a laugh.

"Oh no, it's best he prepares," Niko says, stripping down and heading into a shower stall. He raises his voice as the water comes on. "Besides, I know how to handle the man. Blowjobs are a good distraction."

Teddy snorts, dropping his damp towel in the hamper. "I know way too much about my coworkers' sex lives."

That makes me smile. "I like it."

Teddy raises a brow. "You like hearing about Niko's oral skills?"

"No," I say, chuckling. "I mean...how open everyone is here, you know? There's no artifice."

No pretending we aren't all just people with messy lives who are trying to get by the best way we know how. No posturing or judgment or pretention.

"People here...they're real," I say. Even though it's all a show, the people behind it are *real*. "That's what I like."

Teddy nods, eyeing me a little curiously. "Yeah, I know what you mean."

"How'd you get into porn?" I ask, taking a seat on the bench in front of my locker. I know my own reasons, but I'm guessing we all have different stories.

His lips twitch, an almost sad smile on his face as he sits across from me. "Needed a change of pace, and... I'd been burned by a few too many relationships. This seemed like a decent alternative."

I guess we had that part in common.

"You don't date, then?" I ask just as Alex walks into the room.

The blonde man's eyes swing Teddy's way, his expression brightening. "Ooh, are we talking about Teddy's love life again? I'm just in time."

The bigger man rolls his eyes, although there's a smile on his face. "No, we're not. So you don't even need to start."

Niko comes out from the showers, a towel around his waist, hair wet and hanging to his shoulders. "Small fry, you interfering in others' love lives again?"

Alex grins. "It worked for you."

Niko huffs a laugh, but he doesn't deny it.

"Hey, Niko," Alex says sweetly, taking a seat next to Teddy. "What's Kipp up to these days, hmm?" He flutters his lashes at Teddy, and Teddy covers Alex's face with his hand.

Alex squawks, batting him away. "Rude!"

"You need a muzzle," Teddy retorts, standing up.

Alex looks up at him, seemingly impressed. "Rawr."

"Hey, guys?" I cut in. All eyes swing my way, and I swallow a little, suddenly aware of the fact that I'm still sitting here in a robe with another man's spunk drying on my skin. Not that any of us are unused to that sort of thing. "There's something I wanted to tell you."

"What's up?" Alex asks, abandoning Teddy's side to plop down at my own.

"I won't be here much longer," I say. "I haven't sat down with Jerome yet, but I'll be giving my notice this afternoon."

"Aw, sug," Alex says, squeezing my arm. "I'm not sad *for* you, but I am going to miss seeing your gorgeous face around here. Why the change?"

I shrug a little. "Jason and I are getting serious," I admit, "but that's only part of it. He didn't ask me to quit or anything. I just... I don't need this anymore."

Teddy nods, expression serious. "I'm glad you know your limits, Cas. Porn isn't something you should do past your comfort level."

"That's right," Alex chimes in. "If it's time for you to be done, then it's time, simple as that."

Niko bobs his head in agreement, taking a seat beside us, clothes now in place. "And Jerome will understand. He wouldn't want you to be here if you don't want to be."

I nod. I know all that, I do, but it's nice hearing those things confirmed. Having the support of my coworkers. "Thanks," I say softly. "I'm really glad I ended up here, you know. I'm glad I got the chance to know you all."

Alex sniffs before his arms come around me like a vise. "Damn it, sweets, I'm going to miss you."

I chuckle a little, patting him on the back. "I'll miss you, too."

"*You guys*," Alex moans. "Get in here."

The next second, two additional pairs of arms are surrounding me and Alex is muttering out something about how all of his coworkers are "a bunch of soft-ass cinnamon rolls, I swear."

Honestly, it's perfect.

"Don't for one second think this means you're getting rid of us, honeybunch," Alex mutters against my shoulder. "You're one of us now, you and your beau both, and I *will* track you down if you try to ghost."

"He'll do it," Niko puts in, his head near mine. "That's why Mal never got away."

I huff a laugh as Niko grunts. Pretty sure Alex punched him.

"Sounds great," I sigh.

"Uh, guys?" Emil asks, standing at the doorway with wide eyes. "What's going on?"

"Cuddle pile," Alex answers. "Get your ass in here, boo."

"Uh, I don't think—"

"*Emil*," Alex says sharply.

"Ah, Christ," Emil mumbles, joining the fray, arms coming around me tentatively. "Why are we squishing Cas?"

"Because our lovely Himbo is leaving us," Alex says. "And we're wishing him a fond farewell. He deserves nothing less."

Shit.

"Oh," Emil says. I think he pats my head. "Good luck with...life, Cas. And stuff."

I snort, and some of the pressure around me disappears as the cuddle pile comes to an end. Alex is the last to unwrap his arms.

"Thanks, guys," I say again.

Teddy claps my shoulder. "As lovely as this has been, I need to get going. Seriously, though, Cas, we're always here, all right?"

I give the man a nod, more appreciative than he knows.

"Teddy Bear," Alex calls. "Don't think I've forgotten our conversation."

"What conversation?" Teddy responds, pocketing his wallet.

"About your secret crush," the blonde says.

"I never said anything about a crush."

"You didn't have to," Alex says. "I've seen the way you look at him, you know."

For a long moment, Teddy doesn't say a word. Then, finally, "I'm not interested in dating right now, so…" He shrugs, closing his locker. "I'll see you guys later."

"I don't believe you," Alex calls as Teddy starts toward the door. "You have a lot of love to give, Teddy Bear! You'll make some boy very—and he's gone. *Damn it.* Why are the sweetest ones always so opposed to falling in love?"

Niko chuckles, shaking his head as Alex eyes Emil.

"Emil…" the blonde says.

"Gotta pee," Emil says, disappearing around the corner.

Alex sighs, deflating against the bench.

"Alex," I say.

He looks over at me.

"Thank you for setting me and Jason up. I don't know how you did it, but you couldn't have picked a better guy for me."

He smiles, looking oh so pleased and a little smug. "I'm happy for you, sugar lips. Now, can I be the flower girl at your wedding?"

I choke on a laugh. "Um. Yeah. If we get married, the job's yours."

He looks ecstatic.

"I really need to shower now," I admit, standing up.

Alex snickers. "Have at it." Raising his voice, he says, "You can't hide forever, Emil."

Niko snorts a laugh, ruffling Alex's hair as he passes. "Such trouble." To me, he adds, "See ya later, Cas."

I give the man a nod, and Alex says, "Oh! And we'll need to give you a proper send-off. What sounds best—cast orgy or penis cake? Only one is vanilla."

I shake my head, walking toward the showers as Alex cackles at his own joke, adding something about wondering if he can get a cock-themed party bus. There's a smile on my face as I turn on the water, and it doesn't take long before I'm clean, dressed, and meeting Jerome in his office. Ten minutes after that, I'm standing in front of the Elite 8 Studios sign in the front hall of the building, staring at the yellow neon tubing that welcomed me my first time here.

I'm glad my path wound its way through these halls, however briefly. But now, I'm ready to move on.

After all, there's a whole lot I have to look forward to.

Chapter 24

JASON

"Your finger looks good," I tell Brad, checking over his injury. The stitches are gone now, and even though his skin is still a delicate pink, it's healed up nicely.

"Yeah. Feels weird when I jerk off, though."

I drop his hand like a hot potato. "*Ew*, Brad. So much ew."

He laughs as I shiver involuntarily. "It's not like I was *just* jerking off," he says. "I have washed my hands since then. It's just...kinda numb?"

I nod, plopping onto the couch beside him. "That'll get better," I assure him. "You'll be back to jerking off with full sensation in no time."

"Your bedside manner is superb," my friend deadpans.

I snort.

"Sooo," he says slowly, waggling his eyebrows a couple times.

I frown. "What?"

"*You know*." He bounces his eyes wide, looking as if he's trying to signal me with some sort of morse code.

"What is this?" I ask. "What's happening with your face? Repeat after me. 'My friend Jason is the best. I shall leave him all my warmest scarves and possessions.'"

Brad rolls his eyes. "I'm not having a stroke, Birdie. I'm trying to inquire after your love life. You know, with your *boyfriend?*" He grins, and I can't even be mad at the fool.

"What about it?" I mumble, hiding my smile.

"Are you being purposely obtuse? This is big, isn't it? You and him?"

"Yeah, Bee," I admit.

I think I love the man.

"Does he know about the gene?" Brad asks seriously.

My mood plummets. "No."

"Birdie..."

"Don't, Brad. You sound just like my mom."

I get up off the couch and head into the kitchen. Brad follows me, standing in the entryway as I fill a cup with water. He waits until I've chugged the whole glass before speaking.

"She's a smart woman," he says. And *yeah, yeah.* "Why haven't you said anything to him?"

"I scheduled an appointment for next week," I say, instead of answering his question.

His inhale is quiet, but it's there. "That's good, Jason. Will you ask him to come?"

I shake my head.

"You're making a mistake," my friend says, and his tone is so sure, so firm, I whip my gaze his way. "He's the real deal. And you're going to hurt him."

"I'm trying to *protect* him," I throw back.

"You're trying to protect yourself."

My head rocks back, but neither of us has a chance to say another word before there's a knock at the door.

"That's him," I say, brushing past my friend.

"Birdie," he says quietly.

I stop, hand at the door. "I know, Brad. I love you, too."

There's a smile on Cas's face when I swing open the door. "Hi, Jason," he says—the two sweetest words—and, immediately, some of that tension inside of me spirals away, like dirty water rinsing down the drain.

"Hi," I breathe, matching his smile. I grab the scarf Cas got me, the blue striped one, and wrap it around my neck. *So warm.* "I made reservations for tonight. That okay?"

Cas's smile goes a little crooked. "Of course. Should we go now?"

I nod. When I glance back inside, Brad is watching me, face sad. He gives me a little smile, though, and a thumbs up.

Fucking Brad.

I blow a kiss off my fingers before closing the door. Cas takes my hand, warm and solid and real, and I hold tight, easing out a breath.

"Drive or walk?" Cas asks as we head toward the stairs.

"Drive."

"Color me intrigued," he says, but he doesn't ask where we're going. He lets it remain a surprise.

Once we're inside my car and heading through town, my thoughts turn to what Cas was planning to do today. As soon as we're stopped at a red light, I look over.

"Did you get a chance to talk to your boss?" I ask.

Cas gives me a whisper of a smile. "Yeah. Told my coworkers, too. I have two more scenes on my schedule, and then I'll be done."

I swallow. "And you feel okay about it?"

I've been rolling over the implications of Cas quitting porn all week, alternating between guilt—even though I'm fairly sure the emotion is misplaced—and relief. Part of me feels bad that, in a way, he's quitting because of me. Because of *us*. But ultimately, it was his choice. He told me he's ready to be done.

I would have supported him either way, but knowing I'll be the only person with the privilege of making Cas feel good, of making him fall apart? I don't even know if there's a word to describe how that makes me feel.

Ecstatic. Scared. Awed.

"Yeah, Jason," Cas says. He gives my thigh a squeeze, leaving his hand there as I pull forward into traffic. "I'm okay with it. It was...a bandage, you know? A temporary stopgap. But it doesn't feel the same when I know I have you to come home to."

Damn. So many things about that statement make me want to pull over, crawl into this man's lap, and never fucking let go. I want to promise he won't regret it. That I'll make him happy. That as long as I'm breathing—

The air whooshes from my lungs as my dad's face fills my mind. His skin, sunken and sallow. A breathing tube up his nose.

I flex my fingers, my hand shaking as I take the turn toward our destination. Cas hums beside me as I park.

"What is this?" he asks.

I clear my throat. And my thoughts. "I, uh, thought we could try something different tonight. Cooking lessons."

Cas looks over at me, his eyes wide. "Jason... You picked this for me?"

"Um." *Mouth, so dry.* "Yes?"

"Wow," he says quietly, his hand flexing on my thigh. "Thank you."

"For what, making you work for your dinner?" I tease.

"For listening," he responds.

The look on his face makes me feel more than a little dizzy and a lot warm. "Well, you're always doing nice things for me," I point out. "It's no big deal."

"It is to me," he says, hand lifting to my jaw. He runs the backs of his fingers across my skin, up to my ear, down to my neck, stroking, lingering.

That warmth kicks up a good hundred notches.

"This is what happens, huh?" Cas says.

"What?" I ask, licking my lips. Did Cas get closer?

"When you care about someone," he says. "When they care about you. You pay attention to the little things."

"Yeah," I breathe. He's definitely closer.

"No one has cared the way you do, Jason."

God. How is this man capable of stealing my breath with a few simple words?

I close the final inch between us and kiss him. I can't *not.* I don't know how it still feels new. Like it's our first. Like every time my lips touch his, we're starting all over again.

Maybe we are. Maybe that's what a relationship is. Rediscovering each other over and over again. Falling in love over and over again.

I could see myself falling for Cas time after time, as sure as the seasons. Every spring, summer, autumn, winter, I'll fall. Like the rain, the leaves, and the goddamn snow, I'll fall for Cas without fail.

I'm his. Without question. For as long as I live.

"Jason," Cas says, pulling back, his breath hot on my lips. "Are you okay? You're shaking."

"Yep," I say with a short, sharp nod. I ignore the cough of *avoidance* from my conscience. "I'm perfect. Ready to head inside?"

"Yeah," Cas says, giving me a grin. "Let's get cooking."

When Cas and I head into the building, we're greeted at the door by a perky blonde in a white apron. "Hi, there! You must be our last couple. I'm Tori."

"Jason," I say. "We talked on the phone."

"That's right," she says happily. "And you are?"

"Cas," my boyfriend answers, returning her massive smile. And *oh boy*, Tori flutters her lashes like she's trying to take flight.

I nearly groan. It's been a whole day since someone ogled Cas in front of me. I mentally reset the clock.

Time since last incident: zero minutes.

"Well, come along," Tori says with a giggle. "Your station is right over here."

There are five separate island-style countertops within the space, four of which are already occupied by other couples. Tori leads us to the only empty one before standing back and clapping her hands.

"Welcome, everyone!" our host-slash-chef says. "We're making something simple tonight. Creamy stuffed shells! Ready to make a mess?"

Cas chokes, covering his laugh with a cough as Tori starts explaining the dish we'll be preparing. "We're stuffing what now?" he whispers, sidling up next to me.

I snort. "I dunno, but apparently, things are going to get messy."

"I thought I quit my day job," Cas says.

This time, it's me covering a laugh.

"All right!" Tori says. "Let's get on our aprons."

I turn, finding the two aprons stocked at the back of our station. One pink and one blue.

"I don't think they were expecting a queer couple," I comment, looking around the room. Although *why* the aprons need to be gendered "queen" and "king of the kitchen," I don't understand.

"That's okay." Cas snatches the pink apron. "I look good in pink."

"You look good in everything," I note, taking off my scarf so I can put on the blue apron.

The smile Cas gives me is sweet and softly pleased. "Thank you, Jason."

Fuck. This man.

As Cas grabs a box of large pasta shells, following along with Tori's directions, I tie my apron around my waist. Then I start filling a large pot with water.

"Now we don't want to overcook the pasta," Tori is saying, "because we'll be baking the dish for twenty minutes."

"You know," Cas says quietly, leaning close enough for our elbows to brush. "Once I'm officially done at the studio, you could stuff me with *your* cream."

"*Holy*—" I grab the large pot of water with two hands, steadying it and myself. Because *fuuuck*. Ho-ly fucking fuck. "Sorry," I say aloud to the few people looking my way. "Almost dropped a...thing. I'm good now. Um, thanks."

Cas's eyes are wide when I duck my face away from the others, and his lips twitch. "Okay, Jason?"

"What do you think?" I hiss.

"I think you probably have a lot on your mind," he retorts calmly.

I groan. "You should know."

He simply smiles.

"Happy with yourself, aren't you?" I mumble.

He shrugs. "Yeah, I am happy. This is fun."

"Yeah?" I say seriously, my chest feeling warm. I grab a bowl for the cream filling as Cas sorts herbs. "You like the cooking lesson?"

"Yes," he says, and then, "But mostly, I like *you*, Jason. I like spending time with you."

Shit.

"Mm," Cas says. "There's that blush."

"You're being cheeky tonight," I point out, not minding that one bit. I like when Cas is like this. When he flirts with me. He doesn't do it with others, I've noticed.

Cas chuckles in response to my comment, the sound all low and throaty in a way that goes right to my dick. I'm almost afraid of what's about to come out of his mouth. "You like me cheeky," he says. "Just like you like my *cheeks*."

And yep. There it is. Mind immediately in the gutter.

"Behave," I mumble halfheartedly.

"Now you want to stir that cream," Tori says loudly.

"Oh my *God*," I groan as Cas laughs.

I never knew cooking lessons could be so filthy.

I sneak a peek Cas's way as I dump the ricotta into a bowl, my mind trailing back to one particular thing he said. He's measuring out the herbs now, checking the printed recipe as Tori talks above us.

"You'd, um…" I clear my throat and try again. "You'd want to go condom-free?"

"With you? Yes," he says easily.

Okay. That's… *Fine*. So very fine. Mhm.

"You like that," Cas says. "The idea of marking me."

"Jesus *Christ*," I whisper, lowering my voice as much as possible. "You just…*say* stuff like that."

"Am I not supposed to?" he counters, an amused grin on his face.

I wave my hand a little. "No, you are. That's good. Communication and...stuff."

He chuckles again.

"But cripes, Cas. We're in public. This isn't"—I lower my voice even more—*"foreplay.* We're supposed to be..."

"Stuffing shells?" he fills in, laughter in his tone.

"That," I agree, pointing my spoon at him.

"I think anything can be foreplay."

God, I am never going to get rid of this chub. "Hush up so I can stir this cream without a boner."

Cas's laugh feels like all things right in the world. Like happiness and sunshine and perfect little snowflakes. It feels like...*fuck*. Like my future. And before I know it, my grin rivals Tori's, and everything else—everything but me and Cas and *this*—falls away.

"Now don't forget. You'll want to fill those shells to the tippy top," Tori says cheerfully. "Stuff 'em real full. Your belly will thank you."

Oh, for Heaven's sake.

Doesn't even matter. Nope. This date is perfect.

Chapter 25
Cas

Jason's cheeks are bright as we head up the stairs to his apartment. I think part of it is the cool evening, but most of it, if I had to guess, has to do with that massive smile he's been sporting for the past couple hours.

I'm not sure I've ever seen him look so happy and carefree.

"Too bad we couldn't keep the aprons," Jason says, opening the door into his hall from the stairway. I follow him through. "You looked good as *queen of the kitchen*."

I huff a laugh. "Think I should get that tattooed above my ass?"

"Uh, no," Jason says. "The only thing I want to see above your ass is—"

He cuts off abruptly, but there's no way I'm letting that one go.

"What?" I prod. "What do you want to see above my ass, Jason?"

He clears his throat, stopping at the door to grab his keys out of his pocket. "My hands," he finally mumbles.

I bark a laugh. "Or maybe your name?" I add as a tease.

Jason doesn't take the bait, but I can see the way his neck reddens. I can't help but step close, lips settling over his blush, hands curling around his hips.

"Property of Jason?" I say, kissing his skin.

His breath hitches, and one of his hands moves over top of my own. "You're not property, Cas," he says, his voice almost hard.

I close my eyes and inhale, catching a whiff of vanilla. It seems to linger on Jason's person, that scent. A carryover from the coffee shop, I think.

It's comforting and sweet, just like him.

"No," I agree. "I'm not. But I *am* yours. Willingly."

"Fuck, Cas," he mutters before turning in my arms. He gives me a swift, hard kiss, his hand on the back of my neck squeezing tight. "The things you say."

It doesn't sound like a bad thing.

When Jason lets go, he opens his door, and we head inside. The lights are on in the apartment, as is the TV, paused on some video game I don't recognize.

"Would you ever get a tattoo?" Jason asks, unwinding his scarf. He takes off his beanie, too, fluffing his hair.

I shrug, toeing off my shoes. "I don't know. Maybe? If it was something that had meaning. Have you ever wanted one?"

"Actually, yeah," he answers, much to my surprise. "I've thought about it."

"What would you get?"

"Um. Maybe a caduceus?" He grabs his phone from his pocket, doing a quick search and then aiming the screen at me. "It's a symbol commonly associated with healthcare."

The picture is of a staff, with two snakes twisted up the length of it and wings at the top.

I hum. "That would fit you."

"I almost got it after... after my dad," he says, fiddling with his phone. "But I thought I should probably actually *become* a nurse first."

He chuckles a little at that, but it's a strained sort of sound, and my chest squeezes tight. I wonder if the tattoo has more to do with honoring his dad's memory than actually becoming a nurse. Although maybe the two are one and the same.

I reach for Jason's hand, holding it in my own. "If and when you're ready for it, I'll come with you to that appointment, okay?"

"Oh, thank God," Brad says, walking into the room from the hallway. "You told him."

Jason freezes, his hand reflexively squeezing my own. "Brad," he says tersely.

"No, it's good," Brad goes on. "You shouldn't be alone for this, Birdie."

Jason shuts his eyes. "Stop talking. *Please.*"

"What?" Brad says, gaze pinging between us in confusion. "You told him about the appointment, right?"

"What's going on?" I ask.

Jason slips his hand from mine, rubbing his face.

Brad's expression falls. "You didn't."

"I didn't," Jason answers.

Brad groans, a long, low sound.

"Jason?" I ask, wondering what I'm missing.

"I'm sorry," Brad says quietly to Jason, his tone full of regret.

Jason simply shakes his head and grabs my hand. He tugs me down the hall into his room, shutting the door behind us, and then he paces beside the bed.

"So..." he says, and that's it.

"What's going on?" I ask again, sitting down at the edge of his mattress. "You have an appointment you didn't want to tell me about? I assume it's not for the tattoo?"

Jason shakes his head. "No. I haven't actually thought about that tattoo in a while."

"Okay," I say slowly, watching Jason walk a tight circuit around his room. "Jason, you're starting to freak me out here. What is this about?"

He stops moving, his hands dropping to his sides. He looks...wrecked. "My dad's Huntington's disease," he says.

Oh. Now I'm starting to understand.

Jason swallows several times as my heart beats erratically. "Huntington's," he says before blinking and blowing out a breath. "Huntington's is genetic."

I force my shoulders to come down. "I know."

Jason stills. "What?"

"I know that," I admit. "I...I looked up some info about it after you told me. I hope that's okay. I just wanted to understand, and... I know there's a chance he passed it to you. That you have it, too."

Jason gapes at me, and I go on.

"I assumed you knew, one way or another, and I was..." I blow out a breath, scrubbing a hand through my hair as my eyes start to sting. *Fuck*, this is harder than I thought it would be. "I was giving you time to tell me."

Jason looks gut-punched, but he doesn't say a word. He doesn't look capable of it.

"Your appointment," I utter. "Is it about managing your symptoms?"

He inhales finally, a great big, wracking sound. "*God*, Cas. You..."

"What?" I ask, reaching for him.

He doesn't move. Not even an inch.

"Jason, please," I whisper, knowing I'm about to cry one way or another, and I'd much rather have Jason in my arms when it happens.

Because *fucking hell*. If Jason has an appointment, that means he has it, right? From what I understand, twenty-four is young for symptoms to present but not impossible.

"Please," I repeat, voice wobbling. "Whatever it is, tell me. We'll figure it out, okay? We will. Just *please*. Please come here and tell me."

His breath leaves him in a whoosh, and then he's walking forward, climbing onto my lap and burying his face in the side of my neck. "Do you mean that?" he says, his voice choked. "You knew. You already knew, and... You're not going to leave me?"

I'm not exactly proud of the sound I make, but there it is, all the same. "Why would you think that?"

"You'd be better off."

And no. Just no.

"I would *not*," I tell him firmly, my arms around him tight. He's shaking slightly, but fuck, so am I. "Don't you dare ask me to give up the best thing in my life because I won't do it. You hear me?"

Jason lets out a sob, and then he's crying for real: big, wet tears against my skin. I try to keep myself in check, but it feels like a losing battle. The idea that this man could be taken from me much earlier than either of us deserves is like a boulder against my diaphragm. I can't take a full breath, no matter how hard I try.

I can't lose him.

When Jason speaks, his words are muffled against my neck. "I don't know if I have it. My appointment is for genetic testing. I might not have it. I might not."

My breath hitches, holds, and then leaves me in a rush. "Fuck, Jason," I choke out. "You couldn't have led with that?"

His laugh sounds pained, but he sobers quickly, brushing his face against my shoulder. "I'm sorry, Cas. Fuck, I'm so sorry. Maybe I should have told you. Maybe I'm fucking this all up. But I didn't want you to know. I didn't want you to worry. I thought..." Another great big shuddering sob. "I thought I'd go get the test, and if I didn't have it, then there'd be nothing to worry about."

"Except for the fact that my boyfriend would be hurting all alone," I tell him, shaking my head against the side of his. I turn and kiss his hair. "Fuck, Jason. I want to *be there* for you, okay? I know my life is a bit of a hot mess. I just quit my jobs, I'm going back to school, and I don't really know what I'm doing with my life. I may not be the smartest—"

"Stop that," he croaks.

"—or have my shit figured out, but I'm good at caring. And I care a hell of a lot about you. I... I've been waiting for the person who was made for me, and I'm not about to let a little genetic disease stop me from being with him."

"*God*," Jason sobs. "I'm scared."

"Me, too," I admit. "But we do this together, okay? Then neither of us will be alone."

"I'm sorry I didn't tell you," he practically whispers, burying his face against my neck. "Are you angry?"

I take a moment to truly think that through. "No, I'm not angry, but... Please don't withhold these things from me, Jason. I can handle it, okay? And I deserve to know what's going on."

"Fuck," he says, hands spasming against my back. "You're so much more than I ever expected."

"I hope that's a good thing."

"The best."

It's quiet for a minute before I speak. "Can I ask a question?"

Jason lays his cheek on my shoulder, breath hot on my skin. "Yes."

"Why now? Why didn't you get the test before this?"

He eases out a breath. "You."

"Me?" I ask in surprise.

"Because of you and me."

Because we have a future together. Is that what he's saying? I rub my hands up and down his back, my emotions threatening to overwhelm me.

"When's your appointment?" I ask.

"In a week," he answers, his words slow. Slurred, almost, like he's dead tired. "But the results won't come in for another two after that."

I keep moving my hands along his back, soothing—him and me—as I nod slowly. My throat feels hoarse, but my voice comes out stronger than I feel. "Okay. So we won't know anything for three weeks. Let's not worry about it until then. Like you said, maybe there'll be nothing to worry about, right?"

Jason nods, but then he starts to cry again. I can't do a thing other than hold him tight as he battles with his fears. My tears slip free alongside his, despite my best efforts to follow my own advice, and eventually, we lie on the bed, a patch of salt and grief drying against my chest.

Jason falls asleep before my thoughts have quit spinning, which is why I hear the gentle knock at the door. Brad peeks his head in just after, face drawn tight, and I wave him in.

Without a word, he climbs onto the bed and lies behind Jason, his hand on his friend's back.

That's exactly how we stay for the rest of the night.

Chapter 26

JASON

"Okay?" Cas asks, thumb running over my knuckles.

"Of course," I tell him, nodding quickly. "It's just a blood draw."

"Still," he says.

And yeah. Still.

It's just the two of us in the waiting room at the clinic. The air around us is quiet before Cas says, "When I was seven, my parents brought us to the coast." His voice is soft, soothing, and I wait for more. "We stayed at this fancy resort on the ocean, and it was the first time I'd been in water like that. It was...so much. Beautiful, you know? But the entire time we were there, I was terrified of the undertoads."

"The what?" I croak out around a laugh.

"Undertoads," Cas repeats, and yeah, I guess I heard him right. He huffs a breath, lips twitching. "I thought... I don't know what I thought. That there were giant toad-like ocean creatures waiting to pull me out to sea? Anyways, it wasn't until the end of the trip that Leo figured out why I was so scared of going in the water."

"I'm guessing he explained it?"

Cas nods, his thumb still gracing my skin. "He told me about undertows. About ocean currents and the tides. About the moon, even. I don't remember most of it," he admits. "But I remember him that day. He's always been patient with me."

Admittedly, I'm curious about Cas's siblings. About his whole family, really. The way he talks about them is...complex. He loves them, clearly. But he also speaks of them sometimes as if they're *other*. As if he doesn't belong.

"One part I do remember," Cas goes on, "is how to escape an undertow. You don't swim toward shore. The current is too powerful. You swim sideways, along the beach, until you're out of it. It always scared me, though, maybe even more so than the undertoads. This concept of the ocean being too powerful to fight."

I nod, wondering where Cas is going with this.

He gives my fingers a squeeze. "If it feels like too much, just hold my hand and we'll swim sideways, okay? We can't fight the inevitable, but we can stick together and come out on the other side."

My breath *stings* as it's pulled from my lungs. It aches in the worst, best way.

Cas knew. He already *knew* I might have Huntington's. For how long? Weeks? As far back as that day at the park? He knew, and he continued to date me. Continued to look at me like... Like he is now. Like he's there for me. Like he wants nothing more than to stay by my side.

I want to cry. I want to rant and rail and fucking force him to go, but I can't. I can't give him up. Don't want to. *Won't.* Even if... Even if he has to watch me fight the undertow. And lose.

A nurse calls my name, and I jolt.

"That's me," I say, letting Cas's hand go. He gives me an encouraging smile, and with the warmth of those whiskey eyes boring into my back, I follow the nurse for my blood draw.

"Distract me," I say, my hand gripping Cas's thigh tight as he drives. My other hand is toying with the collar of my sweatshirt—*Cas's* sweatshirt. I bring the fabric up to my nose.

We're on our way back from the clinic, and I can't stop fidgeting. Can't stop my thoughts from running wild. I need to do *something* before I jitter out of my skin.

Cas hums, shooting me a glance. "Want to visit Neddy's?"

"Is that the place where you play basketball with kids?"

"Yeah," he says a little sheepishly. "We don't have to. I—"

"No," I cut in. "I mean yes. Yes. Let's do that."

"Okay," he says with a smile.

"Okay."

Cas gets us driving in the opposite direction, and then he starts to talk. About nothing. About everything. I turn my head, breathing in the subtle scent he left on his sweatshirt and watching his lips move, letting him become my whole world. At least for a little while.

It's chilly when we exit the vehicle, having officially taken the turn into December. Although chilly for Las Vegas is about fifty degrees.

Cas grabs a bag from the trunk, and then he motions for me to join him. The building is pretty nondescript from the outside, but once we get close enough, I see the small Neddy's

Rec decal on the front window. Cas opens the door, holding it as I go through, and then he follows me inside.

"Welcome to Neddy's," the woman inside the lobby calls. A wide smile graces her face when she sees Cas. "Well, hey there. If it isn't my favorite person."

"Queenie," Cas says with a chuckle.

"I see you brought a friend today," Queenie says. "Care to introduce me?"

Cas places a hand on my back as we walk up to the counter. It's warm and reassuring, and I let myself sink into it.

"This is Jason," he says. "Jason, Queenie. Think he could fill out a volunteer application?"

"Of course," Queenie says, grabbing a paper from her desk drawer. She stands up and slides it atop the counter. "You like hoops, Jason?"

I falter. "Oh, uh..."

She chuckles at my non-answer. "It's not a requirement," she assures me. "These kids just need to see that there are adults in their corner. You be good to them, and we won't have a problem."

"I can do that," I tell her, grabbing a pen to fill out the form.

Cas and Queenie catch up as I jot down my info. All the while, Cas's hand stays on my back, his thumb making gentle strokes. *I'm with you*, he's saying. *I'm here.*

When I'm done with the form, Queenie tells us to have fun, and Cas leads me down the hall to a locker room. "I'm just going to change," he says. "Want to come in or stay out here?"

"I'll wait here. But, um... Am I dressed okay?"

I'm in jeans, after all. Not exactly sportsball clothes.

"You're fine," Cas says. "Everyone is casual here."

"Okay, good."

As Cas heads into the locker room, I tug my sleeves over my hands and meander down the hall. The sound of voices gets a little louder as I turn a corner, and I find myself standing in front of an open doorway into what appears to be a large rec room. There are tables set up inside, regular ones with board games or cards on top, as well as ones for table tennis and things like foosball. At least a dozen kids are in the space, ranging in age from late teens down to maybe ten or so.

An adult notices me standing there and gives me a wave. I lift my hand in response when Cas's voice catches my attention.

"Ready?"

Turning, I find Cas striding toward me in a t-shirt and—*ohh*—a pair of gym shorts. These ones are blue, not the shiny silver ones, and they're much less clingy. But that doesn't seem to matter to my brain because all I can remember, taking in those shorts, is Cas that first night I stayed at his apartment. Cas and his plump, perfect ass. Cas and the way he moans when he's on my dick. The way he pushes back against me, cheeks flexed beneath my fingertips.

Yeah, this...

I blow out a breath.

This will be a good distraction.

"Ready," I tell him.

Cas leads me toward the back of the building, and when we push outside, we step onto a fenced-in area of pavement. There's a basketball court off to the right, full of teens and their raucous laughter and jeering, and another to the left. Cas heads that way, toward the nearly empty court where a lone figure is dribbling a ball.

"Hey, Marshall," Cas calls, swerving around the fencing to get onto the court. I follow at his heels, feeling a bit out of place. I don't think I've been in front of a basketball hoop since high school gym.

Marshall, the lone teen occupying the second court, looks up at Cas's voice. He scowls, and I'm so shocked by it, my pace falters. I don't think I've *ever* seen someone look at Cas that way. I've seen people eye-fuck him, sure. Seen it *plenty*, not like I'm holding a grudge. I've seen people literally drool. I even saw one lady walk into a hot dog vendor on the sidewalk because she couldn't stop staring.

But I've *never* seen someone scowl at him. It's so novel I can't help but laugh. Just a little. I think I might like this Marshall.

The teen looks back down at the ground, dribbling his ball before throwing it. Taking a shot? Whatever it is, he lets the ball fly, and it whooshes through the net. Cas, for his part, doesn't look remotely perturbed by Marshall's lack of greeting. He simply grabs another basketball that's sitting at the edge of the court and gives me a grin, waving me forward.

"This is Jason," Cas says loud enough for Marshall to hear. "He's new to the game. Think we could show him the ropes?"

Marshall glances at me then, a quick thing, before his eyes are back on the ground. "Whatever," he mumbles.

Cas looks happy enough with that, his beaming smile never faltering. "Cool," he says, and before I even have a chance to worry about what I'm doing, Cas has his hands around my hips, and he's guiding me toward the center of the court. He gives me a squeeze and then places his chin over my shoulder. "Lesson one. Ready?"

"Um," I manage, pulse skipping as Cas's stubble scrapes my cheek. "Sure?"

He sets the ball in my hands. "Aim for the backboard and shoot."

I bark a surprised laugh, startling even myself. I haven't laughed much this past week, but I push the thought away and hold the ball tight.

"Really, Coach?" I quip, turning my head to see Cas's smile. "That's your brilliant advice? Shoot the ball?"

Cas shrugs, giving me a wink before he steps back. And *ho boy*. You think I'd be used to the winking by now, but I'm not sure I'll ever get used to the way Cas warms me from head to toe with a simple look or touch.

Not sure I want to.

"Go ahead," he says, nodding toward the net. "And don't worry. Everyone misses their first time."

Damn. If that isn't just the sweetest.

Marshall, I notice, is standing off to one side of the court, pretending to be immersed in his own ball. With a breath, I look at the backboard, aim, and throw.

I miss, of course, by a good margin. Cas just jogs over to where the basketball is rolling lazily away and shoots me a smile. "Good try," he says, his optimism like a sunbeam, making the words that could easily sound condescending feel encouraging instead.

"Let me try again," I say, holding out my hands. Cas tosses the ball my way, and I aim a second time. This time, the ball hits the board before bouncing away.

"Hey, look at that," Cas calls, running off after it like a labrador on speed. "Almost had it."

"Try spacing your legs," Marshall says.

I nearly miss his words, as quietly spoken as they were. He's not even looking directly at me, but I'm sure it was him who spoke.

"Like this?" I ask, stepping a little wider.

He shoots me a quick glance, nodding when he sees my feet.

Cas is grinning when he comes back with the ball. He hands it off, and this time, when I shoot, I make the basket. Net? The ball goes through the hole, and Cas cheers like we just won the lottery.

"Nice tip, Marshall," my boyfriend says.

Marshall doesn't respond, but I swear there's a little smile on his lips.

When Cas comes back to me this time, he swoops in close, smacking a quick kiss against my lips. I'm not shocked, exactly, because Cas is frequently demonstrative. But I do look over Marshall's way. He's not watching us, but I get the feeling he's not as unaware of the two of us as he pretends to be.

Cas moves me around the court a couple times, explaining where I'm standing and what the lines on the ground mean. He demonstrates a few shots himself, too, rarely missing. And he includes Marshall. Despite the teen's relatively tepid attitude, Cas isn't to be deterred, and he makes sure Marshall doesn't feel left out.

It's around the fourth time Cas gives me a quick kiss as a reward for making a shot—if I knew basketball came with *those* sorts of rewards, I might've tried it sooner—when Marshall clears his throat.

"You guys together?" he asks before throwing the ball from the three-point line. It swooshes through the net.

Cas answers easily. "Yeah. We're boyfriends."

Marshall nods, dribbling his ball some. He doesn't offer any more, but I swear I see him watching Cas in a new sort of way. Not an *I-wanna-fuck-you* kind of way. Just...curious.

"Hey," I tell Cas when he returns with the ball. I push it back his way. "I wanna see what you can do."

"Yeah?" he says, cocking his head.

"Yeah. Show me what you've got."

He grins. "Up for a competition, Marshall?" he calls out, jogging off with the ball in tow. "Most baskets in a minute wins?"

Marshall snorts. "You're going down, old man."

"We'll see," Cas says, giving me a wink. "Time us?"

With a smile, I pull out my phone, and when I give Cas the go-ahead, he races off. He shoots basket after basket from various positions on the court, giving himself more of a challenge by varying the distance, if I had to guess. He only misses twice, and at the end of the minute, he's made eleven shots.

"Dang," I say, not sure if that's a good score or not but impressed all the same. "Is he any good?" I ask Marshall.

The teen huffs. "He's a'ight."

Cas grins at that, and he comes over, stopping just inches in front of me and pointing at his mouth. "Kiss?"

And how could I possibly refuse?

Cas tastes like the sun when my lips meet his. Like energy and joy and hope, layered over the smell of spice I've come to associate with his person. He tastes like... *Fuck*. He tastes like mine.

When loud smooching sounds come from the court next to ours, Cas and I break apart. A couple teens are at the fence, clearly making fun of us. Marshall throws his ball at them, and they back up, laughing when it smacks the fence in front of their faces.

"Don't be dicks," Marshall yells, ignoring the teen who flips him off in response. He grumbles something else I miss as he picks up the basketball.

Cas and I exchange a look. I can't help but wonder if maybe Marshall himself is part of the LGBTQIA+ rainbow. It ups my admiration and respect for Cas even more. I know he doesn't come here to *spread the gay agenda*, as it were, but... He comes as himself, interacting with these kids because it's something he wants to do, simple as that. It makes him happy—undoubtedly. He has fun—also clear to see.

But he's showing these teens, however incidentally, that queer men aren't one thing. That you can be buff, enjoy sports, be friendly, be kind. That love—*any* love—isn't something to be ashamed of.

He's showing them an example of a man who is settled in his skin, who offers everyone around him a smile regardless of their similarities or differences. He's showing them what it means to be a good human being.

And that...that is pretty damn remarkable.

How did I find this man? Luck? Fate? I'm not even surprised at this point that my attraction to Cas grew. My affection was there from the beginning. From the moment Cas dropped to his knees in front of me, concerned I might have been burned, and I painted his face with whipped cream, it was there.

So no, I'm not surprised I love Cas. Not in the least. It was inevitable, like that big fucking tide, although not nearly as scary. But I do wonder *why*.

Maybe there's a reason Cas and I met. Maybe I really am that person made just for him. If that's the case, I have to believe we'll get through this. One way or another, we'll swim sideways. Maybe we'll have fifteen years together. Maybe much more. But I won't waste them. Whatever sits ahead, I'll grab a hold of that hand Cas is offering and hang on tight.

When Marshall comes back, dribbling his ball, I restart my phone's timer. "Ready?" I call out.

The teen gives me a nod, and for the next minute, he's a whirlwind of smacking shoes and speed. He only misses once, and when the buzzer goes off, he's made twelve baskets, one more than Cas. His smile, this time, is big. And only a little smug.

When Cas and I leave, he swings by the locker room to change. I head down a deserted hall, rolling my phone over in my hand before dialing my mom. She picks up quickly.

"Hey, Jaybird," she says, her warm voice washing over me. For a moment, I swear I can smell freesia.

"Hi, Mom. I have something to tell you."

There's a beat of silence before she says, "I'm listening."

And I think—*I hope*—all might be okay.

Chapter 27

Cas

"Ready for this?" I ask, watching as Jason pulls his suit bag out from his closet. He hangs it on the back of the door where there's a hook.

"Yeah," he says, shooting me a wobbly smile. "Easy peasy. Just meeting my boyfriend's parents. And siblings. And like a whole bunch of people I don't know at a black-tie anniversary dinner. No big."

I huff a laugh. "You met a room full of porn stars and barely broke a sweat. This'll be nothing."

"Right," he says slowly. "*Barely* broke a sweat. Uh-huh."

His tone is light, but he does look nervous, so I roll off his bed and head his way. He sighs when I wrap my arms around him.

"It'll be fine," I assure him. "They'll love you."

"I'm not fancy," he says quietly. "Not even on the inside."

That has me chuckling, although truthfully, that's one of my favorite things about Jason. He's not showy. He's just honest. And real.

"I'll tell you a secret," I say, kissing his jaw. "Neither am I. We'll fake it together, and then we'll come home and ditch the suits. Deal?"

"Deal," he says, lips curling.

I give him one more kiss before heading toward the door. "Be right back."

My outfit for tonight is hanging in the bathroom, right where I left it when I first showed up at Jason's. I pull the pieces on quickly: the pressed button-down, the pants and suit jacket, even the pocket square I find ridiculous but know Leo will comment on if I *don't* wear. Last are my shoes.

After running a bit of product through my hair—styling it neatly back for once—I head from the bathroom.

Jason is right where I left him, except now, he's dressed for the night. His suit is a deep burgundy, which makes me smile because I know he picked the color out for me. He's adjusting his lapels in the mirror as I watch, smoothing the fabric down. He looks so handsome, with his blonde hair on display, all wavy and bright. The long, lean lines of his body under the fitted suit. His hazel eyes, more green than anything in contrast to the burgundy of his outfit.

He looks strong. Sweet. Confident, despite his apparent nerves about tonight.

When he catches sight of me through the reflection of the mirror, his eyes shoot wide, and he spins.

"Cas," he breathes.

"Look okay?" I ask, taking my hands out of my pockets.

He makes an incredulous sound. "*Okay?* You look... No. Actually, just no. You can't go out like that," he says, coming toward me like he's planning on locking me away. He does, in fact, tug me further into his room, but then he just stands there, seemingly at a loss. "You can't..." He groans, spinning.

"What?" I ask around a laugh, looking down at myself before raising an eyebrow. My tux is royal-blue velvet, cut in a slim fit. I always thought it was a little over the top, but Charlotte insists it suits me. "Not okay?"

Jason pinches the bridge of his nose, looking pained. "Cas, every single person you're not related to at that party is going to want to fuck you, and I'll have to fend them off. I only have two hands."

My laugh this time is louder, and it goes on for a good couple seconds while Jason tries not to smile.

"You know," I say, grabbing Jason's hand and kissing his palm, "most people I've been with would've been happy to parade me around like arm candy. Whereas *you*. I think you'd rather shove a bag on my head."

"There are not enough bags in the world to cover you," he deadpans.

"Well, it doesn't matter. Because the only person I want, the only person I'll be going home with"—I give his palm another slow kiss—"is you."

He stutters out a breath. "You're potent."

"You can show me how much later," I say with a wink.

Jason groans.

"Ready to go?" I ask.

He nods, sobering. "Yeah. This will be good," he says, lips forming a shaky smile. "Another distraction."

My chest twinges, and I give his hand a squeeze.

"Sorry," Jason says. "I shouldn't have— "

"No. Any time you want to talk about it, we will, okay?"

He blows out a breath. "Five days."

The words are loaded.

"Yeah, Jason," I say slowly. "Five days."

In five days' time, we'll meet with Jason's doctor for the results of his gene test. The past couple weeks of waiting have simultaneously flown by and crawled. I barely remember my last day at Kinsley Richman. Barely remember my final scene at Elite 8 Studios just yesterday. I've been too caught up in my worry for Jason.

I'm still worried. But, like he said, we have five more days, and I'm doing my best to stay optimistic until then.

Maybe—*maybe*—there's nothing to worry about.

"Come on," Jason says firmly. "Let's do this."

When we get to my parents', there's a valet station set up in front of the house, right at the top of the circle drive. I hand off the keys to my beat-up vehicle, and the guy takes them with a worried look. I don't blame him.

"This is where you grew up?" Jason asks quietly as we ascend the stairs.

"Yeah," I say, wondering what he sees. The opulence? A family home?

A member of the staff opens the door at our arrival, and noise filters through from the rest of the house. A few people are milling about inside the grand foyer, chatting with cocktails in their hands. Jason looks around, eyes wide as he takes it all in.

"Holy cow," he says, blinking over at me. "Cas. You said you were rich, but this…"

Yeah. This is something else.

We pass the people in the foyer, and I lead Jason down the hall toward the back of the house, where floor-to-ceiling windows showcase the yard. More people are milling about out on the lawn and patio, their fancy attire fitting right in with the tux-clad waitstaff walking hors d'oeuvres around on trays.

"It's so…" Jason says.

"What?" I ask.

"Empty."

He winces immediately after he says it, but I shake my head, not minding his observation because I understand what he means. This house is full of art and fine finishings and amenities most people would love to have. And yes, I had a good childhood here. But... It *was* a little empty. Empty of dust and dirt and grime. Empty of messy life experiences like getting covered in flour while baking cookies or learning how to sweep because it was your chore for the week.

I didn't have things like that. And it makes me feel guilty even thinking I was missing out because I know I had it good. And I *know* my parents love me and our family. They provided for us the best they knew how. They weren't absent or uncaring or abusive. They gave us everything within their power to give.

But I never got to be a *normal* kid. I grew up under the weight of expectations, and it shaped me, for a long time, into a person I didn't want to be. I didn't understand until recently that I could be grateful for all I've been given while simultaneously wanting something else.

I think Jason helped me see that. That I wasn't beholden to the legacy left at my feet.

"Oh God," Jason says, pulling my attention. "Is that your mom? You look so much like her."

I follow his gaze out the window, where, yes, my mom is standing next to Leo and Char.

"What do you think?" I say. "Meet the family first or hide away for a while?"

Jason swallows, but he grabs my hand tight. "Meet the family."

My fearless lion.

Charlotte notices us first as we approach. She's dressed in a gorgeous emerald ball gown tonight, and when she smiles, my mom and Leo turn their heads.

"Cassius," my mom greets, stepping forward to kiss my cheek. Her hand squeezes my arm before she steps back.

"Happy anniversary, Mom."

"Thank you, darling. Is this him?"

"Yes, it is. Mom, meet Jason. Jason, my mother, Lori," I say.

"A pleasure," Jason says, looking calm despite how I know he must be feeling inside.

"It's so nice to meet you," my mom says warmly.

I indicate my siblings next. "This is Charlotte and Leonidas."

Leo holds out his hand. "Welcome, Jason. I hear you're a nurse? What a wonderful field to dedicate yourself to."

Jason looks a bit stunned. He shakes Leo's hand, though, nodding and blushing only a little.

"Um, thanks." He accepts a kiss on the cheek from Charlotte next. "It's nice to meet you both."

"Likewise," Char says, her smirk concerning. "Tell me—is my brother as much of a sap as I'd expect him to be?"

"Char," I groan.

Jason's smile widens, some of his tension bleeding away as he huffs a small laugh. "He's definitely the sweetest person I've ever met. I don't think anyone pays attention the way he does. He's always doing things to make me happy, to show me how much he cares." He clears his throat, eyes catching mine. "I'm lucky to have him."

Char's eyes soften, and my mom squeezes my arm again.

"Apologies, but you'll have to excuse me," Leo says, signaling to someone across the yard. "My wife is trying to get my attention. Jason, it was a pleasure to meet you. Hopefully, we can all find a time to sit down together soon. Get to know one another better?"

"Of course," Jason says. "I... I'd like that."

With a nod, Leo heads off, and I run my thumb over Jason's. "We should probably go give our hellos to Dad."

"Of course, darling," my mom replies. "Last I saw, he was in the dining room catching up with a few friends. Circle back around when you can, would you?"

"We will," I tell her.

She gives me another kiss on the cheek before Jason and I head back toward the house.

"They're really nice," Jason says as soon as we step through the door.

I weave us around a couple people before giving him a smile. "Yeah, they are."

"*Cassius.*"

Well, *shit.*

Shoulders tense, I stop and turn toward the source of that voice. I knew, in theory, that Simon might be here. He's been a family friend for years, after all, ever since he and Leonidas were in college together. But I'd hoped he would skip tonight's event in deference to me. To what we had over half a year ago.

I guess he never did respect me all that much.

I spot Simon walking over from the sitting room. If he's remotely bothered to see me in turn, he doesn't show it. There's a smile on his face, and his strides are long and sure. He moves like confidence. Like all the things I once found attractive. Before I found out what was underneath the pretty shell.

He stops just a foot in front of me, head cocked slightly, as if waiting for my reply.

"Hello, Simon," I say, resigning myself to a polite conversation with my ex.

Jason tenses next to me before taking a step forward. "You're Simon?"

Oh, crap.

Simon looks from me to Jason, his brows quirking for only a moment. "Yes. That's me. And you are?"

Good Lord. Jason is *growling*.

"This is Jason, my boyfriend," I tell Simon. And I don't know what possesses me to do it—if I'm threatening Simon to leave us be or warning him away from my boyfriend—but I add, "And he knows all about you."

Simon's eyes narrow. He never once loses his cocky attitude. "Is that so? And what, precisely, does he think he knows?"

Jason takes another step forward. "How about the fact that you're a disrespectful piece of shit who thinks it's okay to take advantage of someone's good nature and then throw it back in their face?"

Whoa.

Simon's eyes flare wide. "Listen, you little—"

"What's going on here?" Leo asks, walking up with Daphne, my sister-in-law. There's a smile on my brother's face, although he's looking between us in concern, clearly having picked up on the tension in the air. Jason is still bristled, standing half a step in front of me, and Simon has taken a step back, as if realizing he might need an exit strategy.

"Nothing," I say in a soothing voice, trying to defuse the situation.

Jason shakes his head quickly, though.

"Jason," I say quietly. "It's fine."

"It's not," he hisses under his breath.

Simon chuckles, holding his hands up. "We're good," he tells Leo. "I'm just meeting Cassius's new boyfriend."

"Get his name off your tongue," Jason grits out.

Holy fuck.

I should *not* find that so hot.

"What is going on here?" Leo asks again, tone harder now. "Simon?"

It's Jason who speaks up, still standing in front of me like my own personal shield. "You should ask your friend about the way he treats his partners. I think you'd be surprised by what he has to say."

With that, Jason walks off, tugging me along for the ride, and I glance back over my shoulder in time to see my brother's confused face turn Simon's way.

"God, Jason," I say.

"No," he retorts, leading me onward. He pauses in front of the family room before walking on, dragging me along to the alcove behind the stairs, where it's quiet. He stops there, finally, facing me in the darkened corner. "I won't apologize."

"I won't ask you to," I say, casing his reddened cheeks and tensed jaw.

"Someone needed to say something. It's not fair what he did to you, and your brother should know."

"Jason," I say again, cupping my hand under his jaw, feeling his heart race against my palm.

He shakes his head, a slow movement. His eyes are on me, his voice whisper-soft. "I'd do it again, Cas. You're worth it."

I ease out a breath, feeling so very warm. "No one has stood up for me like that before," I tell him, kissing his jaw, right above my thumb. "So thank you."

"Oh," he breathes.

My chuckle is soft, and Jason's hand finds its way beneath my jacket, fisting into my shirt.

"Higher," he says.

My smile is immediate, and I lift my lips, kissing his cheek. "Here?"

"Over."

I kiss his nose. "Here?"

"*Cas*."

I bring my lips to his other cheek, kissing him right above the corner of his mouth. "Here?" I whisper.

"Kiss me on the goddamn lips, Cassius, or I swear to God, I'll—" He cuts off, moaning into my mouth as I give him what he wants, his grip on my shirt pulling the corner of it from my pants. He's all fire and combustive energy, and if I didn't have a commitment to be here, I'd tug him back out the door and—

A cough rings out, and Jason jolts back from me, a gasp leaving his lips.

"Well, well," my dad says, humor lacing his tone. "Making out in the corner like a teenager, Cassius? Some things never change."

"Oh. My God," Jason whispers. "Oh my God, oh my God, *nooo*."

I turn around, letting Jason get himself together behind my back as I give my dad a rueful smile. "Happy anniversary," I tell him.

My dad lets out a soft laugh. "Changing the subject, I see. I'll allow it."

"Brad is never going to let me hear the end of this," Jason whispers behind me.

Figuring he's had enough time to straighten himself out, I step to the side. "Dad, this is my boyfriend, Jason. Jason, my father, Tiberius."

"Tiberius?" Jason mutters under his breath, too quietly for my dad to hear.

I hold in my laugh as he steps forward, hand outstretched.

"Nice to meet you, sir," he tells my father. "Sorry about the, ah..."

Luckily, my dad takes pity on him, shaking his hand and giving Jason a smile. "So glad you could attend tonight. I trust the evening is treating you well?"

Okay, so maybe he's throwing a little snark after all.

"Very well," Jason says, blushing.

My dad gives him a nod before letting his hand go. "If you wouldn't mind, Jason, I'd love a brief word with my son."

"Of course," Jason says quickly.

"You'll be okay?" I check.

He gives me a nod. "Yeah. Don't worry about me."

"I'll come find you when I'm done."

My dad gives Jason a thanks, and then my boyfriend walks off, leaving the two of us alone. "Might want to fix that," he says, pointing at where my shirt is hanging loose.

I huff, tucking it back in as my dad leads me over to a bookshelf along the wall.

"I wanted to check in with you," he says. "See how you're doing since leaving Kinsley Richman."

I blow out a breath. "I'm good, Dad." Concern over Jason aside. "It was the right choice. I..."

When I don't go on, he says, "What is it, Cassius?"

"I'm going to be giving away some of the money you and Mom left to me," I tell him. "I'm not asking for your permission because you told me it's there for whatever purpose I want. But... I hope you're not upset by that."

My dad tilts his head, looking at me curiously. "You're donating it?"

"Yes," I answer.

His smile is slow, but it builds steadily, calming the nerves thrumming through my veins. "My boy. You've always had such a big heart. It's a strength, that. A wondrous gift. I'm so very proud of you."

Fuck.

I've been called *soft* before—naive, idealistic—but it never sounded like a compliment. To hear my dad say he values that in me is like aloe on a sunburn I didn't even know I had.

"You're happy?" he asks.

I nod, unable to form a single word.

He clasps me on the shoulder. "Then I'm happy for you. I couldn't ask for anything more."

Chapter 28

JASON

"Look at him," Charlotte says, pointing across the yard, drink in her hand.

I follow her gaze, finding Cas stopped just outside the house. He must be done talking with his dad because now he's helping an older man step down onto the patio, a smile on his face and his arm held aloft as a guide.

"My brother is such a softie," Charlotte says with a sigh. "He's always cared for others more than himself, and no matter how many times he gets hurt because of it, he refuses to change. To harden his heart. He's hopeless. Utterly hopeless."

There's undeniable affection in Charlotte's tone, despite her words, and when I look her way, the smile on her face is one of pure fondness.

"Will you protect that heart, Jason?" she asks, her brown eyes meeting mine, unflinching.

My pulse kicks. "With everything I have."

She hums before taking a sip of her drink. "I like you."

"Hey," Cas says, having reached us. He gives me a big smile. "Sorry about that."

I swallow down the lump in my throat, eyeing Charlotte one more time. The woman is a little scary. "Not a problem," I tell Cas.

"It's getting cold," Cas notes, trailing his hand against my neck as if checking my temperature. His thumb brushes my skin before it falls away. "Want to head inside where it's warmer?"

"Sure," I answer, grabbing Cas's hand when he offers it. "Nice to talk to you, Charlotte."

Cas's sister gives me a wink, turning into a conversation with a few other impeccably dressed guests, and Cas leads me back across the lawn toward the house. I can't believe how massive this place is. It's gorgeous, sure, but it's also imposing. And try as I might, I can *not* picture a young Cas growing up here, running on the perfectly cut grass or swimming in the heated pool. I can't picture him tearing through the wide halls or riding a pillow down the curving staircase.

I know Cas has money. That his parents gave him and his siblings a sizable nest egg each. He told me as much when he admitted he could easily live a comfortable life several times over without working another day in his life.

But Cas doesn't care about his money, not in that way. Apart from the occasional fancy tux, his possessions are simple, not ostentatious. He doesn't throw his wealth around or use it for leverage. In fact, he doesn't seem to like to mention it at all. He wants to go back to school, to learn a new trade and work a job he'll enjoy—one in which he can help people. He volunteers with kids and gives me thoughtful little gifts, not to show off but because he knows I'll enjoy them. He's selfless and kind and genuinely cares about others, even strangers for whom he holds the door.

Cas once told me he felt like he didn't fit. Like he was some outlier because his brain and his heart didn't want the life he'd been gifted.

But I think that's what makes him beautiful. Cas is unlike anyone I've ever known, and somehow, this gorgeous soul turned his megawatt focus on me. I don't want to ever take that for granted. That this man who stops to watch the snow fall finds something worthy in *me*.

"Do you want anything else to eat?" Cas asks, stopping just inside the door.

I shake my head. "No. Can I see the rest of the house?"

He shoots me a smile. "Sure."

Cas leads me past the partygoers, up the staircase we hid behind less than an hour before. He points out the various bedrooms, office spaces, and even the library that overlooks the backyard. When he gets to his bedroom, he waves me inside. It looks nothing like him, not really.

"My parents redid the bedrooms," Cas explains. "There used to be a poster of Dwight Howard on the wall over there."

"Who?"

Cas smiles. "Basketball player."

I can't help but laugh. "Mhm. Wonder why you had that above your bed."

He snorts, and I walk over to the back wall, where double doors lead out onto a balcony. A *balcony*.

"Can I?" I ask.

Cas nods, and I open the door. The air is turning downright frigid, much colder than when we first arrived. It ruffles the curtain some, until Cas follows me out and shuts the door. I can hear the party carrying on just around the corner, but the balcony attached to Cas's room faces out from the side of the house, so there's a little more privacy. Just trees and the freezing wind. I tug my jacket more firmly around myself.

"Should've brought you a scarf," Cas comments, coming to stand in front of me and cupping his warm hands around my neck.

"I'm okay," I mutter, gaze caught up in Cas's whiskey eyes. The Jason of a few months ago would have looked away, looked down at the ground, too nervous or self-conscious to face off with someone as blindingly bright as Cas. But now, I know the man beneath. I know him, and he knows me, and I'm not afraid of that. Even though I'm terrified of so many great, big things, I'm not terrified of *this*.

"Cas, I need to tell you something."

He frowns a little but nods, his thumbs running along my skin. He's warmer than any scarf. More comforting. More secure.

"If I have Huntington's," I say slowly, "I won't blame you if you have to go."

"Jason," he says cautiously.

"Please. Just let me say this."

He sighs but nods for me to go on.

"I won't push you away. Ever," I tell him. "I'm not going to do that. And I'll only bring this up once. But if it gets too hard, if it becomes too much for you, I'll understand." My voice wobbles as I clear images from my head. Memories of my dad. My mom, by his side. My own pain. The many unheard pleas I made for things to be better. Easier. Eventually, over. "I would understand. You didn't sign on for this, Cas."

"Yes, I did," he immediately counters.

My incredulity must show because Cas draws his hands up to cup my jaw, squeezing slightly. He leans close, face inches in front of mine.

"Yes, I did," he repeats. "Relationships *always* come with risk. I told you, back then, I was willing to take the risk with you. I meant that."

"Cas," I choke out. "But you didn't know about this. About me."

"Doesn't matter," he says, shaking his head. "You've always been worth the gamble." His gaze pins me. Holds me and cradles me. "You're the only person I want. Why would I possibly go away?"

I nearly lose it as the words I gave him are tossed back my way. Cas's expression softens, his thumb coming up to drift over my cheek. He rubs away the tear that slipped free, just as a snowflake lands on his nose. Another follows, drifting down and settling on his shoulder, melting instantly.

I look up at the white flakes coming down in a gentle sway, like feathers falling from the sky. Each one unique. Each carved from the Heavens, their lives so much shorter than such beauty deserves.

Cas is smiling when I look at his face. His eyes are wide open, staring up at the sky the same way I had been, and I feel it like a physical thing. A punch to my solar plexus. I love this man. I love the beauty in him. The way he sees the world. I love his smile and his perfect goddamn lips and that soft heart he carries inside his chest. I love the little and the big, and if my life is destined to run short like these snowflakes falling all around us, I won't waste a single moment of what we could have together.

"I love you," I whisper. Cas's head comes down, eyes wide as I repeat myself loud enough for him to hear. "I'm in love with you."

The *smile* that lights his face.

"Jason," he says, leaning close, his lips whispering against mine. "And you think I could ever walk away."

My eyes close, hands finding a home against Cas's hips.

"I love you, too," he says. "*So* much. If we're lucky enough to grow old and gray together, I will love you. And buy you cardigans."

I huff a pained laugh against his lips.

"And if we have ten years instead of fifty," he adds softly, seriously, "I will still love you."

"It might not be easy," I tell him. Because despite what I've always told myself—that there's a chance I don't have the mutated HTT gene—I've always assumed I'd end up just like my dad in the end. "There could be days...years," I add, swallowing roughly, "that are hard."

Cas shrugs ever so slightly. "We'll still make them count. We'll swim sideways."

I inhale shakily, pulling in a lungful of achingly cold air. With my forehead pressed to Cas's, it's easy to close the remaining gap between us and bring my lips to his. Cas meets me in kind, the plumpness of his mouth so familiar to me now. The way he goes high, and I go low, the pair of us slotting together like two halves of the same whole.

It nearly breaks me, the hope I feel. The desperation to give this man good news. To tell him he doesn't have to watch his partner succumb to a slow and debilitating disease.

But I can't give him that. Not yet. I might not *ever* be able to.

"Do we need to stay here?" I ask Cas, my hands shaking against his sides.

He pulls back an inch at most. "No."

"Take me home?"

He nods, reaching down to clasp my hand. I look out at the slowly drifting snow one last time before following Cas through the balcony door.

We swing by to see Cas's family before we go. We wish his parents a happy anniversary again, say goodbye to Charlotte, and Cas has a few quiet words with his brother, promising he'll call soon. It's cold outside as the valet grabs Cas's vehicle, but I don't mind. Not this time.

My apartment is dark when we arrive, lights off and rooms quiet. Brad must be at the gym or out on a date. We head to my bedroom, and I flick on the light before walking over to check on Amadeus. He's coiled over a branch, and his tongue scents the air as I give him a hello.

"Does he need to eat?" Cas asks, pulling off his tuxedo jacket. It does nothing to diminish his appeal, instead adding to it, as the white shirt draws Cas's darker features into startling contrast. The dark brows, the hair atop his head, styled so neat and suave. The richness of his eyes, and his lips, bowed and red.

"No," I tell him, turning from the tank to step Cas's way. "Can I have you tonight? Can I have your cock?"

I need it. I need to be close to this man. Need to feel him, connect to him in every way possible.

Cas's eyes flare at the question, but he wraps his arms around me as I reach him. I slip my fingers beneath his waistband and ping the button free.

"Yeah, Jason," he answers. "But only if it's something you want. I don't *need* to top you."

"I want it," I assure him quickly, tugging down his zipper. "At least, I think I do. I want to try."

"Then yes, of course," he repeats, sighing out when I wrap my hand around his shaft. I pump his cock, running my thumb over the tip.

Cas starts unbuttoning his shirt as I let go to work on my own clothes.

"You had your medical screening?" I check.

Cas underwent biweekly STI testing for his job at Elite 8 Studios anyways, but he got checked again as part of his exit process. He nods. "All negative."

"Then..." I say, losing my voice for just a moment. Cas is naked now, and he brings a hand to his dick, stroking slowly. I lick my lips, quickly shucking the rest of my clothes. "Will you fuck me bare?"

Cas's eyes close in an extended blink before he nods. "Yeah, Jason."

"Okay," I say, an undeniable thrill running through me. "Yeah, okay. That's good."

Cas smirks a little. "There he is."

"Huh?" I ask, making a pit stop at the nightstand for lube.

He steps up behind me, arms wrapping around my body. One anchors at my stomach and the other drifts lower, wrapping around my erection.

"*Fuck*," I hiss out.

"My shy barista," Cas answers, stroking me before nipping at my ear.

I blow out a breath. "Yeah, you still make me feel..."

"What?" he asks, hand lowering to my balls. He palms them, rolling and squeezing.

"*Ahh*. Breathless."

I can feel Cas's smile against my ear. "On the bed, babe. Let me take care of you this time."

And *fuck*. How could I ever say no to that?

Cas takes the lube from my hand, and I hop onto the mattress, rolling to my back. He follows me onto the bed, slinking up my legs, and I have to swallow roughly in order to simply breathe again. He holds my eye as he lowers his lips to the tip of my cock, and then he *smiles*, sinful yet sincere, before taking me into his mouth.

My eyes find the ceiling, a near-incredulous laugh bubbling up from my chest. It's so good. It's *always* so good with Cas.

He hums around me, and my gaze snaps back down as Cas encourages me to tilt my hips. Despite this being my first time on the receiving end of such attention, I know the score, and I pull up my legs to give Cas access, not in the least bit scared or worried about what's to come. He'll take care of me.

Cas opens the lube as he sucks on my cock, barely breaking concentration as he brings a wet finger to my ass. He rubs along my taint and over my hole slowly, giving me time to get used to the sensation. And when I wrap my legs over his shoulders, urging him on, he doesn't seem remotely surprised. He huffs a laugh around my cock and slips a finger inside my ass.

It's not a completely foreign feeling. I've fooled around with my ass before. I just always preferred jerking off or using a cocksleeve over fingering myself. But the way Cas does it, all smooth and sure, has my eyes rolling up and my hands flying to his head. He pulls up to suckle on my cockhead as he works his finger into me, and *fuck*. Just fuck. It's Cas. It's Cas fucking me with his finger, getting me ready for his dick.

"God," I croak out. "I never..."

"What, babe?" Cas asks, popping off my cock.

It jerks at the endearment, and Cas grins, swiping his tongue across my slit.

"I never expected you," I admit, not for the first time.

Cas presses in with two fingers, and the ache blooms slow and sweet across my body. He swipes up my cock with his tongue, eyes on me all the while. "The whipped cream facial was a dead giveaway."

I bark a laugh, which quickly turns into a moan as Cas presses his digits deep. He rubs and searches and...

"*Ah-hah-hah-God.*"

"Mm," he hums, rubbing and circling his tongue over my crown.

"Fuck me," I beg.

"Almost," he says, adding a third finger. The ache is there again, but I welcome it. It's a fullness, a stretch that promises wicked, wonderful things. And as Cas works my prostate again, I know I'm in for *very* wonderful things.

"You're gonna..." I pant out, fingers curling tight in Cas's hair, "gonna get a *real* facial... in a moment... if you don't *ahh.*"

Cas pulls his fingers free, and I let him go, uncurling my legs from around his shoulders. He slicks his cock and then drops over me, lips at my own. I kiss him, tasting myself—*Christ, why is that so hot?*—and his cock bumps my ass when I wrap my legs around his hips like a hug.

"Jason," he says so quietly.

I bob my head. "I know, I know."

Cas nods, reaching down to notch himself against me, and then he pushes. His cockhead stretches me wide, just like his fingers, and there's a moment where I'm almost in disbelief. There's a *dick* in my ass. A very real person, *this* person, the man I love, invading my body like he's invaded my mind and that organ beating surely inside my chest. He stills before long, letting me get accustomed, and I can't say a word. It's too much. *So* very much. I just hold on and nod again when I'm ready, and Cas flexes his hips, inching further into my body.

Those Pop Rocks, remember? That fizzy, exploding moment where everything is grand and bright. Too big to contain. When you experience fireworks inside your very core, and for the briefest of seconds, you wonder if you're about to blast apart at the seams.

I feel it as Cas's hips meet my ass. The momentousness of this moment. Not because I'm bottoming for the first time, but because I know this man feels what I do. He loves me, and I don't know what comes next—where we go from here—but I do know Cas will be there with me, just like he is now. We'll move forward, swim sideways, do whatever we need to do. Those eyes staring down at me, those lips kissing me so sweet, that heart beating against the outside of my chest; they'll be with me.

As Cas starts to move in earnest, my mind drifts away. There's nothing except his cock splitting me open in a way I never knew could feel so good. There's the drag of him inside me, and the way it feels like my nerve endings are lit like morning sun. There's his balls slapping my ass like a deliciously filthy caress and his abs rubbing along my dick. There's the way he grunts when I tug his hair hard and how he picks up his pace just like I need him to.

"Oh, God. Cassius, please," I moan out. "I need..."

Cas lifts up, kneeling and raising my hips higher in the air. He pumps shallowly, his sweat-slick body like erotic art, his cock rubbing against my prostate just like his fingers did. His hand clamps around my dick, pulling, tugging, and...

"Oh, *oh*," I gasp, vision whiting out as I splinter apart like a cannon shot. Cas keeps fucking into me, his cock feeling impossibly bigger, harder, and then he's coating me inside with his cum. It feels hot, shockingly so, and my dick jerks at the baseness of it. Cas's does, too, shifting inside of me as he comes down from his high.

"Fuck," I manage.

"Fuck," he agrees, settling over me. His back is sweaty under my palms, and I run them over every inch of him that I can reach, all the way down to the taut globes of his ass, as our chests heave against one another.

"Next time," I breathe out, "I'm going to come in your ass. That was..."

Cas chuckles as I dig my fingers into his cheeks. "Anything you want, Jason. I'm all yours."

Fuck. If that's not just the most perfect thing.

I inhale Cas's spicy scent as my heart beats like a drum. "I'm so glad all my firsts and lasts will be with you," I tell him softly.

His sigh is the sweetest sound.

Chapter 29

CAS

"Cassius. Thank you for calling."

"Of course," I tell Leo, sitting on the couch in Jason's apartment. Jason is in the shower, getting ready for today, and Brad is out in the kitchen, making himself a late—or, for him, regularly timed—breakfast.

Leonidas is quiet for a moment. "Why didn't you say anything?"

"I'm sorry," I say around a sigh. "Simon didn't want people to know we were dating."

"Not that," Leo replies, sounding almost frustrated. "The fact that he...ended things so callously."

"He told you that?" I ask in surprise.

"Well, I had to pry it out of him," my brother says. "But eventually, yes. When I told him I would get Jason to tell me the whole story if he didn't, he finally talked. What..." He's quiet for a beat. "What did he say to you in that email?"

I brush a hand through my hair, leaning against the cushions of the couch. "Are you sure you want to hear this?"

"Yes," he says, although his voice is small.

All right, then. "He told me it's a good thing I'm pretty because I don't have a lick of common sense. That we were fun but I'm not the type of person one commits to. And he said if I wanted to be useful, I should consider a job in sex work."

Leo is quiet for a long time, his breath coming across the line. I notice Brad peeking his head out of the kitchen, frowning. I give him a little shrug as my brother starts talking again.

"Cassius," Leo says quietly. "I hope you know everything he said to you was pure crap."

I huff a small laugh. "You know... He wasn't wrong about all of it. He just wasn't the right person to appreciate what I have to offer."

The noise my brother makes isn't particularly happy, but he lets it be. "And Jason. Is he the right person?"

"Yeah, Leo. He's my right person."

He hums at that. "Simon isn't welcome in my life any longer. I thought you should know."

"You didn't have to do that for me."

He huffs. "I did, too. You're my brother. I will *always* support you. And the way he treated you... That is not okay. I don't need friends who treat others that way."

"You're a good guy, Leo."

"You are too, Cassius. The best I know."

"I should have told you," I say again. "The way he acted was a red flag, even before we broke up. I just..."

"You see the best in people," Leo replies. "I know. It's one of the things I admire most about you."

Shit.

"Thank you," I say, voice a little hoarse.

"Is Jason there?" my brother asks. "I'd like to give him my thanks."

I look over my shoulder and listen, fully expecting Jason to still be in the shower, but he comes around the corner of the hall, stopping and looking at me.

"Uh, yeah," I say, standing up. "Just a sec."

Jason watches me curiously as I approach. I hold the phone out his way. "My brother Leo."

His eyes widen a little but he takes the device. "Hello?"

As Jason talks to my brother, I head into the kitchen for some water. Brad is still there, chewing on a piece of buttered toast. "An ex said that?" he asks.

I nod, filling up a glass at the fridge. "Yeah. Not one of my finest choices."

He shakes his head, swallowing down his breakfast. "Not your fault, you know. That's on him. You didn't make him an asshole."

I guess he has a point.

"For what it's worth, though, I get it," Brad says. "People looking at you and seeing one thing. Assuming one thing."

"Yeah?" I ask, leaning against the counter across from him.

He nods, setting his plate beside the sink. "Yeah. Although your ex *was* right about one part." His lips quirk. "You *are* pretty."

"*God*," Jason groans, coming into the kitchen with my phone down at his side. "No. Just no. I leave you two alone for *one* second."

Brad laughs as Jason throws a dish towel at his face, but then he sobers, seeing Jason dressed and ready to go. "Are you guys leaving now?"

Jason swallows, handing my phone back. "Yeah."

"Birdie," Brad says quietly. He opens his arms, and Jason steps forward, the two wrapping each other up tight.

I set my glass in the dishwasher, using the excuse to hide my face for a moment as I blow out a slow breath.

"Love you," Brad says quietly.

"You, too," Jason replies. When he steps back, he reaches for my hand, and I give it willingly, holding on tight. "I'll let you know what happens, okay?"

Brad nods, but as Jason pulls me gently from the kitchen, Brad mouths, *See you soon.*

At the front door, Jason layers up in his jacket and scarf. His beanie is light gray today, and he smiles a little tremulously as I brush his hair across his forehead.

"It'll be okay," I assure him. "One way or another, it'll be okay."

He doesn't answer, and I don't push it.

The hospital isn't far, and I park in the visitor's lot once we're there. Jason is silent as we make the trek into the building. Silent as we walk down halls he's well acquainted with. Silent as we take the elevator to the appropriate floor. And silent once we sit in the waiting room. His foot taps the linoleum, his knee brushing against mine.

"I'd like to live in a house one day," I say, and Jason looks over at me. "Not someplace huge. Just something nice and simple, maybe with hedges? I've always wanted a kitchen with a window seat, too. Like, a tiny nook to curl up in when it's rainy outside. Maybe I could read more."

Jason nods, and his tapping slows.

"I like wallpaper, too," I go on. "I know it's kind of cheesy, but I saw this floral kitchen in a magazine once, and...it was so warm. I wanted to live there. Learn how to cook there."

"Stuff some shells?" Jason puts in.

I chuckle. "Exactly. We could make those again. They were good. Or bake cookies, maybe? Have you ever baked cookies?"

"Yeah," he says quietly, staring down at our clasped hands. "I could teach you how to bake."

"I'd like that a lot. What's your favorite kind?"

His smile is small. "My mom makes these double chocolate cookies I've always loved." After a quick beat, he adds, "She'll like you."

"Yeah?" I say, chest warming. "I bet I'll like her, too. She made you, after all."

"Don't remind me," he says with a groan. I'm not quite sure what to make of that, but then he asks, "Do...do you want kids, Cas?"

It's a big question, but I'm not surprised by it. Jason and I have been talking a lot about us lately. About the future.

"I always thought I might," I say. "I'm not there yet, I don't think. I'd like to feel a little more settled before I jump into something so big. But if kids are part of the future you see, Jason, then yes, I would have kids with you."

His lips shift, like he's trying not to cry. "I think it would...depend a lot on..."

"Yeah," I say gently, giving his hand a squeeze.

He inhales a big, stabilizing breath before blowing it back out again. The door opens at the same time, and a nurse calls out Jason's name.

"Shit," Jason mutters, pushing to his feet. I go with him, my hand still in his grip, and we follow the nurse down the hall. She settles us in a small room with couches and chairs. Jason takes a seat on the couch, and I sit next to him.

"The doctor will be in shortly," the nurse says, offering a kind smile Jason's way before leaving us in peace.

"Fuck," Jason mutters, his leg bouncing again.

"Hey," I say, tugging his chin around. His eyes are glassy, and it splits me down the center, seeing the fear on his face. "We've got this."

Jason shakes his head ever so slightly in my grip. "I don't think I have this."

"You do," I tell him surely, placing a kiss at the corner of his mouth. "We're going to sit here on this cushy couch. The doctor will show up. And we'll listen to what they have to say."

"And then?" he asks, voice shaking.

"Then we live our life, Jason."

"Simple as that?" he says, eyes pinging between my own.

"It can be."

The door opens, and I let go of Jason's chin, nearly wincing as his hand tightens on mine to the point of pain.

"Hello, Jason," the doctor says, closing the door behind her. She's a woman in her late forties or early fifties, with a gentle voice and a folder in her hands.

"Dr. Allen," Jason replies, swallowing.

"Would you like your companion to stay for this?" the doctor asks, taking a seat across from us.

Jason nods a little stiltedly. "Yes, please."

"All right," she says, setting the folder in her lap. She doesn't even open it. She must know exactly what it says.

Jason's leg starts bouncing rapidly in the brief couple seconds that pass, and my own heart is loping just as fast, a nauseating pulse in my chest, legs, and arms. I feel heavy, weighed down, but I do my best to slough off the discomfort, focusing instead on the man beside me and what we're about to learn here in this room.

"I'm going to get right into it, Jason," the doctor says, "because I know you're familiar with this disease and all that comes with it. You don't have the HTT mutation."

Jason goes completely still, his leg stopping, a single breath raising and lowering his chest. "I don't?" he nearly whispers.

Dr. Allen gives Jason a smile. "No, you do not."

Jason pulls in a stuttering breath, and then, without a word, he's turning, falling against my chest and sobbing out days, weeks, *years* of worry. His grief, his *relief*, is so palpable that I can't stop my own tears. They spill down my face, fat, wet drops that fall atop Jason's beanie as my lips wobble.

"He doesn't have it?" I ask, needing to make sure I understood her correctly. "He won't get Huntington's?"

"He will not," she assures me over Jason's crying. "The mutation is passed down genetically." A fifty percent chance, I remember. "But Jason's Huntingtin gene is in regular, working order. He won't develop Huntington's disease like his father."

"Thank you," I tell her hoarsely, squeezing Jason tight.

She gives me a nod. "I'll leave you two alone. If Jason has any further questions, please let him know he can come talk to me anytime."

"I'll do that. Thanks, Doctor."

Dr. Allen offers a final smile before quietly exiting the room, and I turn back to Jason, pressing my face against the top of his head as I suck air into my lungs and simply *breathe*. Jason is shaking in my arms, his tears wetting my shirt as mine are his beanie, and I feel... God, relief. So much relief it's painful.

"Babe," I manage. "It's good. It's good, right?"

He doesn't answer, only cries harder, and I hold on to him tight, letting my fear wash away with his.

He doesn't have it. He's *okay*. He's going to be okay. And the two of us... The two of us can just *be*.

We sit in that room for a good long while, crying and holding and comforting. A half hour, maybe. More. At one point, I wonder if Jason has fallen asleep, he's so still. But then, finally, he stirs, shifting off my body and wiping his face with his hands. His tears are dried, cheeks a little red and eyes puffy.

"Are you okay?" I ask gently.

"I am," he says, even though he sounds unsure. "I will be. I don't know what's wrong with me. I should be happy, not crying so much. I just..."

"It's a lot," I answer.

He sniffs, nodding as he sits back. "It's hard to believe."

And that, I understand.

"The doctor said you could talk to her any time," I tell him. "Maybe it would help to see the results yourself."

"You might be right," he says, wiping his face one more time before sighing. "Come on. I should go call my mom."

I don't reply, but I get up with Jason, walking with him to the bathroom, where he splashes water on his face, and then holding his hand as we head back out toward the waiting room. When we get there, Jason goes stock still.

His mom and Brad are inside the room, and they stand quickly. Jason's mom has clearly been crying, but Brad has a smile a mile wide on his face.

"What—" Jason says, and then he's sobbing again.

His mom swoops in quickly, tucking him in her smaller arms. "Shh, honey. It's okay. Cas let us know."

"When..." he says, but that's it.

I texted a short while ago, knowing they were waiting here for the results.

Brad wraps his arms around Jason and his mom. "We weren't going to let you walk out of here alone, Birdie, whichever way it went."

"I'm sorry," Jason hiccups. "I'm sorry I didn't get the test sooner."

"Oh, hush, Jaybird," his mom replies, rocking him back and forth slightly, her own tears spilling free. "You had to be ready. And now..." She lets out a great, big sigh. "Now, hopefully, you can find some peace."

"Yeah," Jason says, reaching for me from within the hug. I grab his hand, letting him tug me close. "Pretty sure I already have that. Pretty sure I have everything I need."

Chapter 30

JASON

"Look at that man," I say dreamily, watching as Cas flips the delicate crêpes he's making. It's been five months of this: cooking lessons and domestic bliss and simply *existing* without a giant cleaver over my head. *Our* heads. "Just look at him."

"Uh, no thanks," Brad replies, holding his hand up like a blinder. "That sounds like a trap if I've ever heard one. You specifically told me *not* to look at your man."

"I don't mean you should check him out," I say indignantly, waving at the fine specimen in the kitchen. "I just..." Cas leans down, using a spatula to examine the bottom of the crêpe, and I trail off. Because *ungh*. That ass. "Yeah, never mind. Don't look."

Brad chuckles, dropping his hand. "You're really hot for that man, huh?"

"Yeah," I breathe.

"They're in sync, your head and your heart," he says almost sweetly, ruining it when he adds, "And your other head."

"Why are we friends?" I ask, shoving Brad to the side.

"You love me," he claims, chuckling.

And yeah. Yeah, I do.

"Hey, can I ask a question?" he says.

I turn from my boyfriend, a difficult feat for sure. "Shoot."

Brad cants his head toward the living room, and I follow him that way, sitting on the couch beside my friend.

"Have you ever...thought of me that way?" Brad asks, much to my surprise.

"What?" I squeak.

"You know," he says, circling his hand. "Have you ever been attracted to me?"

Holy crap.

"Um, no," I say slowly, wondering why the hell Brad is asking this now.

He slumps a little, looking relieved. "Oh, thank God. It's not that I thought you were harboring some secret crush on me or anything, but I think I was always a little afraid to ask. I mean, you're my best friend, so I probably would have tried for you, you know? But I've never taken it up the ass before, and I have to be honest—the idea terrifies me."

I gape.

"I used my fingers once," he says, "but I couldn't get the angle right—"

"*Oh my God*," I moan, falling back against the couch and rubbing my face. "This isn't happening."

"—and it didn't really do anything for me. But I can kind of see what Zeek was talking about with your stomach."

"For Christ's sake, please shut up," I beg.

"I mean, it's nice and smooth."

"Stop. Talking."

"You're not as curvy as I normally like, but that's okay, Birdie. You're plenty sexy—"

"If you don't shut your mouth right this instant, I'm going to give you a papercut, drop you in a shark tank, and *monologue until you're de—*"

"Whoa," Brad says, holding up his hands. "Okay, okay, shutting up now."

Thank *fuck*.

"It's just..." he says, tone serious. "I see how you are with him, Birdie. How you look at him. And I'm so happy for you. You deserve that, you know?"

I nod, my throat a little tight.

"And I didn't want you to take what I'm about to say the wrong way," he adds.

My pulse kicks. "Okay?"

Brad turns to me, his knee bent on the couch between us. "Jason, you're my big love."

"Brad..." I say slowly.

"No, see?" he says, a small smile on his face. "You're taking it the wrong way. Just listen, please."

I nod a little shakily, and Brad goes on.

"Romantic love isn't the only kind out there. Your friendship has meant the world to me. The way you love me? It's a big deal. It's been a big deal to me. You know I didn't really have that before you. I didn't have anyone who was there for me."

I nod again, heart clenching.

"What I'm trying to say is I love you, Birdie. I love you more than I love anyone. You're my best friend. My brother. And I need to step aside now so you can be with Cas."

"Brad—"

"You're a couple," he goes on. "It's you and him. And there will always be you and me, too. I know that. But you guys...you deserve to start your life together. You have a clean bill of health. You're done with school and will be moving into a full-time position at the hospital. He's heading back to college in the fall. You're settling in to this thing you have, and that's great. I'm glad for you. But I don't belong inside that future you're making together. So if you want to live here, I'll move out. Otherwise, I think you should."

"Damn it, Bee," I croak, swiping at my face.

"I know, Birdie. Change sucks."

I nod mutely, embarrassed that my lips are trembling. "I love that man so much," I tell my friend, and he smiles because he knows. "But you're my first love. When I became your Birdie, you became my Bee. And fuck, that sounded cheesy."

Brad chuckles.

"But you're right," I continue. "There will *always* be an us. Any time—" I clear my throat. "Any time you need me, I'll be there, okay?"

"Ditto," he says. And when Brad opens up his arms, I fall into them, squeezing him so hard he wheezes.

When there's a clink beside us, I look over. Cas gives me a gentle smile, leaving plates of cream cheese crêpes on the coffee table before giving Brad and me some privacy.

"And *I-ee-I*," Brad sings softly, "will always—"

"What are you doing?"

"—love you-ooo-oo-woo-oo-oo."

"Oh my God," I groan.

"Will always—"

I shove Brad's face, and he cracks up, sitting away from me.

"*Love you*," he mumbles quickly, finishing the verse.

"Jesus Christ," I complain, a massive smile on my face. "I have the worst friends. The absolute worst."

"Marley, nooo," I moan. "Not you, too."

"Suck it up, buttercup," she says, shoving the present my way. "It's your last day at Hyped. I couldn't let you go without a gift."

I sigh. "Should I open it now?"

"Nah," she says with a concerningly wide smile. "Open it later."

"Thanks, Marls," I mutter, stashing the present under the counter.

"What was that?" she asks, cupping her hand to her ear.

"I said thank you," I practically shout.

"Jesus," a deep voice cuts in, making me jump. "I don't remember the service here being so loud."

"Oh, uh." I cough. "Hi, Dixon."

"Jason," the man drawls from the other side of the counter, one dark eyebrow raised. "I hear you're leaving."

I fidget with my apron strings. "Um, yeah. It's my last day."

Dixon grunts.

"This is Rip, my replacement," I offer, pointing to the half-asleep student standing at my side. I kind of forgot he was there, seeing as he's barely said a word all morning.

Dixon eyes him for half a second before grunting again.

"'Sup," Rip says.

Dixon meets my eye, eyebrow nearly hitting his hairline.

I choke just a little. "Um, Dixon gets a large hazelnut latte every morning," I tell Rip.

"Right on," the guy says, starting the drink order.

Marley snickers to herself as Dixon sighs long and low. He grumbles something about *change*, and yeah. I get it.

"Here," Dixon says, thrusting something across the counter.

I stare at it, bewildered. "What…"

"Just accept it," he says, apparently as bad at *feelings* as me. "You won't be here for Christmas, so I had to get you something early."

I swallow roughly. True, Dixon has always given Marley and me a little something around the winter holidays, but this feels more like a goodbye.

Because it is.

"Thanks," I say quietly, accepting the small box and placing it beside Marley's gift. *This fucking day.*

"Good luck with, y'know, the hospital," Dixon says. "If I ever get a cucumber stuck up my ass, I'll come to you."

Marley, Rip, and I all make strangled sounds. Dixon just smirks.

"Cas, uh, told you that story, huh?" I say, shaking my head before huffing a laugh.

"Mhm," Dixon hums.

"Uh, your latte, sir," Rip says, sliding the cup across the counter.

Dixon looks at him with a completely flat expression before lifting the drink and taking a sip. His eyes pan over to me slowly, and he twitches his brow as if to say, *You're going to make me put up with this crap?* I don't know how, exactly, I've come to understand Dixon's various eyebrow communications, but the simple fact of it sends a twinge through my gut.

I'm going to miss it here. I'm ready to start my job as an RN, I am, but… These are my people. Rip excluded, these are the faces I've spent every morning with for the past four years.

And now, it's time for me to go.

"Have a good day, Marley," Dixon says, drawing me to the present. "Rip." He sounds a little more reluctant with that one. He gives me a nod last. "Jason, see you later."

"Yeah," I respond. *Tonight.* Because no, I'm not losing these people entirely. "See ya."

Dixon turns and heads off, and Rip pours a coffee refill for a customer who came up to the counter with an empty mug. Marley gives my shoulder a nudge.

"Okay?" she asks.

"Yeah, just..."

"Yeah," she says, a crooked smile on her face.

When I clock out of Hyped for the very last time, I pull off my apron and look at it for a long while in the back room. I remember meeting Cas in this apron, when he asked me out and I spilled coffee all over the both of us. The way he tugged off his shirt and then fell at my feet. I remember thinking, even then, that he was striking. Beautiful, really. But I didn't know him at the time, not enough.

I didn't know I'd become attracted to him. I didn't know I'd find a person who so effortlessly accepts and supports me. I didn't know the porn star I'd been watching for months would become the love of my life.

Life is really fucking funny sometimes.

When my phone pings, I roll up my apron and drop it in the laundry. I already said my goodbyes, so I don't do it again. But I do grab the two presents waiting for me underneath the counter, and I bring them home with me.

The text is from my mom.

Mom: Congrats, Jaybird. I always knew you'd do big things. When is your first official shift?

I grab Amadeus out of his cage, letting him explore the bed as I text my mom back.

Me: Monday. It's real now.

I passed my NCLEX exam. I'm officially a nurse.

Mom: Lunch on me this week? You, me, and Cas can celebrate.

Me: You got it, Mom.

I don't bother mentioning Cas and I are already celebrating tonight. I'm pretty sure my mom would enjoy hanging out with a bunch of porn stars *way* too much.

Mom: Love you, Jaybird.

I let out a little sigh.

Me: Love you, too.

"Hey," Cas says, stepping into the room with a smile on his face. He crouches down when he sees Amadeus, giving my snake a little hello. It's the cutest thing I've ever seen.

"Hey, you have fun at Neddy's?" I ask.

Cas climbs up onto the bed, rolling toward me and laying his head in my lap. I drift my fingers through his hair, clean and dry, so he must have showered earlier.

"Yeah," he says. "Marshall brought a friend today."

"Really?"

Cas nods against my thigh. "He's practically a marshmallow these days."

I snort because that's certainly not true. "You must be rubbing off on him."

"Are you calling me soft?" he asks, lolling his head back to look up at me.

I run my hand down his chest, his abdomen, and over his crotch. I squeeze him there, and Cas's cock jerks and swells against my palm. "Not entirely," I answer. He smirks at me, and I let him go. "But in all the right ways," I add, "yes, you are."

Cas hums a little. "Before I forget," he says, pulling something from his pocket. "Here."

I huff. "Gifting is your love language."

"If gifting is mine, eating ass is yours," he says.

I bark a laugh, but my mood quickly sobers when I see the caduceus pin in Cas's palm. It's small and metal, and it reminds me instantly of my dad. "Thank you, Cas. This is...perfect."

Cas doesn't say anything in reply, but his soft smile speaks volumes. He sits up after a moment, planting a quick kiss against my lips before hopping off the bed. "I'm going to make dinner. And then we can get ready to meet the crew."

"Yeah, sounds good," I reply, setting the pin on my night-stand. "I'll be out shortly."

Cas gives the doorframe a gentle knock before exiting the room, and I grab the presents I'd left at the side of my bed. Amadeus flicks his tongue as I open them, slinking up beside my leg.

The first present, the one from Dixon, is a fridge magnet. It says, simply, "Don't fuck with me. I'm a nurse." It makes no sense, and I haven't a clue where he could have found it, but I laugh loudly nonetheless. The second gift from Marley is wrapped carefully in tissue paper. I unfurl the wrapping, find-ing a tiny metal figurine inside. It's a cat, one paw extended, claws out.

I hold it to my chest, a single tear slipping down my face. The good kind.

Yeah. I think I'm ready for whatever's next.

Chapter 31

CAS

"They're here!" Alex shouts, throwing his hands in the air as Jason and I step inside the party bus, Brad trailing in behind us. Alex reaches back, waving frantically at Emil, who hands him a small bag, and then the three of us are being showered in paper confetti, Jason taking the brunt of it.

"Oh geez," Jason says from beside me, rubbing a hand over his hair.

I huff a laugh, helping him get rid of the pink and white paper.

"Guys, you know Jason," I say to all before pointing over at Brad. "This is his friend, Brad."

There's a chorus of "Hi, Brad," from within the bus, one "ow-ow," and one "take it off."

Brad waves wildly, a grin on his face.

I already had my official goodbye party at Elite 8 Studios months ago, but Alex wouldn't be deterred about having a second celebration to include Jason's graduation from nursing school. The whole crew isn't here this time, but several of my former coworkers joined the fun.

Alex claps his hands together once, calling everyone to order. "Now that our esteemed guests have arrived, our night of debauchery can begin!"

There are a few groans.

"What?" Alex asks, deflating.

"Debauchery?" Dixon questions, arms crossed. He's sitting beside Niko. "What kind of fucked-up shit do you have planned for us, you tiny menace?"

Alex grins slowly.

"Dicks," Alex's boyfriend Finn calls out.

"Huh?" Dixon says.

There's a beat of silence, and then Alex snorts a laugh. "*Dicks*," he emphasizes. "Not Dix with an X. I've planned *dicks*. Obviously." He pulls out a tote filled with...dildo crowns?

"Oh my God," Emil says, sliding down in his seat. "I don't want to wear that on my head."

"You could wear this, then," Alex says, pulling out a bright pink jockstrap.

Emil grimaces.

Alex holds it out to Rowan, his other boyfriend. "Grizzly Bear?"

"Alex," Rowan says cautiously, "I don't think that thing would fit up my leg."

Alex bites his lip, nodding slowly as he ogles his boyfriend's thighs. He seems to have lost the power of speech, which is a first.

"Is everyone here?" Teddy asks from further down the bus.

"Uh, no," Niko puts in, looking around. "Where's Kipp? He said he was coming."

"I'm here," Kipp says, coming up the steps of the bus. His short, dark hair is mussed, and he lets out a sigh like he just ran a mile.

"Look!" Alex calls excitedly, glancing back at Teddy and jumping a few times. "It's Kipp. Look, Teddy. Kipp is here. Teddy, it's Kipp."

"Subtle as a freakin' train," Teddy mutters, shaking his head. His lips are twitching, though.

"Yeah, hi," Kipp says, waving to everyone. He sends an up-nod Niko's way before noticing the tote of crowns. "Oh shit, are those dicks?"

Kipp grabs a blue dildo crown, much to Alex's delight, and then crashes down beside Niko, squishing Dixon out of the way. Dixon grumbles, but Niko gives his friend a one-armed hug.

As Alex starts passing out the rest of the crowns, Jason and I take seats next to one another. Brad files in behind us, looking like a kid at a candy store. Marco is here too, and even Bill, one of the cameramen, with his husband. I give them all waves.

"Are we ready to go?" the driver asks, apparently unfazed by the goings-on inside his party bus. We're probably not the wildest thing he's seen.

Alex cheers. "Ready!"

The bus lurches forward, and Alex scrambles into a seat. As we drive toward our first destination for the night, Alex, with Finn's help, passes out drinks. Once we all have something in hand, Alex raises his plastic cup of champagne in a toast.

"To Jason and Cas," the small blonde says. "For one becoming a nurse. And for the other, our precious Himbo, closing his legs and spreading his wings. Congrats, you lovebirds."

"Beautiful," Brad says as a round of "*congrats*" rings out.

Jason leans close to my ear. "Don't think the closing your legs part is accurate, though."

I grin, brushing the backs of my fingers along his thigh. "Certainly not for you."

"God, that shouldn't be so hot," Jason mumbles.

"We're here!" Alex shouts.

Dildo crowns in place, we exit the bus, and the next three hours pass in a blur of blinding neon lights, dancing, laughter, and a surprising amount of dicks, as Alex promised. He busts out dick straws, candy dick necklaces, and a game of pin-the-dick-on-the-porn-star during one of our rides in the bus.

It's pretty perfect, honestly, as far as send-offs go. And Brad, well... He's eaten the most candy phalluses.

During our last stop of the evening, Jason and I separate from the crowd and step outside for some fresh air. The sidewalk is nearly as boisterous as the inside of the club, but we find a spot to stand out of the way. Jason's cheeks are flushed, more from happiness than anything else, and it makes me warm, seeing that. When his eyes catch on something across the street, I follow his gaze.

At first, I think he's looking at the chapel. But then I notice the tattoo parlor next door.

Jason's hazel eyes are bright when he looks my way. "I want to go in."

"Now?" I ask. "Are you sure? There's no rush."

"I'm sure," he says. "Will you come with me?"

I accept his hand. "Anywhere."

Jason and I head to the tattoo parlor together, matching grins on our faces. There's a guy waiting at the desk when we enter. He looks between us, raising a brow.

"Have an appointment?" he asks.

"No, but I want something small," Jason says. "Do you have time?"

"Are you drunk?" the guy throws back.

"I had one drink several hours ago," Jason answers truthfully, looking at me for confirmation, to which I nod to the guy at the desk. "Is that a problem?"

He grumbles a little. "Not ideal. You're not supposed to drink before getting inked, but it's not like folks around here generally listen."

Yeah, I'm guessing getting a drunk tattoo in Vegas is right up there with getting drunk-married.

"Can you at least stay off alcohol for the next two weeks while you heal?" he asks.

"Easily," Jason answers.

"All right, then," the guy says, waving us back. "Come with me."

Back in a private room, Jason shows the tattoo artist a rendering of a caduceus. After drawing it up, the artist transfers the image to the inside of Jason's wrist. It doesn't take long after that—a half hour at most with a little wincing on my boyfriend's part—and then Jason is looking at a permanent reminder of his dad. His eyes well a bit when he glances my way.

The tattoo artist covers Jason's wrist and explains the process of aftercare, but before we leave the room, I speak up.

"Any chance you have time for one more?"

"What?" Jason asks in surprise, head whipping my way.

The tattoo artist rolls his eyes, but he holds out his hand in a gimme gesture. After a quick search on my phone, I find something that looks similar to what I have in mind and show it to the guy, explaining the differences I want. It takes him a little longer this time to draw something up from scratch, and as he does, Jason grabs my hand, pulling me off to the side.

"Are you sure about this?" he asks me quietly. "I thought you only wanted a tattoo if it meant something."

"This does," I tell him, nodding over to the drawing, completed enough now for Jason to understand what it is.

"It's a snowflake," he nearly whispers.

I give his hand a squeeze, smiling when he meets my gaze. "It's our very first I love you."

"Cas," he says quietly.

I bring his hand up, giving his palm a kiss. "I want to keep it with me."

Jason blows out a small breath before stepping against me, chest to chest. He leans up, speaking quietly enough not to be overheard. "When we get home, I'm going to give you something else of mine to keep with you."

My dick jerks. "You mean..."

"My cum in your ass, Cassius."

Fuck. I clear my throat.

"How's this?" the tattoo artist asks.

Taking a step back, I look over at the sketch. The snowflake is drawn in straight lines, formed by geometric shapes. It's simple and precise and exactly what I wanted.

"Perfect," I tell him.

When Jason and I leave the tattoo parlor a little while later, it's with two big smiles and two new pieces of ink. There's a text waiting on my phone from Alex, asking where we are, but before I can message back, he comes bursting out of the club, stopping as he sees us crossing the street.

"There you two are!" he says, absolutely covered in dicks. Dick crowns, dick necklaces, you name it. "Are Teddy and Kipp with you?"

"Um," I say, looking over at Jason. "No?"

"Actually," Jason says, pointing over his shoulder at the chapel. "I saw them go that way earlier."

Alex's jaw drops. "What?" he squeaks before taking off.

I don't even have time to say goodbye, but that's all right. I know I'll see him soon.

Jason and I head inside to let our fellow partygoers know we're taking off. We get plenty of hugs, one suggestive "get it" shouted out from who-knows-where, and a sloppy cheek kiss each from Brad.

Jason snorts quietly as he watches Brad wade back into a throng of horny men. "Fucking Brad."

We grab a cab instead of waiting for the party bus to take us back. At Jason's, we head straight to his room. There's no finesse this time. No slow and sweet about it. Jason pushes me to the bed, draws down my pants—careful to avoid pressure on the bandage covering the snowflake at my hip—and then he swallows my cock. He gets me close to begging before he flips me onto my stomach, proceeding to hike up my hips and eat me out like it's our last night for it. His fingers follow, stretching me open, lighting me up.

When Jason finally draws back, he says, "Stay there. I want to see you open and waiting for me."

"Fuck, babe," I mutter, my cock so hard I'm dizzy with it. Pretty sure there's no blood left in my brain.

Jason removes his clothes slowly, a tease. I can hear the whoosh of each piece, the light thumps as they hit the floor. Can feel the indentation of the mattress as he climbs back onto the bed.

"Cassius."

"Yeah?" I breathe out.

Jason's palms smooth over my ass, followed by the press of his lips against my skin. "This is it. Us."

My pulse fires fast. "Yeah, Jason. It is."

"I love you," he adds, lips dragging across my ass cheek.

"Yeah, babe. I love you, too."

So much. The kind of love that lasts forever.

Jason exhales, a soft breeze, and then he lifts up. Without wasting a moment, he presses into my body, hips slapping my ass.

It feels like coming home.

Jason grips me tight as he fucks me, his fingers careful to avoid my new ink. He doesn't hold back, and I'm glad for it. I want to feel it, this moment. I want to remember, as surely as the lines etched on my skin, what this man means to me.

My shy barista.

My lion.

The only man who's looked inside and wanted me for what he found. I was his first, and I know he'll be my last.

"Cassius," he groans out, grabbing my hands. He presses them to the bed, holding me down. Holding me tight. "You need to come."

"Mmph," I manage, face against the sheets.

He nearly growls, and then his hand is in my hair, tugging. "Stop holding back. Come *on*."

"Fuck," I gasp out, everything in me tightening as Jason grinds against my ass, only to pull almost the entire way out and slam back in. He hits my sweet spot head-on once, twice, and I'm gone, tightening around him and splashing my release onto the bedsheets.

Jason groans, his grip in my hair loosening as he pumps his cum into my ass. I can feel him shaking with it, feel the way his fingertips dig into my skin inches above that *I love you* that sits immortalized in hexagonal ink.

"Cassius," he says again, a plea.

"Yours," I answer.

He sighs.

When Jason pulls out of my body, he doesn't go far. He rolls us onto our sides, him spooning me from behind, and then he shoves my top leg forward. Without a word, he presses two fingers back inside my body, his palm cradling the middle of my ass, and then he just...stays there.

I turn my head to look back at him. His eyes are closed, a content smile on his face.

"Are you just going to hold me all night?" I ask, amused.

"Yep," he answers, blinking open an eye and kissing my cheek. "For as long as I can."

Well, damn. My skittish kitten is a dirty little thing. Not that I didn't know that already.

"Okay," I reply, not minding one bit.

Jason eases out a breath, fingers curling against me gently.

For as long as I can.

Doesn't that just sound...

Well, perfect.

Epilogue

JASON

Three Years Later

"Cas?" I call out.

"In the kitchen."

I snort when I come around the corner. Cas is sitting reclined in the bay window seat inside our new kitchen, Amadeus painting a long stripe up one side of his chest. They're caught in the morning light, and it makes my heart ache, seeing my boyfriend there, looking so content.

"Are you reading to my snake?" I ask, walking over.

Cas gives me a swift grin. "He likes this book."

When I get close, he scoots his butt so I can sit next to him. The window seat is plenty wide, so it's an easy fit.

"I think you're his new favorite," I note.

Cas's smile turns a little suggestive. "What can I say? Your snake loves me."

I huff a laugh. So ridiculous, this man. Ridiculous and *mine*.

Still... "Don't look at me like that," I warn.

"Like what?" he says innocently, leaning close and brushing a kiss below my ear. *Ungh.*

"*Nooo*," I say weakly, placing my palm on his chest. I intend to push him away, but it's such a nice chest. I pet Cas as I tell him, "There's no time for this."

"For what?" he whispers, kissing my neck and then my clavicle.

"For, uh..." *Damn it.* Words. "For me to fuck you over this window seat."

Cas chuckles, tasting my skin.

"You're dangerous," I tell him. "We can't miss our flight."

He sighs a little, drawing back. It's a good thing—it is—but *ugh*.

"You're still not going to tell me where we're going?" Cas asks, setting his book aside. I adjust myself as he picks Amadeus up, the snake curling loosely around his hand and forearm.

"You'll find out soon enough," I tell him. I won't be able to hide our destination once we get to the airport. "But I thought you liked surprises."

"I do when they come from you," he says simply.

My heart hammers inside my chest at that show of trust, and I lick my lips, giving him a small nudge. "Come on. We should get going."

Cas nods, and the two of us head from the kitchen. The *floral* kitchen. I swear the wallpaper is the reason Cas latched onto this house when we went hunting for a place together.

And when he saw the big bay window? Well, I knew he was a goner.

Kind of like I was. For him.

Cas gives Amadeus a gentle finger rub before putting him back in his cage.

"Brad will stop by to check on him," I remind him.

"I know," he says, securing the top. "Doesn't mean I won't worry."

This man.

I link my fingers with his and pull us toward the front hall where our suitcases are waiting. The glass snowflake Cas gave me all those years ago hangs against the window beside the door. It glimmers in the light, and beside it, on the adjacent wall, is the canvas Cas painted of Dick Dog. They're both treasures and made the move with us.

The drive to the airport doesn't take long, but my pulse hammers away the entire time as Cas hums along to the radio beside me. *Distraction.* Distraction would be good.

"Did you get everything set for that charity auction?" I ask.

I catch a hint of his smile before refocusing on the road.

"Yeah. Celeste said she's expecting a record turnout. The guys might have something to do with that."

He chuckles, but I know how much it means to Cas that his former coworkers from the studio participate in his fundraisers. Sometimes they simply help with setup or marketing the events, but this time, the men *themselves* are being auctioned. Not sexually, of course, but for community service.

The mental image of Dixon scrubbing someone's floor in a maid's uniform makes me snicker.

"And your DPT program?" I ask, giving Cas's thigh a quick squeeze. "Are you ready to start that when we get back?"

"Yeah," he says. "It might be hard, but I'm ready."

After three years back in undergrad, Cas earned his bachelor's in physiology. The next step is a Doctor of Physical Therapy program. Cas is hoping to specialize in pediatrics, and honestly, I think that sounds perfect. He's always been good with kids.

"I think you'll do great," I tell him.

He gives me a smile.

My pulse kicks back up as I pull into the airport, and I have to remind myself to calm down. We won't even be at our destination for hours.

Cas and I grab our bags, lock the car, and head inside. I keep a hold of the tickets all the way through security, but once we approach our gate, I know there's no more hiding the surprise. Well, at least part of it.

Cas looks around as we slow, and I wait, practically holding my breath as his gaze swings over the screen above the flight attendants at the check-in counter.

"We're going to Iceland?" he asks, his wide gaze panning to me.

"Yeah," I manage, swallowing around my nerves. "Is that okay?"

"Yeah, Jason," he says, looking at me like... Like he always looks at me. His grin widens. "Maybe it'll snow."

My chuckle sounds nearly manic. *Counting on it.*

As Cas and I find seats to wait for our plane, my phone pings. I grab it from my pocket.

Brad: Good luck, Birdie! You got this.

God, I hope so. I hope I have this.

Me: Thanks, Bee.

Brad: If you get nervous, just remember that man once let you edge him for an hour in a Macy's dressing room. If that's not love, I don't know what is.

Me: I wish I'd never told you that story.
Brad: Too late. I will always remember.
Brad: And stop sighing at me.
God, he knows me too well. But I can't resist...
Me: Step on a fire ant hill, Brad!
I nearly jolt when they call boarding for our plane.
"Ready?" Cas asks.
I nod decisively, tucking my phone away. "Ready."
The trip to Iceland takes a little over ten hours. Cas and I both sleep a bit on the plane, and when we arrive at our mountaintop resort, it's nearly six in the morning local time. The two of us stop for a moment once we exit the taxi, just staring out over the picturesque landscape. The sun crests the peaks of the mountain, snow blankets the ground and floats gently down through the air, and warm lights welcome us from inside the cabin-style lodging.

"Wow," Cas says, the first to step forward, our bags at his sides.

I follow quickly, heart thundering along as my boots leave prints in the snow. The staff was expecting our early arrival, so we're quickly shuttled to our room. Everything is white and gray, like fluffy clouds, and a private hot tub steams just outside our back door. Cas's head is on a swivel as he looks around, and he opens up the slider, stepping outside next to the tub. He looks up, his form illuminated lightly in the early morning light, and my breath catches.

When he glances over his shoulder at me, a few snowflakes on his dark hair and a smile on his face, I can't do a thing other than join him.

"Jason, this is beautiful," he says, eyes closing toward the morning rays. It's cold. Cold as balls. But I'm sweating as I watch the play of expressions on Cas's face. Joy. Happiness. Calm.

"Cas," I say lightly.

He opens his eyes, head turning to me. A snowflake lands on his eyelashes before melting. "Yeah?"

I palm the box in my jacket pocket, but then I still.

What if he says no? *Oh God*, what if he says no, and we're stuck here together for an entire week in absolute awkwardness on a snow-covered mountain? Where will I go? I'll die out there, trying to fend for myself. Why didn't I pack more scarves?

"Jason?" Cas asks. "You just squeaked."

"Yeah, uh..." I blow out a breath.

He won't say no.

He won't.

I pull out the box, dropping to one knee with as much confidence as I can muster. Cas inhales sharply.

"Cassius," I begin, looking up at this man. This man I love with everything I have. "You once told me you liked looking at the snow because it made you feel important. And I remember, when I was sitting across from you on that very first date, I wanted you to look at *me* like that. I wanted to be important to you."

Cas swallows roughly, those whiskey eyes warm and bright, and I go on.

"You stole my breath the moment you walked into my life. And you did see me, the same way you let me see you. I fell, undeniably, a snowflake drifting down to Earth. But you fell with me, so it was okay. I knew I'd have you by my side for the journey."

Cas wipes his cheek, wipes away the tear there, and I pop open the ring box. His breath stutters as he looks at the band nestled inside. It's engraved with the same geometric snowflake that sits tattooed on Cas's hip. Our first *I love you*. But certainly not our last.

"Sometimes," I say hoarsely, "life is short. That's not always something we can control. But with you, my life is so very full. I love you, Cassius. And I want to spend every moment of this life I have falling with you. Would you marry me?"

"Fuck, Jason," he says, dropping to his knees in the snow in front of me. His hands come up to my cheeks, shaking slightly, but I can see the words he's going to say before they spill off his tongue. "Yes. *Yes*, I'll marry you. Of course I'll marry you. I love you, babe."

"Yeah?" I croak.

"Yeah," he says, nearly a laugh. "Did you think I'd say no?"

"No, I just..." I let out a giddy breath. "I was nervous."

His expression softens at that, hands coming down to cradle my neck. I grab his shirt, tugging him close.

"My little lion. Don't you know I'm already yours?" Cas says before meeting my lips gently. It's dizziness and relief and so much yearning that I lose myself in it. In this man.

My fiancé.

Whoa.

When Cas draws back, he looks a little dazed, just like I feel. "Maybe I should send Simon a thank you card."

"What?" I nearly growl.

Cas laughs. "If I wasn't Himbo, I might never have met you. I wouldn't have known Dixon. I might not have ever walked into Hyped."

My breath leaves me in a rush. "I never thought of it like that."

"So you agree we should thank my ex?" he asks.

"Uh, hell no," I get out, tightening my hand on Cas's shirt. "That guy can go fuck himself."

He chuckles. "Fierce," he mutters, sitting back and looking down at the box in my hand. "So are you gonna put a ring on it or what?"

I laugh wetly, pulling the band from the dark velvet. Cas holds out his hand as I slip the ring on his finger, and I brush the pad of my thumb over the snowflake on top.

"My forever *I love you*," Cas says quietly, a gentle smile lifting the corners of his mouth.

"Yeah, Cas," I breathe out, reaching up to run my thumb along his lips. *Those* lips. The top. The bottom. Each perfectly formed. Each able to speak their own *I love yous* with the simplest of curves or brushes. "This is it. Our forever."

The End

About the Author

Information about Emmy Sanders and her complete list of works can be found on her website. Subscribe to her newsletter, join her Facebook reader group, Emmy's Enclave, and connect via email or social media:

www.emmysanders.com

Find online:
www.facebook.com/emmysandersmm
www.instagram.com/emmysandersmm

www.ingramcontent.com/pod-product-compliance
Lightning Source LLC
Chambersburg PA
CBHW070438300726
48975CB00007B/1966